TWISTED PRETTY THINGS

SHADOWS OF LONDON #1

ARIANA NASH

Twisted Pretty Things, Shadows of London #1

Ariana Nash ~ *Dark Fantasy Author*

Subscribe to Ariana's mailing list & get the exclusive story 'Sealed with a Kiss' free.

Join the Ariana Nash Facebook group for all the news, as it happens.

Edited by No Stone Unturned Editing.

Proofread by Marked and Read.

Cover design by Natasha Snow.

Edited in US English but retains some UK spelling as part of the character of the work.

Version 1 - July 2021

www.ariananashbooks.com

"What a charmer," I muttered, taking a drink from my glass. My shadowy corner tucked away at one end of the packed bar in Leicester Square was the perfect place to keep an eye on my target—a man in his forties, currently entertaining a small crowd several tables away.

Reedy, in a slate-grey suit, the target had his new friends laughing and the drinks flowing. His wandering hands for the women hadn't gone unnoticed either, but a few jealous boyfriends were the least of Gareth Clarke's problems. On the outside, Mister Clarke was a typical London city boy, just out for a pint. No harm done, mate. But that Gareth Clarke was a mask. The real Gary was a pencil pusher, whose idea of adventure was wearing a red tie instead of the grey pinstripe he'd worn for the last twenty years. The divorced Mister Clarke had recently bought himself a Porsche and hired routine visits from high-end escorts. And right now, he was running up a bar tab that had the staff bending over backwards to tend to his every need. Maybe Gary was having a mid-life crisis, or maybe it was more to do with the fact Gary was an unregistered latent who happened to be cash-rich and have an artifact in the pocket of that cheap grey suit, making him as harmless as a nuclear bomb.

Gary laughed, triggering his friends to laugh too loud with him. I wasn't sure which of us was the sadder man. Him for having to pretend to be something he wasn't, or me, drinking alone on a Friday night. I was here for work, but this *was* me most nights.

I waved the bartender over and had him top up my drink. Gary's agency file suggested that once I'd introduced myself, he wouldn't put up a fight, not physically. A stiff breeze could blow Gary over. But being a latent, he had certain abilities—known as a *trick*—which made him volatile, and when amplified with an artifact, that trick had the potential to be explosive. Charming Gary could flatten Leicester Square to rubble. Which was why I had eyes on the unassuming Gary Clarke, and why his mid-life crisis was about to come to an abrupt end.

Approaching him inside the bar was too risky. Too many bystanders. Too many unknowns.

Luckily, Gary was a creature of habit. His exploits during the last few weeks suggested ten minutes from now he'd leave the bar, hail a cab, and head toward Piccadilly. That was when I'd have a quiet word. In an ideal world he'd see the error of his ways, hand over the artifact, and let me escort him to the local cop shop for processing.

In my two years since leaving the military and landing an agency job, no latent had ever given up without a fight. And as a latent myself—registered—I didn't begrudge them their attempt at freedom. But freedom for unregistered latents was not how things worked in London. Boxes had to be ticked, forms filled in, and latents tracked and tested and controlled, for their own safety.

Gary picked up his jacket and made motions to leave. His crowd begged him to stay, offered to buy him more drinks. One woman had her hand planted on his arse, staking her claim. She whispered something in his ear and her hand slipped around Gary's hip, seeking more intimate parts.

He grinned, laughed, brushed her off, and made for the door.

"Now we dance." I downed my drink and started after him.

The packed crowd by the door briefly blocked Gary's exit. A few awkward shuffles and polite smiles, and he slipped between them. I shoved through in his wake. If I lost him now, he'd be in a cab and gone.

A tall, dark-haired prick who didn't believe in manners barged in front of me. He was out of the door ahead me, stalling my progress by a few crucial seconds. Spilling onto the pavement, I spotted Gary a few strides way, his arm up, hailing his usual black cab.

There was never a cab around when you needed one, until the target wanted to make a break for it.

A few steps and I'd be on him. I swept my jacket back, revealing my agency ID badge fixed to my belt, while simultaneously sinking my left hand into my pocket, seeking my deck of cards.

"Hey, man?" an American voice called out. The prick who'd shoved in front earlier jogged by me on the pavement toward Gary, his hand out. "You dropped this."

I got a glimpse of dark eyes, a smooth but sharp jaw, long legs inside pressed dark trousers, all wrapped in one of those three-quarter length wool coats only male models look good in—the kind of Hollywood glamor that opened the same doors that get slammed in my face. And all right, I might have taken my eye off the target longer than I should have because when I found Gary again, recognition had widened his eyes. He knew the American and they weren't friends.

Gary dropped his hand into his pocket—reaching for the artifact.

"Gareth Clarke," Hollywood began, "you're being detained under the Unregistered Latent Act, Nineteen Seventy-Eight—" He produced a pair of shiny cuffs from his coat pocket.

Oh hell no. Hollywood wasn't stealing my target.

I slipped a card from my deck, sent a measured pulse of trick through my fingers—sizzling just enough power into it—and launched the card through the air, between Hollywood and Gary. The card hit the parked cab and exploded like a military flash-bang, raining sparks over the cab's glossy black paint. The cabbie put his foot down and sped away from the curb, leaving Gary and Hollywood gaping in my direction.

"Now I have your attention," I said. "Gary, mate, I'm Agency. Hand over the artifact and—"

Gary bolted. Hollywood shot me a look as though I'd just stolen his Oscar. Too bad, he shouldn't have tried to poach my mark.

I flew after Gary. He sprinted across the road, through

slow-moving traffic. Headlight beams swept over his legs and mine, and horns honked.

He splashed through puddles and ran like fucking Seabiscuit down Leicester Square's bustling streets until veering right, slinking into a narrow, uneven cobbled side street. The streetlight was out. At least it was a dead-end.

Gary met the brick-faced wall at the end of the alley and turned on his heel. The sprint had mussed his hair, and a flickering mask of fear and desperation contorted his expression. A bad combination. His hands shot to his head and yanked. Gone was the suave, charming Gareth Clarke from the bar, the lie. The fun and games were over. Latents didn't get nice things to play with.

"Easy, Gary." Withdrawing a card in my left hand, I charged it up, sending rippling yellow light over the dank alley walls, illuminating us. "That artifact you've got, you know it's not safe, right? Just hand it over and I'll say you cooperated. No harm done."

Gary breathed hard through his nose, teeth bared. He dropped his hands—putting them closer to the artifact in his pocket.

If I didn't talk him down, then me, this alley, and anyone nearby was about to be blasted into the afterlife. Artifacts and latents went together like fire and gasoline. I just had to keep him from grabbing whatever artifact he had in his pocket.

"Nobody has to get hurt, all right?" I inched closer.

"They can't know I took it!" he whined, pacing the small alley from wall to wall. "If I give it to you, they'll find out!"

We could have a nice chat about everything when he handed over the damn artifact. "Come quietly and—"

A backfire from a passing car boomed. Gary suddenly dropped, like a doll tossed away. I blinked, thoughts slow to catch up. Gary lay sprawled on the ground, eyes open —unseeing. A puckered hole marked his forehead.

Not a backfire. A gunshot. After years in the military, I should have known the sound, but guns were rare in London.

Hollywood strode into the alley, coat flaring. He lowered his muffled smoking gun and grimly regarded the dead man.

"This is London, arsehole. We don't execute latents here!" I flicked a charged card at his pretty face, meaning it.

Hollywood ducked and the card exploded against the alley wall behind him, blasting us in brick dust. He frowned at the hole in the wall then ran *at me*.

Shit, he was a blur. I pivoted, avoiding his wild left swing, but not the butt of his gun as he whipped it across my jaw. Stinging pain lashed my face. It might have been enough to knock me down if I hadn't grown up in a house where having the shit beaten out of me was a weekly event. He expected me to fall, because when I smiled instead and spat blood in his face, shock had him reeling. He didn't expect an East End lad to fight fair, did he? He was out of his depth on these streets. My next right jab split his lip and rocked him backward. I'd have followed through with a kicking if his gun hadn't come up, pressed under my chin, and abruptly put an end to the scuffle.

I froze and lifted my hands. "You gonna shoot me, Hollywood?"

Hollywood sneered, and even angry his face was all

pretty. Perfect dark eyebrows pinched together. "I wasn't here."

"Fuck off then."

He stroked the tip of his tongue over the split in his lip and those long-lashed dark eyes dropped to *my* mouth. Deep, dark pupils dilated. *Hello*, Hollywood had the hots for beating on London men. In other circumstances, I'd have been game, but this prick had just executed an arguably innocent man and there was still the matter of the artifact. It needed to be recovered before falling into worse hands than the late Gary's.

Distant sirens wailed. Shit, we'd be having company soon.

Hollywood wiped a dribble of blood from his chin, and—taking his gun from under my chin—he backed up. In a whirl of coat, he was gone.

I dashed to Gary's side and checked his pulse, in the slim hope he still breathed. The headshot was terminal. Gary had been dead before he'd hit the ground.

"Bastard!"

My job now was to locate the artifact. Until it was secured, the scene was still dangerous. Rummaging through his jacket pockets yielded a wallet, a phone, but no artifact. I scrabbled around for any more pockets or jewelry or something buzzing with psychic energy. There *had* been an artifact. I'd brushed by him earlier, playing as if I'd accidentally bumped into him, and felt the familiar throb of the artifact. But he didn't have one on him now.

My heart hammered.

Had he dropped it? Scanning the alleyway was fruitless. Rubbish littered the edges and the debris from my earlier blast covered much of the ground. It was here though, it had to be.

"Armed police! Don't move!" A troupe of black-clad armed coppers spilled into the alley.

Tires screeched and blue lights washed over the scene, highlighting the hole my card had blown in the wall and the body at my feet.

I sighed. My night was now fucked. Rising, I lifted my hands and squinted into the glare of half a dozen torches. I probably had a few rifles aimed at my head too.

"I'm Agency," I said coolly. "Kempthorne and Co. There's an artifact on-scene." Not that they'd care. Private agencies tasked with keeping London free of magical latent-enhancing artifacts didn't mix well with traditional policing. London's Metropolitan Police figured we were one piece of paper away from the people we tracked for a living—which in my case, was technically true. The Armed Response Unit and their officers routinely bullied artifact agents off what they considered their patch.

Two firearm officers ran in and checked on the deceased Gary. "Man down. Single GS," one of the AFOs reported into his radio. That spooked the rest who swarmed me like ants. Hands swept over all my best parts, searching for weapons. They didn't know I was a latent, which was a blessing. Had they known, I'd have been facedown already, eating concrete.

"I'm unarmed. I didn't kill him. No gunshot residue. Like I said, there's an artifact nearby. It needs to be located and secured. If you'd just let me do my job..." Nobody was listening.

Someone found my deck of cards—just an old deck to

them—and returned it to my pocket. Another pair of hands found my ID and grunted, "Kempthorne and Co."

"Move your arse." A shove in my back had me stumbling toward the police van. I was their bitch now and I'd better cooperate, or I'd find my face meeting the pavement multiple times.

The AFO bundled me into the back of the van.

Alexander Kempthorne, Head of Kempthorne & Co Artifact Retrieval Agency, would have my arse for this, and not in the good way. The target was dead, and I'd lost the artifact in question. As failures went, that was a solid one.

The van doors slammed shut, plunging me and my AFO escort into a surreal quiet. I had a long night of paperwork and interrogation ahead of me.

That prick, Hollywood, owed me a damn good explanation for why he'd executed my target. If I ever saw him again.

2

B eing thoroughly roughed up and worked over by the Met's forensic team and underpaid detectives was right at the top of my least favorite ways to spend a night. It happened more often than I'd have liked. Whether they had it out for latents, or agents, wasn't clear. Or maybe I ticked the box for both, entitling me to special treatment. Whatever the reason, Kempthorne must have pulled his strings because I was released the next morning, instead of spending forty-eight hours in a cell. As Gary was an unregistered latent, they'd take my forensics, bag and tag it all, throw his file into a drawer, and probably never open it again. The whole thing was a song and dance we all knew would go nowhere.

By the time I'd ridden the commuter tube and trudged back to 16a Cecil Court, a thick drizzle had descended over the twee pedestrianized Victorian street.

I dug around my pockets for my key to the side-door, figured the cops still had it, and hit the buzzer. I'd have liked nothing more than to shower, crawl into bed, and sleep for the rest of the day, but as I lived at the Kempthorne & Co office, there was no avoiding the dressing down coming my way from the boss.

Cecil Court, also known as Booksellers' Row— London's quaint little street full of bookshops—appeared harmless. Tourists couldn't get enough of the Harry Potter ambiance. They visited a slice of Ye Olde London, splurged on some rare books, and went home with a few London bus fridge magnets. And none of them had any clue Cecil Court also housed one of three independent Artifact Retrievable agencies commissioned by the Crown to do what we do best—trace, retrieve, and neutralize psychically charged artifacts, keeping them off London's streets.

The intercom screen flickered and Gina's rings of tightly curled dark hair and plucky round face appeared. "Dom, you look like shit," she said around a mouthful of toast.

"Wow, thanks. I lost my key. Let me in, will you."

She buzzed me in and I trudged up the creaking wooden stairs to the second floor. Gina, Robin, and I were all Kempthorne's agents. We also shared the apartments over 16a Cecil Court. Kempthorne himself had half a dozen houses all over London and was forever flitting between them. His top floor loft apartment at Cecil Court was one of his favorite haunts, but off-limits to the rest of us.

I'd barely gotten my coat off when Robin popped her head around the door. Her auburn hair was ponytailed painfully tight. She poked at her big glasses, sliding them back up her nose. Robin rarely smiled, and always scowled at me as if I'd ruined her day. It wasn't personal. She didn't smile for Kempthorne either. But this morning's deep frown didn't bode well. "Kempthorne wants to see you. In the basement."

Better to get it over with. I grabbed a custard cream from the packet lying open on the kitchen island, ate it in a single bite, and plodded back down the stairs, avoiding the shop level, descending into the basement. Kempthorne & Co also sold books. Two years and I was still trying to figure out why, when they had enough to keep them busy with tracking down artifacts. Maybe Kempthorne just liked books.

The basement's racks of shelves held a jumble of dead artifacts—neutralized and no longer harmful—from the mundane, like a pebble, to modern tech, like mobile phones. Pendants, talismans, tablets, jewelry, wired timer devices that looked suspiciously like they could have been actual bombs at one time, and more than a few creepy dolls. They all filled the shelves. Robin could put her hand on any item Kempthorne wanted, so there had to be some order to the chaos.

A muttered curse drew me toward the back of the basement. Shelves holding old artifacts gave way to stacks of books and an ugly floor-standing 1970s lamp, the kind with tassels. The lamp was hideous, and a fire hazard. But like most things in the basement, it had its place.

In front of the old lamp, seated at an antique desk, was Alexander Kempthorne. With his head bowed and his attention glued on a coin pinched between his fingers, he didn't notice me approach, giving me a chance to take him in. Which, honestly, was always a fucking treat. His dark hair, short at the sides, longer on top, flopped effortlessly over his forehead. One stray curl always escaped his efforts to restrain it. Too many times I'd almost reached out to flick the lock back. Luckily, I'd stopped that impulse before it got me in trouble.

He and I were the same age, early thirties, but from opposite sides of the tracks. I'd grown up on a council estate and had learned how to survive the urban jungle. He'd grown up in a Surrey mansion and had probably gotten a pony for his sixth birthday. I should have hated him, out of principle, but after I'd been booted from the military under bullshit medical grounds, his agency had been the only one willing to take on a licensed latent with my past.

He'd rolled his white shirtsleeves up past his elbows, revealing a fine pair of forearms, tanned golden from whatever exotic place he'd recently returned from. An old-fashioned watch that had cost more than I'd earned in my lifetime glinted on his wrist. Yeah—I should have hated him. For multiple reasons. One of those being he was as hot as sin and had shown no signs of being interested in men, or women. Anything with a heartbeat hardly registered on Kempthorne's radar, but give him an artifact to riddle out and he was in love. He was so far out of my league, we were on different continents. But none of that mattered anyway because posh guys weren't my type.

He studied the coin between his fingers like it held the secrets to world peace. My first week, I'd walked in on him staring at a fork with that same level of intensity. It turned out the fork had been an artifact, and he'd been trying to get the measure of its strength. Almost impossible to do for non-latents, like him.

"Here." Kempthorne flicked the coin at me.

I snatched it from the air. Its psychic kick hit me in the chest, tugging on my trick, and stole a gasp from my lips, leaving no doubt the coin was an artifact. "Bloody hell." I dropped the coin into my left hand and shook out the tingling from my right. "Some warning next time?"

"Highly charged?" he asked, eyebrows lifting, widening piercing blue eyes. The kind of blue that changed with his moods. Right now, the blue was light and warm, but I'd seen them glacial cold. Those times, he was best avoided.

"Very."

"Hm." He sat back in the old, creaking chair and steepled his fingers against his lips, returning to his thoughtful state. "Tell me about it, Dom."

Breathing in, I studied the coin. Now I was ready for it, I could guard against the psychic leakage. It appeared to be a simple pound coin. One of the round ones, not the newer twelve-sided version, making it several years old. Its psychic burn tingled my fingers. All artifacts, old and new, started out as everyday items. The coin had started life as just another coin. But at some point, a psychic shockwave had blasted it, staining it, turning it from a coin into an artifact. The more psychic shock an item absorbed, the more powerful the artifact. The coin was perhaps mid-range.

As London was as old as dirt and had been through countless historical atrocities—the Great Fire, the Blitz—the city was rife with artifacts. Most had been taken off the streets by agencies. Some were traded secretly at high level auctions and shuffled between hands alongside high-end art—which was how I figured Kempthorne had gotten into the business, seeing as he lunched with people who had Rembrandts on their walls. Murder weapons made typical artifacts and were more obvious to spot than the obscure items that slipped through the net. Like Kempthorne's coin.

This little coin had witnessed something horrific in its past. It had soaked up the shockwave, making it ripe pickings for latents. Little artifacts like this one were like illicit drugs to latents. We couldn't resist them, even as they destroyed us.

Kempthorne's dark eyes fixed on me, demanding to know *everything* in that penetrative way of his. His intense gaze could smolder the pants off a priest—such wasted talent. I shook that unhelpful image free and focused again on the coin.

I wasn't just any latent. As an authenticator, I could see echoes of the event that had turned an item into an artifact. Useful for tracing an artifact's owner, or should someone want to authenticate an artifact's provenance. My specialty was confirming if an item was real or a fake.

Closing my eyes and shutting off outside stimuli, I focused on the cool metal pinched between my fingers and slipped into the *sight*. It didn't take much—the coin was noisy. *A woman's scream. The flash of a knife. Blood on my lips. A punch to the gut.* Breaking the sight, I blinked, refocusing on Kempthorne still sitting, patient and motionless in his chair. "Murder," I said. "A young woman in her teens." The memories flashed, trying to reassert themselves. "She's wearing a ring and a pink top, maybe a hoodie?"

He didn't react, unsurprised by my findings. "Murder weapon?" he asked.

"Carving knife. Stabbed in the chest multiple times." The knife would have become an artifact too, but the cops squirreled murder weapons away from crime scenes.

"ID on the killer?"

I set the coin down on his desk, earning his raised eyebrow. The more I held on to it, the more the psychic energy leaked into my fingers and the louder the bloody thing got. The longer I held it, the more at risk I was of never letting it go and losing my mind to its whispers. Artifacts with their ability to boost psychic energy were tempting, and resisting temptation was a weakness of mine. "I'd need more prep to see the killer, if I see him or her at all."

I'd do it, he paid my wages, but not while he was staring at me like he could see into my soul and wasn't sure if he liked what he saw. That shit was distracting.

He rose from his chair, retrieved the coin, dropped it into a leather pouch, and placed it into the small archaic-looking safe fixed into the basement's back wall. As I was the only latent on the staff, he locked the coin away to keep *me* safe.

The coin was a test and the case probably old and already solved. He'd spring tests on me sometimes. Usually, when I least expected it—like before I'd had my morning coffee, or when I was engrossed in an unrelated case. Authenticators, like absorbers—latents who leeched power off others—were rare (most got personal with the business end of a shotgun) and I couldn't figure out if he thought me a fraud or if he was just studying me under a microscope. I'd have taken it personally if he didn't pull the same kind of off-the-cuff tests on Gina and Robin, keeping them on their toes.

Falling onto the old military stance of a soldier at ease, with my hands clasped behind my back, I waited for the bollocking we both knew was coming.

"You lost the artifact," Kempthorne said, focusing on me now his coin was safely locked away. His tone had turned cold enough to lower the temperature in the room. With his sleeves still rolled up and his hair ruffled, his look would have been casual on anyone else. In two years, I'd heard him raise his voice once and only then through the walls while he'd been on a call with some poor bastard who'd ended up having a really bad day. But the edge was always there, like he might snap and flip a desk at any moment. Maybe this was my moment.

"The target had it on him in the bar," I explained. "He must have tossed it when he ran."

"You weren't watching him the whole time?" A muscle in his cheek flickered.

"A third party obstructed me."

Straightening, he folded his arms. "The mysterious American who executed Mister Clarke. I read your police report. Is it possible he retrieved the artifact?"

How did Kempthorne get his hands on the police reports so quickly? The right handshake with the right people, probably. Kempthorne had his ways. I wasn't sure all those ways were legal, but he got the job done and seemed to be on the straight and narrow, which was as good as it got for London's agencies.

Did Hollywood have the artifact? Hollywood had

been out of sight for several minutes while I'd chased Gary down. "It's possible."

He fished a mobile phone from his pocket, flicked through a few photos, and handed it over. The image on-screen was Hollywood dressed for dinner somewhere shiny and posh, schmoozing with a young blonde woman who seemed familiar and another middle-aged man. Hollywood's smile dazzled. He wouldn't have looked out of place on a red carpet surrounded by paparazzi.

The picture had been taken from a low angle to keep the photographer from being spotted.

"That's him," I confirmed. "You know him?"

Kempthorne turned the phone off and set it back down on his desk. If he was pleased or surprised, his expression didn't show it. "Did you learn anything during the altercation in the alley that you may have omitted from your police report and would like to tell me now?"

That was a wordy way of asking if I'd lied to the Met. "He has a mean right hook and a split lip, and he executed Gareth Clarke like the man was nothing."

Kempthorne frowned. "That can't have been an easy thing to witness."

I shrugged. I'd process it later, with a bottle of wine. "Before shooting the guy, he quoted the Unregistered Latent Act, which suggests he's agency-trained. Obviously US-based, given the accent."

Kempthorne's lips twitched with a tiny hint of personality that had my tired, foolish heart tripping over a beat. The twitch was his version of what would have been a full-blown smile on anyone else. Was it wrong that I wanted to see that smile turn into a genuine grin? Dammit, I must have been tired if I was getting distracted.

"Get some rest," he said, picking up on my waning enthusiasm. "Meet me in the shop at eight p.m."

That sounded like a dismissal, but where was my reprimand? My screw-up had killed a man. If I'd been quicker, or spotted Hollywood before he'd got the drop on me, I could have brought Gareth Clarke in without incident. I'd failed and a man had died.

Kempthorne noticed my stalling and lifted his gaze. "Was there anything else, Dom?"

"No, nothing else." I backed up and tripped over a stack of books. Kempthorne was already too engrossed in the files on his desk to notice.

I was halfway down the hall when he called out in his clipped upper-class accent. "Domenici, wear suitable dinner attire."

Hearing my surname on his lips sent my mind plunging deep into a well-worn fantasy where Alexander Kempthorne growled my name for reasons that had nothing to do with artifacts and everything to do with getting really personal on top of that large desk of his. Shaking those images from my head before they could take root, I huffed a laugh at my own foolishness. I was tired, that was all. And Kempthorne had a mysterious magnetism that constantly triggered my curiosity. The man was trouble in a suit, and tonight, we were going on a work-date to flush out an American assassin.

3

I didn't own any kind of suit that wouldn't make me look like Kempthorne's valet, so Gina put in a last-minute call and hired a tux. Kempthorne had disappeared sometime during the day, like always, leaving Gina and me to run the agency while Robin monitored the shop. The phones were quiet, but a couple of calls came in. One latent acting "suspiciously," — which usually meant the neighbors didn't want them living next door— and a suspected artifact had been handed in to the Science Museum. I scribbled the last one in the diary for the following day.

My tux arrived at seven, leaving me an hour to get cleaned up. The shop was closed and Gina was rustling up something for dinner when I appeared in the kitchen, all suited and booted, fighting with a ridiculously complicated bow tie. I should have asked for a clip on.

Gina whistled and swooped in, knocking my hands aside to fix the tie. "When was the last time you wore a suit?" she asked, her fingers working beneath my chin with practiced ease.

"Can't remember." At court. I was seventeen and pleading with a judge for lenient sentencing. I'd gotten three months in the nick and had gone straight into the military after release.

Robin, seated at the table and swiping her fingers across a tablet, peeked over the rim of her glasses. "That tux is costing the company as much as our electric bill. Do not get it dirty, John."

If she was using my real name, she meant it. "No, ma'am."

Gina snorted. "He's with Kempthorne at some posh dinner." Bow tie fixed, she patted me on the chest and beamed. "What's the worst he can do? Drop caviar on it?"

"Exactly." Robin tutted. "I mean it. Ruin it and it comes out of your wages."

I resisted the urge to mention how Kempthorne could afford it and straightened my cuffs, fighting my rattling nerves. "How do I look? Like Kempthorne's rent boy?"

Gina snorted. "Hot AF." She sighed. "All the gays in Soho are gorgeous. It's so unfair." She wasn't wrong. It had taken Gina a week to hit on me and discover that, as lovely as she was, her efforts were wasted. I'd gained one hell of a friend, though.

"It's those Italian eyes." With a mock-swoon, she returned to the stool at the breakfast bar and sipped her coffee, her grin growing.

I rolled my Italian eyes—courtesy of my father, who had tried to beat the gay out of me. Clearly, that hadn't worked.

"Are you on the pull tonight?"

"Gina," Robin grumbled. "Give the man his personal space."

I grinned at them both. "When aren't I on the pull?"

Gina laughed and Robin scowled through her glasses. Robin was the backbone of the business. Nothing got by her. She made sure all the i's were dotted and the t's crossed. She had to be hard to tame Kempthorne into signing checks. After two years, I'd grown fond of her grumpy ways like you grow fond of a Siamese cat you know wants to murder you but can't figure out how.

"No fraternizing on company time," Robin added.

"Who am I going to pull at some posh dinner anyway? The staff?" In this get-up, I'd probably get mistaken for the waiter.

"You might be surprised." Gina waggled her eyebrows. "I hear Kempthorne's lot get up to all sorts of kinky—"

The sound of a car horn drifted in through the open window. Right on time. Grabbing my deck of cards, I slipped them into my trouser pocket, said good night to the girls, and headed out.

I'd seen Kempthorne a handful of times outside the office. Once, when he'd collected me from the A&E after a retrieval case had turned more violent than anyone had prepared for. I'd tried not to bleed all over his sleek car's leather seats all the way back to Cecil Court. Another time, we'd crossed paths in the same park. I'd spotted him having a heated discussion with a woman. They'd both seen me smile a hello. It had spooked her enough to leave right after. Kempthorne had then made painful small talk and abruptly left. That meeting had intrigued me for weeks. Then there was the time he'd spotted me getting into a cab with a guy I'd pulled in Soho and had seemed *surprised*. Gina must have filled him in on my preferences afterward because nobody had asked where I'd been that weekend, and Gina always grilled me the second I snuck back home early on Monday mornings. All of us bunking under the same roof meant secrets were hard to keep—unless your name was Kempthorne. He hoarded secrets like the rest of us hoarded the office pens.

So this work-date was the fourth time I'd seen Kempthorne anywhere outside of the office. His black Lexus idled at the curb. Through the open passenger window, I caught sight of his hand on the gearstick, sleeves rolled up.

He didn't say anything, but the second I slid into the leather passenger seat the corner of his mouth ticked. The scents of leather and polish and whatever cologne he wore drifted around us—something woody and masculine. Seductive. Christ, was it hot in here?

He flicked the indicator on and pulled the car into traffic.

"Nice wheels." The words were out before I could think of something less stupid to say. Kempthorne had multiple cars. The one I'd tried not to bleed on had been an Aston. The Lexus was probably his *dull* car, even if the thing glowed inside like its DNA was half spaceship. It was the kind of car that got its wheels nicked if it lingered too long in the wrong part of town.

"Thank you." He sounded amused. Maybe. I couldn't read him, and any time I tried, I error-coded out.

The AC hummed. London reeled by. Traffic lights, red double-decker buses, black cabs.

"No rain tonight," Kempthorne said.

"No, looks dry."

Well, this was fucking awkward.

Throw me into a warzone with psychic assassins, government-sponsored latent-sucking leeches, and I was in the zone, but stick me in a posh car with Kempthorne and I forgot how to brain.

Sparkly and vibrant London glittered as the Lexus's tires rumbled over potholes and patches in the road. "So, where are we going?"

"A dinner with a *friend* of mine. She has a professional interest in artifacts." He said *friend* in the same tone he could have said enemy. Color me intrigued. What kind of friends did a man like Kempthorne have? Golf buddies? Secret handshakes? Was I being an asshole assuming all posh gits hung out in the same circles?

"Are you sure you want me along? I'm not exactly your usual..." Male date? Companion? What was this?

"My usual...?" he asked, with a hint of sly.

"I'm from the College of Cockney, not Eton." I didn't have the plummy accent, for starters.

That little uptick of the lips. I couldn't tell if he was secretly laughing at me or with me. "I wouldn't have asked you to come if I didn't want you to."

Oh well, all right then. He knew what he was getting into. I wasn't about to apologize for who I was or where I'd come from. I just hoped his friends didn't mind an East End army lad eating their hors d'oeuvres because I planned to devour all the mini morsels.

"You think Hollywood will be there?"

"Hollywood?" Kempthorne changed the Lexus down

a gear and pushed her forward, increasing speed through the light traffic.

"The American."

"Ah. Yes. He'll be there. He's made himself rather conspicuous in certain art circles."

Art circles and artifact circles were one and the same. I could believe Hollywood would have made an impression. The man wouldn't have recognized subtle if it looked back at him from a mirror. "Just so we're clear. He killed a man in cold blood and we're about to have dinner with him?"

"Is it really the killing that bothers you? Some could argue you've done the same. Multiple times."

He stared dead ahead. The lights of Piccadilly stroked over him, moving shadows around his face. His eyes still sparkled though, as if part of him thrived in the dark. "Under orders," I said.

"You think your Hollywood acted alone then?"

"He's not *my* Hollywood and maybe. Gareth was scared, dangerous definitely, but he didn't deserve a bullet between the eyes. I was talking him down."

"And if you were wrong and he'd used his artifact, you'd be dead, along with half the residents of that street."

And here was the bollocking. All right. Fine. I'd had this coming. "You hired me to hunt unregistered latents and bring artifacts in. If you think I'm not up to the task, drop me from the agency." I sounded like I had the balls to walk away, but he couldn't hear my heart rattling behind my ribs. I needed this job. I needed the purpose. I needed Gina's backup and Robin's no-bullshit rules. The military had fucked me in all ways. If I didn't have

Kempthorne & Co, I was a ghost. I couldn't go home. An authenticator in the East End? The gangs would've been all over me, and I knew me, I wouldn't be able to resist all that temptation for long. It'd kill me. And probably others.

The Lexus stopped at a set of temporary traffic lights on red.

"You lost the artifact," Kempthorne said.

I wedged my elbow on the door and propped up my chin. "I'll get it back." I was beginning to think Hollywood *had* taken it. It could have been left in the alleyway, but the Met would have found it and informed Kempthorne. That really only left Hollywood.

"What do you think of undercover work? Morally?" he asked, rapidly switching topics.

"You mean pretending to be something I'm not to get the job done? It depends on the perceived risk. If the threat is substantial, then undercover can be a discreet way of ending a difficult scenario."

"You ran undercover ops in the military?"

Could he know for certain? He knew a whole lot. Knew things he shouldn't. But there was a difference between sweet-talking the Met's chief and getting his hands on classified military files. "Not me. I was just a grunt."

The lights turned green and the Lexus purred its way toward Vauxhall Bridge. The Thames always looked sexier at night, when it was an oily line snaking through London instead of a brown soup. I watched the waters flow as Kempthorne drove us toward Chelsea's leafy streets.

We'd been silent for some time by the time he pulled

into a sweeping drive. A pair of double automatic gates opened, letting us glide through. "I want you to get the measure of Hollywood," Kempthorne said. "Find out what you can about him. Do and say what you have to so he trusts you. Are you all right with that?"

A valet opened the driver's door and Kempthorne climbed out.

I threw my door open, then grinned at Kempthorne over the car's roof as he adjusted his jacket. "Am I all right with lying to the prick who fu—screwed me over, executed a latent, and stole our artifact? I'm sure I'll manage."

Kempthorne strode around the front of the car and adjusted his cuffs. He slipped on a shining pair of opal cufflinks with deft fingers and ran a hand through his hair, somehow managing to perfectly align those dark locks but for the irritating lick of a curl.

This might have been the first time I'd seen him dressed in a tux and bow tie and he fucking *dazzled*. I'd seen him in suits, mostly the morning after whatever he'd been up to the night before, so he'd always been scruffy and disheveled. But not here. Here he shone, the epitome of masculinity and money, all fine lines, crisp tailoring, and smooth silk shirts. The only other thing on that street more impressive was the Chelsea mansion behind him, with its stucco columns framing Georgian windows, all lit from within by the sparkle of grand chandeliers. I swallowed hard and fiddled with my own sleeves, hoping I could find some more bravado hidden in the seams. Yeah, this was a terrible idea. How was I going to blend in *in there*?

What if this was some awful joke to make me squirm in my hired tux that didn't quite fit and never would?

Kempthorne was odd at times, but not malicious, and he had no reason to torture me. Although, he probably had no idea what bringing me here, to a place like this, was doing to my messed-up head.

"Dom?"

"What?" I answered and swallowed again, trying to clear the gravel in my throat.

He arched an eyebrow. "You're sure you're all right with this?"

"I'm fine." I could bullshit anything and grinned to prove it. "One more thing..." Christ, it was unseasonably hot tonight. I tugged my collar away from my neck. "If anyone asks, we're here as work colleagues?" Was he almost smiling again?

"As friends."

Oh. Right. Okay. I could run with that. Male friends going to a fancy dinner together. Uh huh. That was a thing the wealthy did?

"And you're my authenticator."

And there it was, the real reason he had me tagging along. To show me off to his artifact-loving rich pals while getting the lowdown on Hollywood. Kill two birds with one stone. I was his latent trophy. I'd been used for worse. "Great."

The tick of his lips became a smile this time.

We climbed the steps side by side. I caught Kempthorne watching me from the corner of his eye moments before a pair of huge white doors opened, inviting us into a whole different world.

4

I was a disaster waiting to happen. Part of me wondered if Kempthorne knew it and got off on throwing a cat among the pigeons. I scooped up a champagne glass and trailed alongside him, grinning through his introductions and making polite small talk that had my cheeks aching. If I could just get through the night without making some half-arsed comment or breaking something expensive, I'd call it a win.

Kempthorne was a surprise I hadn't seen coming. Not only did he outright smile, but he *laughed* a deliciously rich laugh. I hadn't even known he *could* laugh. I'd come to a party with a stranger. Who was this different Kempthorne?

I was trying to figure out why his switch in character bothered me so much, when the American entered, dressed like the devil in a dashing all-black tux, minus the horns and tail. A woman in a clinging red dress looped her arm through his. They made such a delightful pair that the whole room must have swooned.

I downed my champagne in one.

"You're snarling," Kempthorne muttered, suddenly at my side.

I jumped and turned, finding him close. The damn place with its chinking glasses, polished floors, and fake laughter had my nerves shot. I grabbed a new glass of bubbly from a passing waiter, guzzled half, and didn't care that Kempthorne raised an eyebrow. "Don't look," he said. His hand settled on my shoulder, sending a jolt of lightning through me. The unexpected contact further unbalanced me. "He's coming this way. I want to see his face when he recognizes you."

I was game. Anything to distract me from the very visceral feel of his hand burning its way through my hired tux.

"Alexander Kempthorne," the American said.

Kempthorne's fingers dug into my shoulder, turning me. Just as I got Hollywood in my sights, Kempthorne extended his hand. Hollywood—focused all on Kempthorne—shook hands and freed his megawatt smile.

"I don't believe I've had the pleasure," Kempthorne purred.

"Kage Mitchell, and this is my—" Hollywood's gaze skipped over me and then zipped back. A polite smile plastered over his abject shock, but we'd all seen his reaction. "—My er... girlfriend, Annie Evans."

"Charmed," Kempthorne said.

Annie smiled, but there was a shrewdness to her eyes that suggested she was reading us as much as we were assessing her. "It's a pleasure to finally meet *the* Alexander Kempthorne."

Kempthorne preened and dropped his hand from my shoulder. "Ah yes, well don't believe everything you read in the papers."

They all tittered their high-society fake laughter.

I thrust my hand toward Kage—that name, really? "Have we met, mate?"

"I don't think so." He chuckled the fakest laugh there and grabbed my hand with enough force to grind bone.

"Maybe you just have one of those familiar faces?" I tightened my grip. "What happened to your lip?"

The handshake went on a few seconds too long, making his girl's smile twitch. What was Kempthorne making of all of this? His presence simmered beside me, just out of sight.

Hollywood finally freed my hand and touched his lip. "A car door."

I played at looking sympathetic.

"This is my associate John Domenici," Kempthorne butted in.

"What happened to your chin, John?" Hollywood asked, gesturing at his own chin around the area where he'd pistol-whipped me.

"This?" I scratched at my chin. My darker Italian skin hid most of the bruise but he knew it had to be there. "It's nothing. Can hardly feel it."

"Tripped, maybe?" Hollywood skimmed his dark eyes over Kempthorne. "I hear there's an authenticator among us?"

"Indeed," Kempthorne's voice rumbled.

Nobody said the obvious, that I was the authenticator. It wouldn't have taken much for Hollywood to figure it out. He already knew I was a latent. He'd seen my trick in the alleyway.

"I'm surprised to see an agency owner here," he went on. "Aren't most UK agencies strict and law-abiding?"

"Oh, we are. When it suits us. But some artifacts go missing. It's in their nature to hide and that sometimes calls for *different* methods." Kempthorne's smile turned predatory, staying far from his eyes.

"Their nature?" Hollywood mocked. "You talk like they're alive?"

"I believe some—the more powerful—develop something of a presence, yes. A religious person might call it a soul."

Hollywood chuckled and his arm ornament tittered. "In the States, artifacts are tools."

"And weapons?" I asked.

A measure of glee brightened Hollywood's eyes. Clearly he got excited over guns and artifacts.

"Anything is a weapon in the right hands." He turned his back and joined the crowd.

Kempthorne watched him, trying to peel the man's layers off with his stare. "I want to know everything he knows about London artifacts. Why he's here, who has hired him, and if he has Gareth Clarke's missing artifact."

"With an ego like that, he's just waiting to spill all so we all know how smart he is." Like the rest of the people here, preened and proper. So full of themselves. I finished my second glass under Kempthorne's intense gaze. "What?"

"Money doesn't make a man good, Dom."

I frowned at the line, so out of the blue. Did he mean himself, or the people here? Before I could ask, he added,

"Get close to Kage. You'll know when I need you." And with that cryptic gem, he handed me his glass and slipped out of the nearest door, vanishing like a ghost.

I was going to need more champagne to get through the night, especially if I had to buddy up with *Kage* for most of it.

The host had left a spread of tiny canapés, which I made a beeline for now that the others were helping themselves. Kage found me halfway through my third glass of bubbly, eyeing the black, bead-like things on my tiny hors d'oeuvre.

"Caviar," he said, assuming I had no idea what I was looking at.

"Right." I popped it into my mouth and devoured it in one bite. Salty.

Kage flashed his paparazzi smile, while cutting in and blocking me from the rest of the table, and his stare made it clear it didn't have anything to do with preventing me from devouring more of those tasty morsels.

"You with Kempthorne?" he asked, cradling a champagne glass in his hand and eying me down his nose.

I picked up another colorful miniature meal. "We work together." The tiny morsel went down a treat. Working together was better than *working for Kempthorne*, which made me feel like the rent boy all over again.

"I mean, are you *fucking* him?"

I inhaled, choked, and coughed all at once. Hollywood grabbed a jug of water, sloshed some into a glass, and handed it over. I drank that sucker down, recovering enough composure to see Hollywood fighting a grin at my expense.

"Better?" he asked.

"Yeah," I croaked.

"Well?"

"Am I..." I pursed my lips and swallowed. "No. He doesn't—He's not into er... men."

"But you are?"

Hollywood clearly didn't have a brain-to-mouth filter, or didn't care. "Mate, what's it to you?"

He raised his hands in surrender. "Just feeling you out."

"Feeling me out for what exactly because the last time we met you held a gun to my head."

He smiled like he knew all the secrets. "That wasn't personal."

"Pulling a gun on someone is pretty bloody personal." I inwardly kicked myself. I was supposed to be *friendly*. I was also better at my job than this, but the glitzy party had thrown me off my stride.

Hollywood lost some of the sparkling grin and asked, "Military, right?" When I didn't reply, he roamed his gaze over the parts of me he could see. "You stand like a soldier, at attention even when you're at ease. In the club, you watched all the exits. You always have a way out." He leaned closer, bumping my tiny plate of canapés. "But the way you fight, that's what gave you away. Ruthless. Fluid. *Efficient*." Hollywood said that last word achingly close to my lips. His fine eyes had a depth that pulled me in, like he and I had seen similar horrors and survived them. Christ, he was pretty. Plump, pink lips aching to be stroked under my fingers and tongue. Soft dark lashes framing amber eyes someone could easily get lost in.

"My delightful guests," the host's bright voice chimed. Kempthorne had introduced her earlier as Joanna

Devere, his *friend*. Joanna looked like someone's posh grandma, the tall, rake-like kind who smiled as she planted poisonous plants in her manicured garden to poison the neighborhood cats.

The crowd turned toward Joanna but Hollywood stayed still, boxing me in. "No exit this time," he whispered, raking his gaze over me as though undressing me with his eyes. I hadn't forgotten his reaction in the alley. This was definitely foreplay.

When he turned to face Joanna, I exhaled, remembering how to breathe. Other parts of me had begun to sit up and take notice. Parts that would soon be impossible to hide if I didn't clear my head.

Luckily, Joanna was waffling about a special guest that I had no interest in and with my mind clearer, the semi I'd been sporting began to wilt.

"Mister Domenici?"

All eyes turned to me, including Joanna's. She beamed, expecting *something*. Hollywood raised his eyebrows and smiled slyly, enjoying my alarm. Shit, it was like being back in basic training, when the CO had singled me out as the reason our squad had fucked up, making all our lives hell for the next six hours.

The authenticating! I was here for *that*. Right. Bloody hell, where was Kempthorne? This was all his *thing* and the prick had left me in the thick of it.

"Right. Yes." I cleared my throat, set my little plate of tiny morsels down, and tugged on my sleeves, buying myself precious seconds to think. "The authenticator. That is er... me."

"Follow me, please, Mister Domenici," Joanna said, urging me to follow her through the double doors.

All the sparkly people watched as I sidestepped around them and hurried after the host. They probably wondered where Kempthorne had dug me up from. Their second thought would also likely be that I was faking it. A few psychics with the dregs of psychic ability got by telling fortunes and communing with "spirits", but their talents for reading the past in an artifact wasn't enough to call them authenticators. At best, they were a party trick. Which was what these people thought they were about to see.

But Kempthorne didn't seem the type to go to all this trouble for a party trick. He'd want the fireworks. A tingling began in my fingertips and my deck of cards felt heavy in my pocket, each card itching to fly.

Steeping into a grand, high-ceiling room, I counted fifteen potential positioned artifacts on a long dining table. To the untrained eye, they looked like junk. A button, a watch, a twisted piece of rusted metal, a child's soft teddy bear that I wasn't going anywhere near—kids' toys were the worst kind of artifacts to authenticate. Happy ever afters didn't leave psychic burns behind.

"Mister Domenici, what do you make of my selection this evening?" Joanna asked.

Kempthorne still hadn't reappeared. I was on my own.

I eyed the selection while mentally guarding myself against their relentless thrumming. "I can tell you straight away that you have two artifacts amongst those that are off-the-charts illegal." In the wrong latent hands, Joanna's innocuous items could do a whole lot of damage, making them sought-after in black market auctions, especially to criminal elements.

"Is that a problem?" Joanna asked.

"No, I'm here aren't I?" Thanks to Kempthorne, who was beginning to piss me off. He'd dumped me in an illegal dealers' little get-together and made himself scarce, probably for plausible deniability. Sly bastard.

"Can you select the more potent artifacts for us and tell the room about them?"

Fucking show and tell? Christ. Time to get on board with the illegal shit then. I couldn't even use gloves to keep my fingerprints off the items. Breathing deep, I calmed my heart, distracted by Hollywood leaning against the table and crossing his arms, his gaze on me, not the artifacts.

The twisted piece of metal screamed for attention. Shaking out my fingers, I picked that up first and hissed through my teeth. It was hot, all right. A smattering of images bombarded me all at once. *Fire. Men screaming. High pitched whistling—like steam escaping. Rubble falling. Water, fire, and banks of rolling steam.* Wincing, I set the piece back on the table. "Nineteen forty-one, the last days of the Blitz. Somewhere near St Paul's. Nasty piece of work, that one. Potent."

Joanna's old eyes lit up with the promise of a prize. She'd make a ton of money at auction for that piece.

"And the other?"

The wretched teddy bear. I scowled at the beady-eyed horror film prop. It didn't scream like the twisted metal had. This one didn't want to be found, but it was too late for that. A horrible, wet, heavy throbbing beat off its limp, furry limbs. "Are there any other latents here?" I asked, taking my eyes off the artifact and delaying as long as possible.

Blank faces all 'round. Now they were all intrigued.

"Why?" Hollywood asked. Propped against the table and so relaxed he looked as though he owned the place, he waited for my reply.

"The next artifact is what agencies refer to as dirty."

A few gasps rippled through the small crowd. They'd have a story to tell everyone at polo on Sunday, or wherever rich-people gathered to gossip.

Even Hollywood looked surprised. He glanced at the collection of items, trying to pick out the right one. If he wasn't a latent, he'd have a hard time finding it. And if he was a latent, but wasn't an authenticator, he wouldn't know which item was hot enough to be a dirty, not with any certainty. It was part of what made authenticators special, and what often killed them.

"What makes an item dirty, Mister Domenici?" Joanna asked, like a teacher testing how much I knew. Next she'd have me juggling balls for their entertainment. Kempthorne had a lot to answer for.

"An extreme level of psychic trauma." I silently begged her not to ask me to elaborate. We were all adults here; we could figure it out.

"And that's dangerous because?"

"The dirtier an item, the hotter it becomes, and the harder it is to control its amplifying effect on a latent's trick." I had a dirty deck of cards in my pocket, but those weren't as hot as the teddy bear.

"So, you'd classify one remaining item as an extremely potent artifact. Something that would be quite valuable to the right people?"

Christ, these people were assholes. And so was

Kempthorne for having me find Joanna a weapon she'd sell to some other prick on the black market.

"I think that's enough." Kempthorne appeared at the back of the crowd like he'd been there the entire time. I shot him a glare, which he ignored in favor of smiling at his friend Joanna. The smile was empty and a long way from friendly.

"Come now, Alexander." She laughed. "You can't have your man leave us in suspense. We simply must know which item is dirty."

Hollywood turned to see if we were all about to witness an argument. Most eyes were on Kempthorne, so they missed one of the guests lunge across the table, his hand outstretched toward the dirty teddy bear. I dove for the artifact. Old military training kicked in, mentally preparing me for the artifact's shockwave. But my fingers swept through air. Squeals from the guests cut off in horror. The small, grey-haired man held the bear up in both hands and stared at it like he'd won the lottery. Too bad his ticket was about to kill him.

A sickening, heavy psychic beat from the artifact rolled through the room, so hot and cloying even the non-latents recoiled.

"Get down!" I barked.

Heat swelled and psychic energy filled the room, plunging us all into a thick, suffocating quiet.

The guests tried to scatter through the doors. Some screamed, some stared openmouthed, perhaps knowing it was already over.

A white-hot, silent flash stole my sight and hearing. Numbness spread, until a ringing began in my ears. Dust cloyed my tongue. My vision blurred back to me, revealing a view of the floor I was facedown on. Blinking my senses back together, I tried to shift upright, but a heavy weight pinned me down. My own thudding heart tried to beat its way out of my skull, through my ears.

The weight on my back shifted and someone's elbow or knee jabbed me in the hip. I grunted a curse and spat grit. Alarms shrieked nearby, maybe in the room with us —my head was too full of broken bits to make sense of it all. Hollywood's face filled my sight, his dark brows pinched together and his lips formed words I couldn't hear. A cut above his right eye dribbled blood down the side of his face. He should get that looked at before it ruined all his pretty. I blinked and he vanished. Maybe he'd been a dream?

As the pounding between my ears tried to split my head open, I flopped over, onto my back.

The fine high ceiling was now a gaping hole. A bed from the floor above had slipped forward and wedged between splintered floorboards. The rusted-red splatters all over the walls were all that was left of the latent who'd grabbed the bear. Poor bastard.

Kempthorne's angry face hovered over mine. Somehow, this was my fault. He growled something, grabbed my arm, and hauled me up enough so I could prop myself on a hand, then he left to check on the twisted remains of the body a few strides from me. Joanna hadn't survived.

Carnage came to mind. The once opulent dining room was now in shreds.

It took too long to gather all my wits and shove them back into order enough to climb to my feet and check on the remaining guests. Paramedics poured in minutes later, followed by the Met, who demanded Kempthorne and I answer their interrogation while standing on the glass-strewn lawn. With the night's chill setting in and the immediate questions over, we returned to his car.

Kempthorne had a scratch on his cheek and he'd cursed at his broken watch, but he was unhurt. We were both lucky to walk away, considering how close we'd been to the latent.

"Kage left before the police arrived," he said, gripping the steering wheel hard enough to make it creak. At 3 a.m., the London streets were almost empty. Kempthorne was making use of the space to put his foot down and race home. He muttered something about only the guilty running.

I dropped my head back and closed my eyes. The ringing in my ears hadn't entirely faded and now a headache had joined the party. If we could just get home, I'd crawl into bed and deal with all the fallout tomorrow. Like why Kempthorne was even involved in such a reckless gathering.

"Fuck," Kempthorne spat. His upper-class accent made the word sharp. "He won't get away with this."

"Hollywood didn't do anything," I mumbled, rubbing the ache at my temple.

"He wanted those artifacts."

"Maybe. Probably. But if he hadn't been there, I might not be alive."

Kempthorne frowned. Shadows gathered on his face but his anger was fading, replaced by worry. "He saved you?"

I nodded. The weight on my back had been Hollywood. He'd tackled me out of the blast radius, probably saving my life.

Kempthorne rammed the car into a lower gear and lurched the Lexus faster through the streets. "You should know. You were the target, Dom."

Me? I snorted. "Right." But Kempthorne wasn't laughing. "Who knew I was going to be at some posh dinner, besides you?"

"It wouldn't have been difficult to deduce. As soon as I put the word out I was bringing an authenticator, your name would have come up. There are certain factions in London who are very aware of you and your talents. I've mostly kept you shielded, but an ex-military authenticator does not go unnoticed in London for long."

Wait, was he serious? "Did you suspect something like this would happen?"

"Not *that*."

"But something?" He hesitated. The bastard. "Let me get this straight." I twisted in my seat, making sure to stare *at* him. "You brought me into your elite circle of artifact dealers knowing someone was going to pull some insane stunt and you didn't warn me?"

He glanced over then pinned his glare on the road again. I couldn't read him well, especially in the dark with the shifting light, but there was a soft sheepishness to his expression, maybe even guilt. "I wanted to rattle loose figures who have been undermining my efforts to secure certain high-end artifacts. Your name just happened to be a way to garner more intrigue."

"High-end like that fucking teddy bear?" He knew that dirty artifact was going to be there. He knew I was walking into a situation far more dangerous than cocktails and fucking caviar on tiny pieces of toast. Christ, the asshole had used me as bait. "And where were you, huh, while your friends were measuring me for a casket?"

He flicked the steering wheel, and lurched the Lexus around a corner, kicking out the rear end in a slide, narrowly missing a bollard. "They're. Not. My. Friends."

"Slow the fuck down!"

He slammed his foot on the brake, anchoring the car to the road. Tires squealed and the car rocked to a dead stop at the end of Cecil Court. Okay, we were done for the night. I leapt from the car like the bloody thing was on fire. Whirling, I ducked my head back inside and glared at the man who had just put my life on the line and used me for some bullshit secret case. He stared back, his face guarded, but his arctic-blue eyes blazed their fury. "The next time you want to fuck me over, the least you can do is prep me first."

I slammed the door on his shocked face and made it four strides before the horror of what I'd just said hit me in the guts, tripped my feet, and ruined a good storming off. My gut screamed apologize, my head said fuck that.

Tires screeched and the Lexus roared away.

At 16a Cecil Court's door, I braced a forearm on the doorframe, realized I still hadn't picked up a spare key, and hit the buzzer. My tux was shredded, Robin was going to kill me, and tomorrow, Kempthorne would probably kick me out on the street for fucking up his case and getting one of his not-friends killed.

It was safe to say, our work date had been an epic disaster.

5

One perk of living where you work was the lack of commute. No sane person wants to ride the Tube twice a day. However, a major downside was having to look the boss in the eye before you've had your first morning coffee and after his actions had almost blown you to bits, for which you'd tossed a scorcher of a gay insult in his face. I had every right to be pissed off, but by the time I dragged my arse out of bed around midday the next day, I was too banged up and feeling sorry for myself to continue the argument.

Gina greeted me with a sympathetic wince and plonked a mug of hot coffee on the kitchen table in front of me. Robin was manning the shop, which was for the best. She hadn't said a word about the tux, or anything. She had glowered over the rim of her glasses when she'd seen the state of the tux and tutted, which was honestly worse.

Gina took the chair opposite me at the table. The kitchen was where most of our unofficial meetings happened. Even Kempthorne liked to linger in the light and airy space at the heart of 16a, with a cup of tea and a packet of Rich Tea biscuits. But not today. Wherever he was, it wasn't near me.

"Feeling better?" she asked.

"A bit."

"I postponed your museum job until five." She cradled her own mug of coffee, sipping occasionally.

I nodded, keeping quiet. I might not be employed at 5 p.m.

Her knowing brown eyes peered at me through the steam rising from her mug. Gina was one of the most expressive people I knew. Her face betrayed her every thought. She always laughed with all her heart, or her fury made all her pixie cuteness warp into a hard mask of don't-fuck-with-me. But right now, the sad eyes and concerned frown were chipping away at my effort to remain stoic.

"I'm all right," I said, with more conviction. "Just sore." In more ways than just the bruises.

I'd given them the summarized version of events— bad artifact, bad crowd, big explosion—and left them to find out the rest on the news. Robin hadn't looked as though she had any patience for hearing how I'd also given the boss a mouthful, so I'd kept that to myself. But Gina had a knack for reading between the lines and wasn't buying the *I'm fine* line.

"I left Kempthorne pretty pissed off last night," I finally admitted.

"Did you have a spat?"

A spat? I chuckled. "Yeah, no. Kinda. He took me to

that dinner party knowing something dangerous would shake lose and didn't warn me."

"I'm sorry."

"It's not your fault."

"I know but Kempthorne... he kinda has tunnel vision sometimes and he forgets we're not in the tunnel with him, yah know?"

"I get it." And I did. I knew what he was like. I should have seen an ulterior motive behind all the glitzy stuff, and missing it was on me. I knew better than to trust the top brass. "Before I got kicked from the military, an op went bad. Our CO was a grade-A dick. His intel was full of holes. Me and one other on my team got out, but the rest..." There was more to it, but she didn't need to know the personal details. "I don't do well with being lied to."

"There's probably a really good reason why he didn't tell you."

"Yeah, he's a prick."

Gina began to laugh, until she froze with her gaze locked over my shoulder. There's an expression people had when they knew they'd been caught out, and she had that look right now—big eyes, lips slightly parted—as though she wanted to crawl under the table and hide.

"Gina." Kempthorne's commanding voice filled the kitchen, and my heart stopped. "I have a meeting with Detective Inspector Barnes in five minutes. Can you make sure she finds her way upstairs?"

I didn't look. Couldn't look. Probably should look. Clearing my throat, I plastered a fake smile onto my face and twisted on the stool.

Kempthorne filled the doorway. Rain glistened on his

dark wool coat. Sharp blue eyes avoided looking at me, fixing on Gina instead.

"Hi. All right?"

"Dom." Now his glare cut deep.

The insult I'd thrown at him came back to me in crystal clarity. I might as well have told him to *butter me up and spread me, Daddy.* Heat warmed my face. Christ.

"How are you this morning? No concussion?" He sounded reasonable, like we hadn't raged at each other last night. Maybe that was the best way to play it.

"I'm fine. You?"

"Yes. Fine. Apart from my watch…" He showed us his empty wrist. "I've asked Robin to have it fixed." After glancing around the kitchen as though it was the first time he was seeing it, he cleared his throat. "The DI will be here soon. After the meeting, Gina, please close the shop and gather everyone there for three p.m."

"Close the shop?" Gina echoed.

"Yes. Thank you." He vanished in a swirl of coat.

Gina caught my gaze and winced.

"I just called the boss a prick while he was standing behind me." I groaned. "That just happened?"

She shrugged. "I'm sure he's been called worse."

"Uh huh. And are those people still alive?"

Chuckling, she got to her feet, taking her coffee with her. "Relax. He likes that you're honest. Most people aren't with him. They know he's loaded and try to befriend him, you know, just for the kudos of knowing London's third richest bachelor, I guess. It's kinda sad."

I rolled my eyes. Yeah, poor Kempthorne. He probably dried his tears with fifty-pound notes.

She sobered and muttered, "Did he look pale to you?

Maybe I should make him a sandwich?" While she was invested in feeding the boss, I used the time to fold my arms on the table and bury my face in them. Could this day get any worse?

This was it then, my last few hours working for Kempthorne & Co. It had been a good run while it had lasted. I'd tried to make it work, but like most things in my life, it had crashed and burned. Latents didn't get decent jobs with good people, we got sent into warzones and treated like cannon fodder. I'd been a fool to think Cecil Court would last.

Glancing at the clock revealed it was late, early afternoon. I had an hour and a half to kill before getting sacked. "I need some air." A walk around Trafalgar would help clear my head.

"Dom, wait," Gina called after I was already out the door. "You'll be back at three, right? And don't forget the museum!"

"Yup, I'll be there." Until then, I needed to get *out* of Cecil Court and out from under Kempthorne's shadow. After throwing on my jacket, I left 16a and hurried through the sea of intrepid tourists, dodging their oversized umbrellas shielding them from the drizzle.

Not much could beat the charm of London in the rain. Old stone buildings crowded up against granite sidewalks, cracked and wonky with age. Posh Georgian terraces huddled against the sharp, jagged lines of new-builds. Traffic hummed. Tires splashed through puddles. Iron railings gleamed. Black cabs and London busses cycled around Trafalgar like the beating veins that kept London alive.

I walked without a destination, passing Trafalgar's

enormous lion sentinels, and strolled down into St James's Park where squawking parakeets fought with the squirrels for breadcrumbs.

Finding a suitably moody tree, I planted my arse on the wet grass among its roots and watched mist swirl above the gloomy lake. Perfect. I could sulk here for a while.

If Kempthorne decided he was done with me, what the fuck was I going to do without the agency? If I went back to the East End, it wouldn't be long before my old life dug its claws in—the same damn life I'd gotten out of by joining the military. Artifacts weren't just a boost to a latent, they were bloody addictive. The rush of touching the forbidden, the high of all that power. Mix it with the East End criminal element... My heart raced just thinking about it, and not all of it was fear. I'd narrowly escaped before. The madness I'd seen on the grey-haired man's face before the artifact had blown him to smithereens, I'd seen on my own more than once. A look that said it was fucking worth it just to watch the world burn. A dangerous look.

Sinking my hand into my pocket, I pulled out my tattered deck of cards and summoned my trick. A faint glow framed the entire deck. The trick's tease of power tingled up my fingers. This artifact wasn't the most powerful, which suited me just fine. Despite the psychic trauma that had created them, there was comfort in holding them. I'd had them beside me for so long, the cards and I were one and the same. They were a part of me, a part of my past. A past I couldn't ever go back to.

"Hey—"

I had a card between my fingers and aimed at Hollywood's head in a blur, and just as quickly twitched my wrist *away*—training kicking in so I didn't take his head off. The military had been good for my control, at least. "You followin' me?"

He spread his hands, trying and failing for an innocent look. "Just walking by."

"Right, London ain't that small, mate."

His mouth tried to find an apologetic smile but missed its mark and found sly instead. He wanted something and as he'd saved my arse the night before, I owed him. I patted the grass beside me. "It's wet."

He sat, not caring about the wet grass and mud, and stared into the misty fog swirling over the lake. "I see why you like it here."

"It's nice when it's quiet. Best avoided when full of tourists." Why was he here? I kept him in the periphery of my vision and drew a knee up, resting my wrist on it, going for casual while also having my deck of cards within reach. I couldn't see a holster on him, but his long black coat probably hid many surprises. "How's your forehead?"

"Two stitches." He frowned, creasing the little butterfly bandage over his eyebrow.

"Shame to scar all that." I waved at his face. "Women everywhere will cry themselves to sleep."

He snorted and leaned back, propping himself up on his elbows. His coat fell open, revealing a thick cable-knit sweater that would've looked like a dad jumper on me. Somehow, it was hot on him. Long legs, slim figure, but not without muscle. He'd make a dustbin liner the height of sexiness. Bastard.

"Thanks," I said. "For the save last night."

His quick smile was gone after a second, but a little mischief still sparkled in his eyes. "Despite what you think, I'm not a bad guy."

"Uh huh." I had to laugh. "That's exactly what a bad guy would say."

His smile stayed this time, and it really was the kind of smile that he knew was irresistible. "A month in London and I've seen more artifacts clustered here than any city in the US."

"London has a lot of psychic trauma. Not long after I started at Kempthorne's, I was in a pub with the team, and I tripped over an artifact used as a doorstop. A chunk of iron straight out of the Great Fire and the idiots were using it to hold a door open. The bloody thing lit me up right there."

The shock on his face said he knew exactly how dangerous it could have been. "What happened?"

He seemed genuinely interested, and when he wasn't trying to take my head off with his fists or shoving a gun under my chin, he almost looked *normal*. Just a guy, same as the rest of us. "I got my hands on it like it was the Holy Grail," I admitted. "Nobody was taking that sucker away until I'd burned through it, me, and half of London." The images it had shown me were forever branded into my memory and half the reason I woke drenched in sweat some nights. "Kempthorne was there. He talked me down. I don't remember much of it, honestly. If another latent had found it, one without my training, the pub would be long gone. Just goes to show how much the agencies are needed."

"He's quite something, huh? Your Kempthorne."

"He's something all right." What that something was,

I hadn't figured out. He wasn't a latent. He hadn't shown any signs of losing his shit over an artifact. But he knew artifacts like latents did. How to handle them, how to avoid them. They were his life. And he was definitely walking the wrong side of the normal line.

"You had no idea there were going to be artifacts that hot there last night, did you?" Hollywood asked. Long-lashed eyes watched me think. Unlike Kempthorne's glare, that skewered its victim, Hollywood's was softer, asking not demanding. He patiently waited for the truth.

"No," I admitted. "And I don't like surprises."

Hollywood followed my gaze toward the swirling mists. The occasional flash of color darted through the mist—parakeets darting from tree to tree. We fell quiet, but there was no pressure to fill the silence, no awkward small talk. It was... nice.

After a little while, he asked, "Know anywhere nearby that serves good coffee?"

Was he asking for himself, or for me to join him? Would I go for a coffee with him? Kempthorne had told me to get close, but that was before I'd yelled at the boss.

I pulled my phone free and checked the time. "I'd help you out, but the boss is about to fire me and I really shouldn't be late *for that*." Standing, I brushed the wet grass off my arse, catching Hollywood's lingering gaze. He didn't care I'd caught him checking me out either and looked up with a sly smile on his lips. He stretched out his long legs, crossing them at the ankle, sprawled like a feast for the starving. And my dry spell was beginning to give me ideas, such as straddling those long legs, shoving him onto his back, and kissing him breathless. But he had a girlfriend. And there was also the fact he'd killed a latent in front of me.

Then saved my life...

Hm. This was getting interesting.

"Why is he firing you?" Hollywood asked, after I'd lingered too long.

"I yelled, told him how to fuck me right, instead of whatever BS that was at the party last night. I'm not sure he took it well."

Hollywood's dark little laugh played havoc with my curiosity. "Maybe he'll surprise you?"

I chuckled, backing up. This was definitely flirting, but I really did have to get back, and putting some space between Hollywood and my libido seemed like a good idea. "Like I said, I don't like surprises."

"I'll remember that."

"You gonna stalk me some more, Hollywood?"

He mock-frowned. "I might."

Laughing, I turned away before whatever this was pulled me right back to him. It was time to face the music, but at least I didn't feel as lost as I had when I'd started on my walk. Hollywood showing up might have had something to do with that.

6

Detective Inspector Olivia Barnes came out of 16a with her nose buried in her phone, narrowly avoiding a collision with me. On reflex, I apologized. So did she. We both chuckled shallow laughs and then recognition sparked in her blue eyes.

"It's John, right?" Swapping her phone to her left hand, she thrust out her right to shake.

"Dom, actually." We shook. Her firm fingers gripped mine with feeling. "Only my mum calls me John," I said, trotting out the same explanation I told everyone.

Dark pixie-cut hair framed an oval face that should have made her cute, but her height gave her presence, and the way she held herself—upright and confident— spoke of someone familiar with giving orders and having them obeyed. Fine lines gave her age away as over forty. She must have turned some top brass heads to make DI before her fifties.

"Alexander's mentioned you." Her smile suggested

the mentions were mostly good. "You must be getting used to civilian life now? What's it been, two years?"

"Time flies," I hedged, stepping into the hallway.

"Nice to meet you, John."

"Dom."

"Of course." A tightness gathered those fine lines at the corners of her eyes, thinning her gaze. But her attention soon dropped back to her phone and she power walked her way back down Cecil Court, disappearing into the flow of tourists.

More recently, the DI had begun to drop by, coming and going from Kempthorne's top floor apartment where they had their *meetings*. I figured there was more to their relationship than just the professional. It would explain how Kempthorne & Co often wriggled out of the Met's clutches when other agencies got bogged down with endless paperwork.

Robin had closed the shop and pulled down the roller blinds, blocking the view of the street. With five minutes to go before Kempthorne showed up, I browsed the shelves of rare books, keeping an eye out for any psychic tickle at the back of my senses. Books were always around people, and people were the main source of psychic burns that caused artifacts. Especially used books. They sometimes took on souls of their own. Maybe that was the connection between Kempthorne & Co and books? Or maybe he just liked books?

Kempthorne joined us right on time at three, carrying a tray of biscuits, a pot of tea, and a stack of cups. None of the cups matched, and he spilt the milk as he set the tray down on a coffee table in the middle of four shabby-chic armchairs.

"Jammie Dodgers!" Gina tore at the packet of biscuits like a latent trying to get to an artifact. Her prize secured between her fingers, she flopped into a chair. Robin took a seat and immediately poured us all tea, then produced a sealed letter addressed to me and stamped with the Institute of Registered Latents seal. The sight of the IRL logo always ran icy fingers down my spine.

I folded the envelope into my trouser pocket. Nothing needed to be said. Inside the envelope would be a politely worded letter inviting me to my annual competency check-up, followed by a warning that if I didn't attend, I'd be fined and sent away for re-education, then maybe thrown in psych prison. Nice.

Kempthorne poured all of his impressive six-feet-something height into a flower-print armchair, with a hint of a smile lifting his lips. He gestured for me to take a seat.

"Before we begin, there is a very important matter I wish to discuss," Robin said, setting the tone. I stilled, expecting the bill for the tux. "Who keeps eating all the custard creams? I buy a packet, and the next day, they're gone."

Off the hook for the tux, I shrugged off my coat and laid it over the back of my chair, then noticed the room had gone quiet. Why was everyone looking at me? "What? I don't even like custard creams."

"Well, it's not me," Gina said and nobody bothered to ask Kempthorne since he already had that focused expression that suggested he was deep in thought and our trivial issues were of no concern of his.

I helped myself to a biscuit—a Ginger Nut—and got comfortable. Robin glared. I showed her my biscuit wasn't a custard cream and smiled, then popped the whole biscuit into my mouth. Her eyes narrowed.

"I've kept you all in the dark long enough," Kempthorne began. *This should be interesting.* "The accident last night and the risk to Dom's life were unacceptable. I personally regret I allowed the situation to progress without better preparing all of you, but especially Dom, who I am convinced was the main target of the dirty artifacts on display. Luckily, Dom has exemplary control. Unfortunately another latent did not." As he'd spoken, his gaze skimmed us, lingering on me a little longer. "Dom, you have my sincerest apologies."

Huh. So... I wasn't getting fired? "Thanks."

A brief pause filled the shop, peppered by the occasional muffled laugh or chatter from tourists from outside.

"The Met have tasked us with rooting out a particularly slippery artifact dealer," Kempthorne continued. "DI Barnes had asked that we keep our involvement as low-key as possible, but after last night, that cat is out of the bag."

"That's why you had me set up all those evening dinners in Chelsea?" Robin asked, leaning forward.

"Unlicensed auctions in the guise of dinner parties, yes. Someone well-connected is buying an alarming number of artifacts at these auctions, using proxies to bid."

"You think Hollywood is one of these proxies?" I asked.

"That's my suspicion, yes. We haven't retrieved Gareth Clarke's lost artifact and Kage Mitchell has been a conspicuous presence at multiple auctions."

"Hollywood?" Robin asked.

I filled her in on everything we knew about Kage Mitchell, which wasn't much. He showed up on my job, killed my target, and probably got away with the artifact, plus he liked to schmooze at auctions with Kempthorne's posh-lot. He's prominent in the artifact-trading world, making a name for himself by charming all the knickers off the ladies. And he'd saved me from getting blown to bits. I left out the part where I'd met him for a chat in the park less than an hour ago.

"DI Barnes has confirmed that whoever has likely hired Mister Mitchell is running circles around the Met and quite literally getting away with murder. Murder Squad is on Gareth Clarke's untimely demise, but their case is hampered by lack of a murder weapon, and Dom being the only witness to an *American*."

"C'mon, nobody in the bar saw Hollywood charge after Gareth Clarke?"

"No."

More like the cops hadn't bothered to follow up on any witnesses. "Typical. The Met aren't going to give two shits about a dead latent anyway."

"That is unfortunately an accurate assessment," Kempthorne agreed.

"Is the person behind buying the artifacts new to London?"

"No." Kempthorne sighed, stirred his tea, but left it on the table and leaned back in his chair. "I've been aware of someone in the background of a few high-end auctions for several years. An anonymous figure with very deep pockets. They're extremely careful to remain unidentified. Lately, they've upped their game and their budget.

But trying to root out any information on them is proving to be impossible. Joanna was my best lead."

And Joanna was very dead.

I leaned in and set my cup down on the table, tea untouched. "You think they got wind you were onto them and had Joanna killed?"

"I think they deliberately planted that dirty artifact out in the open, knowing exactly what would happen. The dirty artifact was meant for you, as a clear message for us to back off. They likely weren't aware of the unregistered latent among the invited."

Robin snorted. "When have we ever backed off?"

"Exactly." Kempthorne smiled, and it was sly rather than friendly. "There is no better way of having me fully invested in stopping them than threatening my agents. I won't stand for it. Now it's personal. Robin, I want you to go back through everything we know about Gareth Clarke. Take another look at his movements. He got the artifact from somewhere. There will be a trail to follow."

Robin nodded. "On it, boss."

"Gina, there's an auction happening Friday night in Covent Garden. Our target will likely be bidding, and it's a stone's throw from here. I've emailed you the details. I want to know every inch of the location, every back door, basement window, and every camera. Find out who is visiting the premises and why. I've also emailed you everything I know about the auctioneer, a Mister Devi Ahuja, a property developer who fancies himself an artifact dealer. Liaise with Robin and find out where Mister Ahuja lives, where he buys his coffee, everything about the man."

This was what I needed. A real case. Something to get

my teeth into. My heart tripped over itself at the thought of tracking down this bastard whose actions were killing latents. Like the rush from heading out on an op, tooled up and with a good team at my back. Doing something, action. Purpose. There was nothing like that feeling.

Kempthorne's intense gaze fell to me. Yes, give it to me. I grinned. Bring it on. Anything. I was chomping at the bit.

"A word upstairs?"

Ah. Not what I'd been expecting.

He stood, told Gina and Robin to proceed, and vanished out of the door. I stared after him. Upstairs wasn't good. I'd never been invited *upstairs*. Upstairs was Kempthorne's loft apartment. None of us went up there. It was his patch. Maybe I was getting fired, after all.

Gina cast me a sympathetic look, as though she knew I was walking to my own funeral. Robin had already left the shop floor and would be in position behind her computer screen, feverishly tapping the keys to dig out all the dirt on the auctioneer.

"I guess I'll be right back." The threadbare carpet on the stairs should have been replaced years ago and the pendant bulbs were all grimy, casting a grim yellow light on my ascent to the attic. He wouldn't have made a point of apologizing only to then sack me, right? Although, it could have all been for show. Make it appear as though he cared when in reality, he just wanted the latent off his team.

I counted the thirteen steps up and knocked.

Kempthorne opened the door and quickly returned to the spread of papers covering every inch of a glass-top dining table straddling a vast open-plan kitchen and lounge area. Steel and glass sparkled beneath long, stylish loft lights. Exposed timber beams and brick gave the place a back-to-basics no-nonsense feel that was Kempthorne to the bone. Velux windows let in London's shifting light and one tiny dormer window peeked out over Cecil Court. It was all too easy to imagine Kempthorne seated in the chair by the window, book in hand as London's moods passed by outside.

"I won't keep you," he said. "I know you have an appointment at the Science Museum soon."

"I've got time." I drifted toward the table. No way was I missing the opportunity to see inside Kempthorne's place or to get a glimpse of exactly what he was doing when he disappeared up here.

"You're new to the team." He scooped up multiple forms and documents. A few color prints caught my eye. A blonde girl, young, mid-teens, full of smiles, surrounded by three smiling Labradors. She looked familiar but before I could place her, Kempthorne swept everything into a heap and rustled it all into a tight pile. "Two years next Wednesday?" he asked.

"Is it?" I bloody knew it was. I'd marked the date in my phone's calendar. Two whole years. I'd expected it to last no more than two months.

"Keeping you in the dark regarding the case wasn't personal," he said. "I had to be certain you were trustworthy."

I frowned. "Have I given you reason not to trust me?"

"You don't trust easily?" He stilled and straightened, hearing more in my tone than I'd meant to reveal.

Had Gina mentioned my failed military op to him?

"I've trusted the wrong people in the past. So, no, I don't trust easily."

"Neither do I."

"Then we're on the same page."

He hesitated again and setting the stack of papers aside, he leaned against the table and sighed. "You should know there are elements to this case I am deliberately keeping from you. Again, it's not personal. It's just..." He stroked his chin, scratching over a shadow of whiskers. "Just not yet."

"Okay. You're the boss. I don't expect to know everything, just the things that might get me blown to bits."

He chuckled, lightening the mood. "Well, I'll be sure to keep you abreast of future explosive situations."

"You're expecting more?"

"Just know I trust you, Dom, within my own personal limits." His slippery smile had me feeling as though I was always a step behind him. "And I hope you feel you can trust me in return."

Kempthorne trustworthy? Everything about him was a mystery. He came and went as he pleased, leaving us in the dark most of the time. He sometimes rocked up at 2am, disheveled and glassy-eyed. His moods shifted like London's weather, sometimes dark and stormy, sometimes bright and carefree. But with the cases, with us, with everything Kempthorne & Co, I *did* trust him. The rest of his life was his own personal business. "I do trust you, actually. With work."

He sighed. "Good. That's good. Oh, and I want you all over Kage. He'll make a mistake and you'll be there to catch it."

"He's all mine." A little too much glee leaked through

my grin.

He nodded, smiling with me. The seconds turned to minutes and the quiet began to stretch thin. "Right. You'd best get to the museum then."

I headed for the door. "Oh, I meant to ask..." He looked up from his stack of papers and that infuriating lock of hair flopped over his eye. "At the dinner, you said something about money not making a man good. What was that all about?"

Kempthorne's real smile melted all the leftover ice in his glare. "I simply meant you're worth more than any man there and you needn't have felt uncomfortable."

"Right, okay. Uh huh." For some inexplicable reason, I laughed. Maybe because his words were doing odd things to my insides. What did any of what he'd just said *mean*? It was nothing, right? Just posh talk. "Er thanks." *Christ, kill me now.* "And er. I was out of line. With the thing. That I said. About the er—" I waved helplessly, clutching at words that wouldn't come.

"Yes, well, so was I—out of line. So we'll call it even."

His soft smile rewired my brain and short-circuited my thoughts-to-mouth processing, leaving me speechless. That smile was a different breed to the one he'd tossed around the party, like this man was very different to the one who had schmoozed his way through that upper-class crowd. He'd been adamant those people weren't his friends, as though it was important to him that I know that. As though he... despised that part of himself.

Two years, and I'd thought I knew how Alexander Kempthorne worked, but the more I discovered about him, the more mysterious he became.

t museum.
Back at 7.
I'll pick up Chinese?

I hit send on the text to Gina and wandered about the plush little office, full of stuffed animals—not the cute kind—and posters declaring climate change was the next mass extinction event and reminding latents to *Get Registered! For your own good!* What it didn't shout about was the IRL's small print that urged anyone to *call this number & report suspicious latent activity!* Subtle.

The curator's assistant, a dour man who grunted two-syllable words, had left me rattling around the office unsupervised five minutes ago.

Doors slammed somewhere in the museum's many corridors, most of them empty now the museum was closed for the night.

My phone pinged a message:
Special chow mein,

Robin says n e thing hot.

K will be back. Get him crispy duck.

I snorted a laugh—of course Kempthorne wanted duck. He probably shot them at the weekends.

The door opened and a stocky man carrying a mahogany box entered. He shuffled about trying to close the door behind him and breezed to the desk, where he put the box down and stepped back, eyeing it warily. He wasn't a small guy either. His suit jacket wrapped around big shoulders. Dark skin gleamed under the pale office lights. He'd make good money with that body as a doorman in Soho, just so long as nobody brought an intriguing wooden box. His anxiety would have been amusing if we weren't dealing with an artifact.

"Hi." I offered my hand. "Dom. Kempthorne and Co."

"Er, yes. Doctor Anthony Taylor." His hand was warm as he took mine, keeping an eye on the box the whole time. "Thank you for coming. We get them sometimes. Usually they're dug up from the archives. Overlooked for years, you know?" He waved at the box, still maintaining a safe distance. He clearly believed whatever was inside was genuine. I was about to ask more when he plowed on, explaining, "It came like that. In the box, I mean. And we have a couple of latents on the staff—that's how we knew to call you. Can't be too careful." He pointed at one of the posters on the wall behind the desk, declaring any unidentified packages or containers should be treated with caution and an agency contacted for retrieval. Here I was.

I studied the box. Leather-clad with thick latches. Old, well-travelled. With a single embossed letter gleamed on the lid. *M.* "Have you opened it?"

"I'd rather not."

So he hadn't seen inside. "How did it arrive exactly?"

"Security found it in the main concourse after closing two days ago. We tried the cameras, to see who had left it, but the footfall was busy. Could have been any one of several thousand. We're lucky a latent didn't fall over it."

Leaving an artifact out in the open was reckless, or malicious, like leaving a bomb in a public place. If someone had wanted it gone, they only had to call an agency. The chance of anyone setting it down and forgetting it was also slim.

The box was its own problem. Whatever was inside could be too weak to emit any kind of heat, but my instincts told me the box's lining was keeping it muffled.

"Do you mind if I leave you to it?" The doctor hurried toward the door. "Just to be safe."

"Sure. I'll handle it. Just wait outside and I'll be right out." The door clicked shut behind him, leaving me alone with the box and its unknown artifact. If the artifact had already been exposed, I could have mentally prepared myself. But opening boxes or containers was never fun.

Surprises.

I hated them.

"Okay, baby." Reaching toward the box's twin latches, I flexed my fingers. "It's just you and me." First, I had to authenticate it as an actual artifact and not junk. Then I'd bundle it back up and take it back to the office for disposal, or, if it was dirty, I'd call in the non-latent clean-up crews who dealt with the real dangerous shit. The artifacts even I couldn't handle.

This was easy. I'd done it for years, removing artifacts

from the military playing field. Like bomb disposal. There was nothing to it.

Flick.

The latches clicked open under my thumbs.

Wetting my lips, I breathed, settling my heart and mind, just like the military had taught me. It was all about control. Just so long as I was in control and calm, my emotions neatly tucked away, I could withstand almost any psychic blast.

I flicked the lid open. Inside lay a bed of red velvet and... nothing. The box was empty. "What the—"

The door lock clunked.

Abandoning the empty box, I dashed for the door and tried the handle. It didn't budge. "Hey!" Banging a fist against it didn't help. Nobody came.

Doors didn't lock themselves. Someone wanted me in there. Why? I backed away from the door and scanned the room again. Nothing screamed a threat. It was just a stuffy office. So why go to the trouble of getting me here only to lock me in with an empty box?

Museum gone tits up, I texted Gina. *Locked in office.*

My phone rang.

"You're what?" Gina asked, sounding pissed that her dinner was going to be late.

"There's no artifact. The meeting was a setup. I'm locked in a back office."

"Why?"

"I don't know." I pinched the phone between my chin and shoulder. "Wait. Give me a sec. I have an idea." Sliding a simmering card from my charged deck, I ran it down the door seal. Smoke sizzled off the wood. The card got hung up on the lock. Pouring more trick through my fingers, it buzzed brighter, fighting through the metal.

"I've got it," I told Gina. "Doctor Taylor is about to—"

A pen rolled under the door and bumped against my shoe. One of those old, nibbed fountain pens, missing its lid. The entire world and my place in it narrowed to a single, mesmerizing point. The pen. I sucked in a breath, heard Gina call my name from somewhere far away.

Somewhere inside a small voice warned me to back away slowly. Get as far away from the pen as possible. Leave the fucking building, if I could. But a much larger part of me *really* wanted to pick up that glossy black pen and caress it close.

Artifact.

So... pretty.

Dirty.

"Shit," I whispered.

"What is it?" Gina demanded. *"What's going on?"*

Tiny little thing. Pretty little thing. Twisted pretty thing. I just had to pick it up and I'd never have to follow orders again. Wouldn't need to rely on others. No more worry. No more temptation. Just pick it up and everything would be easy. It was what I was meant to do... Like, destiny?

"Dom!—Robin, call Kempthorne—"

I hung up the phone, slipped it into my pocket, and stepped back. The light from my sizzling card licked along the pen's casing. Maybe it wouldn't hurt me. I could just pick it up, try it on for size. No harm done. Withdrawing my trick from the cards, the light snuffed out. I casually returned them to my pocket, crouched, and stretched trembling fingers toward the pen.

My mobile rang.

My fingers twitched an inch from the pen. *Grab it.* I could light up London like New Year's Eve.

The mobile's ringing grew shrill, incessantly poking at my mind, trying to distract me from this very important thing. Then the ringing cut off, and the silence was bliss. Yes, nobody had to know. I could just scoop it up and listen to its secrets. And it had many. I could already feel them trying to escape through me. Trying to be heard. They'd been silent for so long. It *needed* me.

The door rattled on its hinges. Someone was trying to get in. They would stop me. I couldn't allow it.

My fingers skimmed the pen's casing, igniting a blast of mind-fizzing power. I wrapped my fingers around it. More power bloomed through my skin, into my hand. *Christ, yes.* The thing was singing to me, demanding to be released. I could do that; I could set it free and have it all. The door rattled again, then boomed. Wood splintered. *No, no, no, they can't have it!* I whirled away, searching for somewhere to hide even as the power burned through every bone in my body, lighting me up from the inside out. I was made for this. The pen was mine!

Someone hit me like a truck, slamming me into the shelf. The stuffed animals in their glass cages rattled. One toppled, smashing across the floor.

Hands swooped in and grabbed mine, still clutching the pen. *Oh, hell no. It was mine!* A snarling mouth and fierce amber eyes came between me and the pen—Hollywood—then his fist came up and smacked me evenly between the eyes. I rocked backward, sprawling. Fingers levered open my fist and the pen was gone—yanking out its power and taking half my strength with it. I staggered upright, breathless, trembling, recoiling from the horror of what I'd almost surrendered to. *Shit, shit, shit.* Control. I'd lost it. Completely.

I couldn't be here.

I couldn't be near it.

I bolted out of the door and down the corridor. The need to go back, to retrieve the pen, to grab Hollywood and wrap my hands around his throat—it tried to turn me on my heel. Urges and desires split me in two. *Run! Go back!*

Outside the museum, in cool air, I slumped against a wall. Tilting my head up, cold, wet rain kissed my hot face. My heart was trying to pound its way through my ribs, but it was slowing. So were my breaths. *Just breathe.* I had this... The pen was gone. Everything was under control. *Breathe and push the madness away.*

My phone rang. Maybe it hadn't stopped ringing. I dragged it from my pocket. *Kempthorne.* Shit. "I'm good —" I croaked into it.

"I'm on my way," the boss growled. In the background the Lexus growled too.

"It's fine. Don't. I'm fine. Really. Just startled. I don't have it anymore."

Hollywood burst through the museum doors. Hands empty. Did he have the artifact on him? In his coat pockets? He saw my sudden, frantic gaze and slowed, expecting me to jump him for all the wrong reasons. I wanted to. Maybe for the right reasons too. Shit, my head was a mess.

"—Dom?" Kempthorne growled again.

"I'm all right, okay?"

Hollywood descended the steps slowly, eying me like

someone eyes a predator. He showed me his empty hands. He'd dealt with twitchy latents before. Probably had trained for it. Slow and steady. No sudden movements.

Just breathe.

"Come into the office," Kempthorne said. "Dom?"

"I will. I am." Christ, what was I saying? I had to focus. "It's all good. I'll see you at the shop." I hung up before he could argue and straightened as Hollywood approached, plastering my back against the cold, hard wall. "If you have it on you, don't come another step."

He lifted his hands. "I tossed it. I don't have it. You'd sense if I did, right?"

The artifact had to be dealt with. But not by me. I winced, rubbed at the bridge of my nose, and messaged Gina to send a cleanup crew to the museum. *Dirty artifact.* She immediately texted an *okay* back and said she'd deal with it. I turned my phone off and lifted my gaze to Hollywood, who now stood close enough to absorb all my wandering thoughts. We glared. Him judging. Me accusing.

"Did you see anyone inside?" I asked.

"Anyone *like...*?"

"Shit, I dunno. Acting suspiciously? Like they'd just fucking tried to kill me."

"No, but I was focused on stopping you."

Ugh. I couldn't think. But I did know Hollywood had just stopped me from having an even worse evening. "How'd you find me?"

He pulled a face. "I may have been following you."

I snorted. "Creepy. But thanks."

He huffed a laugh, then without saying a word, he

hailed a passing cab. I could have argued, could have walked off, should have waited for the cleanup team to arrive and gone back to Cecil Court to face the boss, but I got in the cab instead and rode with Hollywood in silence toward the sparkling glass-clad high-rises of Canary Wharf.

8

We didn't speak in the cab. What was I going to say? How I was a fucking idiot who couldn't control that mammalian part of my brain that wanted to destroy everything I got my hands on. I should have been better. I was *trained* to be better. But the damn pen had taken me by surprise. Whoever had rolled it under the door had known it would. I'd let my guard down. Rookie mistake.

The cab pulled up outside a shiny new-build apartment block in Docklands, with large windows overlooking what had once been bustling docks in the Victorian times but was now a square "lake" surrounded by painted steel cranes, more art than function. Docklands used to be the beginnings of the old East End, and back in the 90s it was an abandoned industrial eyesore. A shit-ton of money later and some lucrative tax incentives had turned London's Docklands into a swish, modern playground for business meetings, exhibitions, and waterfront apartment complexes.

I followed Hollywood through an apartment building's bright, echoing foyer, into a mirrored elevator. The glass reflected the guilt on my face from multiple angles.

The numbers above the door counted up. What the fuck was I even doing here?

"You okay?" he drawled, so American.

I was supposed to say I was fine, it was nothing. But that would have been a lie and I didn't much feel like lying to the man who had just saved me from potentially blowing the science museum to smithereens. Or, at the very least, causing a whole lot of shit for Kempthorne to clean up.

"Yeah, I'm okay."

Neither of us believed it.

Hollywood's pretty face gathered a frown. "When was the last time something like that happened?"

"Military. In training. You learn your limits real quick in Psy Ops." *Or you die,* I added, unspoken.

The elevator still climbed, taking its sweet time. Where the fuck were we going, Narnia? I tapped my fingers against my thigh. Crackling tension was palpable. Everything he'd seen back at the museum, he must have thought me one twitch away from the unhinged latents I helped talk down. That kind of fuck up would get me unregistered—Hollywood could report me. It'd be his word against mine, but as I was the latent, nobody would believe me.

Fuck.

I shouldn't have come. Hollywood had leverage over me. He was neck-deep in Kempthorne's case and I was not in the right headspace for any of this shit. "I should probably go—"

Hollywood stepped closer, bringing my thoughts to a sudden stop. I straightened, hand dropping toward my cards. Those amber eyes gave me a head-to-toe once-over, like he was deciding which prime cut to devour first.

"I can think of a way to take your mind off it all."

A small sensible voice in my head told me to shut him down before everything got more complicated.

"I don't think—"

His fingers skimmed my cheek, tempting me closer until there was nothing between us but my crumbling doubts. "So don't," he whispered against my lips, then chased those words by teasing his mouth over mine, inviting, not forcing.

There was a moment where I could have pushed him off and resisted, but it came and went, and then I had his coat in my fists and my tongue down his throat. He shoved, slamming me back against a mirrored wall, rattling the elevator. Suddenly, he was everywhere, plastered against me, his knee between my thighs—pinning, claiming—a hand on my chest, holding me still, the other at my neck, thumb caressing. It wasn't a kiss, more of a desperate clash of mouths. I leaned into him, fighting his mouth with mine, tasting mint. Lips and tongues met and swept. And somewhere in all of this was the realization that I should go back to Cecil Court where I'd face a thousand questions. I should report my own indiscretion like a good, well-behaved latent. But fuck that. Hollywood was kissing me and I needed more.

The lift doors swept open, spilling us into an empty corridor. Hollywood grabbed my hand and hauled me to a shiny black apartment door, then slammed me against it and attacked my mouth mercilessly. Fuck, he was hot and everywhere and desperate—or maybe that was me.

He broke the kiss, unlocked the door, and in a few steps we were inside. The lights stayed off, painting an open-plan apartment in shades of grey. Big windows framed a sparkling London. I might have appreciated it more if Hollywood hadn't been drawing me to him like gravity.

He ran his hands over my shoulders, shucking off my coat and trapping my arms at my sides, keeping me from touching him while his hot mouth branded my neck. The man was intense, like a raging wildfire burning every-thing it touched. And Christ, I needed it. Needed *him*. I had a hand on his chest, feeling his every breath heave while soaking up his heat.

He tugged at my belt, pulling off the agency ID badge with a wicked grin. Now he'd freed my arms, I marched him back and pinned him against a cupboard in the kitchen area. His smile dared me to take it further. I clasped his throat loosely with my right hand, holding him still, and parted his lips with mine, sweeping my tongue in. He shuddered and moaned for more and when I didn't oblige, his pretty eyes flicked open and fixed on me. In the dark, those eyes shone all their demands.

This wasn't a romance. It was two men trying to fuck away a whole lot of complicated shit, no strings attached. And I was there for it.

The storm that was Hollywood's lust lulled. I hovered my mouth over his, just out of reach, and as I held him back, he attempted to nip and close the gap, trying to steal a new kiss. A slight snarl pulled at his lips. He didn't like to wait.

I wet my lips, secretly reveling in the way he watched my tongue. Fuck, the sudden rush of lust was one thing, but this moment of calm before the storm broke again was so fucking hot that I was having a hard time thinking around my throbbing cock.

His leg hooked around mine and yanked, rocking me off balance. In a whirl, he grabbed my wrist, shoved it down, and twisted it, pirouetting me in some fancy move I hadn't seen coming.

I buckled under him and found myself bent over the island countertop. "Ugh, fuck."

Hollywood locked my arm behind my back and ground his stiff rod against my arse, prompting a hungry groan to bubble up my throat. *Christ, yes.*

He loosened his fingers on my wrist and whispered in my ear, "I almost wish I was a top."

Bottom, top, I was game for anything. I did prefer to bottom, but only with serious lovers, which others had taken advantage of in the past, assuming I'd lie back and take a railing. "We're not there yet, Hollywood."

He sucked my ear between his teeth, then nipped hard, igniting a dart of pain that turned into pleasure and went straight to my balls. "That name."

"You don't like it? Hadn't noticed." I twisted, trying to get a look at him, and sure enough, his face had turned even more intense in the moody, unlit apartment. Like maybe sex or murder was on the cards. A skittering thrill tightened my chest and surged lust through my veins.

He ran his free hand up my back, under my shirt, fingers skimming my spine, then flipped direction and headed south, around my arse, sinking his fingers into my pants to find his prize. Or was it my prize? Because the second his touch skimmed my cock, I lost all ability to think. Hard and aching, I'd leaked enough for him to slide his fingers freely. Now I was the one moaning for more and he obliged, tightening his hold, working my shaft.

"You don't like to lose control." The breathless words fluttered over my ear.

His hand delivered strokes of pleasure that had me half out of my mind, but I wasn't too far gone to let him have his way. I'd been working my free arm under me and levered up, forcing him to stumble back. I turned, braced a hand either side on the countertop, and arched an eyebrow, daring him to come back for more. His gaze dropped to my exposed cock. His smile twitched and he sauntered away, shrugging his coat from his shoulders to dump it over a chair in the lounge area.

He wasn't going to be baited and this might have been the hottest game of cat and mouse I'd ever played. Only there were two cats here, and both of us would probably get hurt.

Standing in the middle of the room, he worked at his shirt buttons, backlit by the nighttime skyline. The bastard knew how gorgeous he was. Where he had a swimmer's physique, I had muscle enough to march over there, scoop him up, dump him onto his back on the couch, and fuck him with his cock in my hand until he came all over himself.

His mobile rang, buzzing inside his coat pocket. He cut the thing a glare as though he'd toss it out of the window in the next second. "Shit, I have to take it."

I shrugged and leaned against the island. Whoever was on the end of that line better be having a life-or-death crisis.

"Kage," he answered, voice flat as he turned away. "Now? All right."

I used the distraction to examine my surroundings. The large, open space was all lines and edges. No personal touches. No framed photos or prints. The place was bland, like a hotel room. Temporary. He wasn't staying in London for long, at least not in this apartment.

"On my way," he said and hung up.

Ah. Our hate-fuck was over.

He cast me a frown before collecting his coat and sauntering over. "Sorry, English." He cupped my face in his warm hand and ran his thumb across my bottom lip before placing the next words there. "Places to be."

"People to kill?"

He hesitated. Maybe my comment had hit a sore spot. His mouth smothered mine, his tongue thrust in, and he was kissing me like this was his last night on earth. All push and pull, full of desperation and need. Sensing he was about to withdraw, I thrust a hand in his hair and kissed him back, unleashing some of my own frayed frustration at having this—whatever it was—brought to an end before it had properly begun.

The kiss soon ended. He bumped his forehead against mine, eyes peering deep into my soul, saying things without words, then he pulled from my grasp. "Leave when you like. The door will lock behind you." And with that cold goodbye, he left.

In the quiet that followed, it took a few moments to brush off the tingling lust and try to bundle my thoughts back into some reasonable order. All right, so I was here, in his apartment, with his permission. He knew who I worked for, and he'd still left me alone. So, snooping through his things seemed like a reasonable course of action.

He lived alone. I learned that much. One plate in the dishwasher, along with a single wine glass and single set of cutlery. The takeout boxes in the bin suggested he didn't cook. His bathroom was neat and tidy, with everything in its place. The bed was made, sheets tucked in. It was all so ridiculously plain it could have been staged. Or he had somewhere else, some other place where he was himself. Because this apartment wasn't a home.

Rummaging through the bedside drawers revealed a notebook with a few cryptic letters and numbers scribbled inside. I flicked through the pages, snapping a few pics with my phone, and then saw my name in Hollywood's tight, neat handwriting. *John Domenici. Military PO 384. Medical discharge. Why? AK & Joanna Devere. M? Clarke = mule. AK knows?*

AK was clearly Kempthorne. PO stood for Psy Ops, the elite team I'd been a part of until the military booted me out. Joanna was the dead woman from the auction. But what was M? Hollywood seemed to think Clarke was a mule—someone used to ferry illegal artifacts around London, which would explain how he'd gotten an artifact. I snapped pics of his notes and immediately sent them to Gina.

Was Hollywood doing his own investigating? What if he wasn't working for the top man? What if, like us, he was trying to figure out who the top man was? Or maybe I was clutching at straws because he'd saved my arse multiple times and kissed like a fucking dream.

My phone pinged.

G: *Where are you? Are you okay?*

It was time to face the team.

9

By the time I'd retuned to Cecil Court it was too late to talk about work. Gina let me in and told me the debrief could wait. I showered, fell into bed, and slept like the dead. The next morning, Gina and I met for breakfast at our favorite little café—The Rouge —a few minutes' walk from the shop. Neutral ground.

"The real Doctor Anthony Taylor was found tied up in a storage room," she said around a mouthful of breakfast muffin. "He didn't see who attacked him."

So the man I'd spoken to in the science museum's office wasn't nervous because of the box and its potential contents, he'd been nervous because he wasn't supposed to be there. "And the empty box?"

"He has no knowledge of it, apparently."

The whole thing was a set-up. "CCTV?"

"Kempthorne and Inspector Barnes are on it."

They'd see Hollywood on that footage, and me losing my shit. I frowned out of the café window at the passersby. The sun made our little corner of London gleam. It looked surreal. Life went on regardless of all my personal shit.

Kempthorne had grilled me that morning. *Where was I, why did I have my phone off, they had needed me at the museum to find the artifact. I'd neglected my duties as an agent.* And I'd gotten a double dose of Kempthorne glare, which had made part of my soul shrivel.

"Someone lured you there, hoping you'd go nuclear," Gina said.

"It was close, G." I hadn't revealed how close. Kempthorne probably suspected from my tailspin afterward. "Like, really close." Like maybe I should reschedule my Institute of Registered Latents competency appointment to next week, just in case this was the beginning of a slippery slope toward latent sickness. I didn't want to go out like that. Half mad and crowing about the voices, until finally succumbing to an artifact's deadly allure. Those latents, the ones I tried to help, they were victims. Long ago, in another life, I'd vowed never to be a victim again.

"It wasn't your fault."

It would have been if Hollywood hadn't slapped me about enough to get the pen free.

"Hey, you're here now, right?" She grinned, and with her, in the sunshine, and the sounds and smells of the café, everything did feel better. "So…" she crooned. "You were in Kage Mitchell's apartment? He just let you in, huh?" She lifted her mocha cup to her lips and raised her eyebrows.

"Yes, exactly," I said. "He let me right in, then left, so I could rummage through his sock drawer. Was there anything useful in the pics I sent?"

"M might refer to the M on the box?"

I'd wondered the same, but it was a longshot. There were plenty of Ms in London. "Maybe."

"What do you think he meant by *AK knows*?"

I shrugged. "Maybe he thinks Kempthorne is on to him—which he is."

She sipped her hot drink before setting it down and frowning at me. "Kage was right about something. Gareth Clarke was a mule. I hacked into his social media account —he used his kids' names as a password. He checked in all over London, in weird places, like the meat markets, then he'd show up around Chelsea around the same time Robin has been booking Kempthorne out of the office at one of his *special dinners*—AKA illegal auctions—and Clarke was getting in trouble at work for showing up late. My guess? He was spiraling." A spiraling latent was someone losing control of their trick. On the slippery slope to latent sickness.

"Or someone was turning the thumb screws, scaring him."

"A mule is dangerous work for a latent. Why not hire a non-latent to move artifacts? Seems counterintuitive. You don't give a crack addict cocaine to distribute."

I blinked at her analogy. "Know much about cocaine, do you?"

She beamed. "I saw it on Line of Duty."

She was right, though. Employing a latent to ferry artifacts around London was asking for trouble. Nobody would do that unless they had another reason to scare the man. "Maybe it was personal. Like Gareth Clarke owed this anonymous buyer something? I bet the top man *knew* Gary. He could be somewhere in Gary's file."

"Maybe I should look for Ms in Gary's file?"

It was a lead, albeit a slim one. "And look for any crossover between Gareth Clarke and Kage Mitchell. Maybe that hit was personal too?"

"So, you slept with the sexy American assassin then?"

Dammit. *"No."* I'd smiled before I could stop myself.

"Oh my God." She almost dropped her muffin. *"You did!"*

"No, I didn't." I straightened, trying to find the moral high ground. Somehow it always eluded me. "Technically, that's not what happened."

She nodded. "Oh, I get it. *Technically* he's gorgeous though. The pair of you? His body, your eyes. Ugh. But the intel we dug up on him says he's dating some daytime TV presenter. Kage Mitchell is as straight as an arrow, *apparently*." She leaned into that last word.

I chuckled, remembering all too easily how Hollywood had tasted and exactly how his lips had felt on mine. Then there was the hard press of his cock. "He's definitely *not* straight."

"Sweetie, with your looks, you can bend anyone is all I'm saying."

"Yeah, well, it's for the job."

"Just make sure it stays that way. Or just don't tell Robin."

I winced. "Didn't plan to."

Her warm face got all soppy with sympathy. "I don't want to see you hurt."

There was no danger of that. I'd been there before, and it wasn't happening again. Ever. "Thanks, but I've got it. I appreciate it though."

"Hey, we all care about you. Even Kempthorne, though he's rubbish at showing it. You're one of us."

"Like a cult?" Not many people had cared in my life. I wasn't sure what to do with the strange sensation of knowing I might have actual friends.

She laughed loud and free, reminding me that some days, the sun did shine and there were good people left who still looked out for one another.

Over the next few days, Robin built a dossier on the auctioneer and Friday's imminent auction, while Gina staked out the premises, feeding all the intel back to Kempthorne tucked away in Cecil Court's basement. I didn't want to push my luck with Hollywood and stayed away from his apartment, ignoring the urge to drop by. Robin's search had been extended to encompass Kage Mitchell, which made for some interesting reading material while I waited for Friday to roll around.

Thursday night, with the Chinese I'd promised finally ordered and delivered, the team sat around the kitchen table, scooping food out of plastic trays to fill our plates. Kempthorne had rolled his sleeves up and even had a cool beer open. Gina was spinning a tale about a party she'd once been to where the cops showed up and had been mistaken for strippers. I chipped in with a few rowdy Psy Ops stories, making out I missed the life, when I didn't. The missions—I missed their buzz, but not the politics behind them.

Talk soon turned to business, with Robin briefing us on the property developer-turned-auctioneer, Devi

Ahuja. Kempthorne warned the auction on Friday was more professional than the cozy dinner we'd attended on Monday. Security would be visible and tight. Which meant we were less likely to get caught in an artifact blast.

"It's taken me months to get to this level," he said, leaning back in the chair.

Months of selling artifacts we'd retrieved on the side, buying his way up the food chain. We all knew how it worked.

"I'm reconsidering taking you," he said to me.

That killed the mood. "What? If it's because of the museum, I had no time to guard—"

"It's too dangerous."

I almost choked on a laugh. Dangerous? How could I politely put that a Covent Garden auction was a long way from raiding a latent-terrorist cell. "Thanks, but I've been in tougher spots than a dodgy auction."

He reached for his beer. "If someone slips you an artifact, and we don't catch it in time—"

"And I go off like I nearly did at the museum?" I finished for him.

"The museum was a public place," he replied. Still level, still calm. "Whoever planted that artifact meant for you to lose control, taking the museum and the company's good name with you."

And there I was thinking he was concerned for my wellbeing. "And we wouldn't want to risk the company name, would we." My smile was cheap, but he bought it. Gina wouldn't have, which was why I wasn't looking at her. "I can handle an auction. The pen was a sucker punch. I'll be prepared for it this time."

"Joanna's and then the museum? You're clearly seen as the company's weakness—" He jolted and glared at Robin beside him—the source of the under-table kick.

She smiled at him, then switched her smile to me. "I think what Kempthorne is saying is that as one of the very few authenticators in London, and with Kempthorne's notoriety, you're an obvious target."

She meant I was a *liability*. "All the more reason for me to be there. Whoever is trying to threaten us, we can't be seen to be backing off."

"And Hollywood will be there," Gina piped up.

"Speaking of Hollywood—uh, Kage Mitchell." Robin opened her phone and flicked through her photos, then handed it to Kempthorne. He assessed the images and handed the phone to me. The pictures showed Hollywood outside the bar near Friday's auction location, standing around, chatting, smiling, being his charming self. And look at that, he didn't burst into flames in daylight.

"I've clocked him there with his lady friend, the TV presenter, every day," Gina said, sipping her beer.

"That bar is a well-known celebrity haunt," I said.

"And right next to the site of the largest black market artifact auction this side of Christmas," Kempthorne said. "That's no coincidence."

"What if we're looking at this all wrong and he's not working for the top man? What if he's trying to root them out, like we are?" All three of them started at me with various degrees of judgment on their faces. Kempthorne took a drink, probably to hide his sneer. Gina winced, thinking I had some romantic hang-up for Hollywood. At least Robin appeared ready to listen. "He's Agency," I added, "and all right, they do things differently overseas—"

"They don't register latents in the US, they detain them, whether they're stable or not," Kempthorne said with grim finality. "Indefinitely."

"But he's not there, is he? He's in London."

"Because someone is paying him to be here, executing our targets."

Kempthorne wasn't wrong, but he wasn't right either. "If the same person who is trying to take me out is paying Hollywood, I'd be dead, along with a whole lot of other people and the company name." They all believed that, which was concerning. If I'd believed Hollywood wanted me dead or wanted us gone, I wouldn't have climbed into a cab with him or let him wrap his fingers around my cock. There was more to the man than some hired gun, but he hid it well. The records Robin had dug up hadn't helped. He'd started out training to join the FBI, dropped out, bounced between jobs for a while, and then picked up a role in one of the largest agencies in the US. The US branches made English agencies look like kids playing dress-up. But they also had a nasty habit of *accidentally* killing latents when trying to bring them in. Like Hollywood had executed Gareth Clarke.

I needed to get in the man's head, but so far, he'd done a damn fine job of keeping me out and getting into mine.

"Whatever. I'm coming to the auction," I told Kempthorne, flashing him a grin. "You'll have to fire me to stop me."

He smiled back, with some warmth. "That can be arranged, you know?"

"Was that a joke, boss?"

His deeply rich chuckle sounded weird in the small kitchen. I couldn't recall a time I'd ever heard him laugh inside the house. Even Robin looked alarmed.

We cleared the table, loaded the dishwasher, and retrieved all the details and documents we had on the auction and its auctioneer, then combed over them, looking for anything we'd missed. Around eleven, Gina called it a night, with Robin yawning and following soon after, leaving me studying the floorplan of the auction location and Kempthorne reading up on Kage Mitchell's file.

The wall clock ticked and Cecil Court was quiet. A nice kind of quiet, like a heavy quilt lay over London for the night.

"I have the pen," Kempthorne said.

My heart flip-flopped, trying to leap up my throat.

"It's lot five in Friday's auction," he added.

He was selling it. That was his ticket into the auction. He'd probably offered up something else originally, to get him through the door, but the pen was dirtier than any artifact I'd dealt with as a civilian. And that made it desirable. Oh Christ. "All right."

"Can you handle it?" He put the papers down, giving me his full attention, and not for the first time I wished I could read what was going on behind those eyes.

Could I handle it? I'd dealt with worse, but I'd been prepared. "I think so, as long as there are no surprises."

The answer didn't have him relaxing. He continued to peer through me, wanting *more*. Waiting for an explanation.

"At the museum." I sighed. "It was already under my

nose before I had a chance to mentally guard against it. You remember the doorstop incident down at the pub? Like that. If I see it, if I know it's coming, I can handle it, all right? Just don't put it in my pocket." I tried to make a joke of it, but he wasn't smiling.

He rose from the table. "I won't lose another good agent, Dom. Make sure you're prepared."

Wait. What? He'd lost an agent? *When*?

He retreated toward the door and ran a hand through his hair, then threw a soft apologetic smile over his shoulder and left for his loft apartment. Two years and nobody had said a damn word about another agent at Kempthorne & Co.

I'd ask Gina tomorrow. There was no way she'd hide that under direct questioning.

I flicked off the lights and headed to my room.

I'd been up an hour, had showered, and was leaving my room to make breakfast, when the old floorboards creaked behind Gina's door. I knocked, trying not to wake Robin down the hall.

"Who is it?"

"Who do you think it is?" Robin never knocked and the idea that Kempthorne would disturb any of us before ten a.m. was laughable.

Gina opened the door. Bundled up in towels, one on her head and one around her middle, she tossed me her bottle of nail polish. "Do my nails, will you?"

I sat on the edge of her bed while she spread her fingers on the dresser. The last time I'd painted her nails, we'd been about to head out for a wild night in Soho. Over eighteen months later, glitter still glistened in all the shop's crevices.

I waited until she was comfortable, and I'd already painted a nail before asking, "You didn't tell me Kempthorne lost an agent."

She covered the crack in her smile well, but I'd been watching for it. "It was years ago."

"I didn't read anything about it when I started working here." And I'd trawled the corners of the Internet to dig up anything and everything on all three of them. Which was easier said than done. Like me, their pasts were either suspiciously dull, or they'd been professionally careful over the years.

"It wasn't here," she said. "Kempthorne worked for another agency back then. He was maybe, I don't know... early twenties, fresh out of the academy. Good, but cocky. Robin knows all about it."

"But *you* didn't tell me." I focused on painting, keeping a steady hand. "I thought we were tight?"

She pulled the towel off her head with a huff and ruffled her hair, filling the air with the smell of strawberry shampoo.

My attempt to accurately paint her nail slid sideways. "Stay still."

"I am."

"Do you want this nail looking like shit?"

Sulking, she settled back down and sighed. I flicked my gaze up; she frowned and twisted her lips. "It's like this—there are things we don't talk about, okay? Personal lives, for one. It's like a Cecil Court rule."

"You're always sticking your nose into my personal

life," I said lightly while stroking more polish over her nails. She knew: One, I didn't have much of a personal life, and two, we confided in each other anyway.

"Because yours is too interesting."

"And Robin's isn't?"

"Not really. She has family up north, I think. She doesn't talk about them much. She doesn't talk about anything much. I was so relieved when you started here. You have *no* idea."

"And Kempthorne? Why aren't you all up in his face asking who he's dating like you are with me?"

She arched an eyebrow. "Because I'm not an idiot and I like my job."

I chuckled, giving her that one. Kempthorne was about as friendly as a bear trap. "Yeah okay. So, back to the missing agent."

"Oh right, yeah. When did he tell you?"

"Last night. He said he didn't want to lose another agent."

"Oh."

Her tone had me looking up. "What happened?"

"She was a latent. The pair were top of their class at the academy, which for a latent isn't easy."

"Tell me about it." I knew that feeling. Not that I was the top at anything, but trying to swim against the tide was exhausting.

"She got partnered with him, and an op went wrong. I don't know much, just that she got hold of an artifact too hot for her to handle and—" She cut herself off. "I guess you know how it goes."

"No wonder he's twitchy around me." Why had he hired me, knowing that a latent on the staff was a liability? The whole point of the agencies was to suppress and control latents. The more I thought about it, the more his employing me didn't add up. But here I was, painting Gina's nails. Against the odds.

"It's not you. He's just like that." She poked at her bouncy hair. "He cares. And I think he blames himself for what happened to her. He's never said anything, but I just get that... vibe. He quit that agency and started Kempthorne & Co a few months later."

"Was it his fault?"

"I don't know," she said, lowering her voice. "He doesn't talk about it, so we don't talk about it. Okay?"

"Fine." I gestured for her other hand and worked my magic on those five fingernails.

Once they were all painted, she admired them with a grin. "You've got a steady hand. Now let me do yours?"

"Hell no."

She pouted. "But you looked so good with rainbow nails."

I laughed her off before she could attack me with polish and abandoned her to her morning routine. Kempthorne hadn't lost just an agent, he'd lost a latent. Someone he'd known for years. That couldn't have been easy.

Entering the kitchen, I found Kempthorne propped against the countertop in the kitchen, hot coffee in one hand, staring across the room, out of the window. The air smelled faintly of soap and his damp hair had darkened from chestnut to black. He'd swept it back, accentuating all the fine angles of his face. In pressed trousers and a crisp shirt, he looked good enough to eat, reminding me exactly why I tried to avoid post-shower Kempthorne.

"Hey."

He blinked and pulled back into the room. "Morning, Dom."

When he wasn't lost in thought and frowning, he looked younger, making it easy to forget he was the boss. We could have been just two guys of the same age who happened to sometimes share a roof.

The whole living/working arrangement was odd at times. It had taken some getting used to. But I wasn't ever getting used to Kempthorne all sleepy-eyed and bed-tousled in the mornings. Like this, he was temptation personified and my track record with temptation wasn't great.

I reached behind him. "Can I just grab the er... the kettle there?"

He sprang from the counter, set his hot cup down, and was a whirl of motion. "The auction begins at ten," he blurted. "I have lunch with an associate at two. I'll be out of the office this morning. Don't go into the basement."

Halfway through making a coffee, I froze. The only reason he'd warn me off the basement was if the pen was down there. "Don't say it." My heart already pounded.

"It's just—"

"I don't want to know. Don't tell me."

"I should probably lock the basement door," he added.

"It's fine." I poured hot water into my cup and grabbed the milk from the fridge, keeping my hands busy and my back to him. "Is it secure?"

"Yes." His voice was close. He'd drifted closer toward me.

"Then it's fine." Christ, I glanced over my shoulder as he was turning away, his lips and brow pinched in worry. Because of the dead latent agent. I wanted to tell him he wasn't going to lose me, or Gina or Robin. "Nothing is going to happen. It's probably in the safest place right now. Go do your thing. We'll be here for tonight." His fine eyebrows dug in and he looked up. "Trust me," I said. "It's fine." I wasn't going anywhere near the basement. "Look, if I can contain and transport an artifact through a Syrian firefight, I can avoid a bookshop basement." It sounded good, in theory.

"Call me," he said. "If you find it getting *difficult*."

I had a quip lined up but swallowed it after seeing the seriousness on his face. "Thanks, I will." Only then did he relax. He left not long after and the front door *thunked*, signaling he'd left the building. Did he really care, or was it all about the company? We hardly knew each other, so what did it matter? He didn't have to care for his employees. He just had to pay our wages. Still, I was beginning to realize this life, this shop, his business, it was more than just a job, or something to keep a rich guy from getting bored. It was a mission to him.

And people died on missions.

10

I had my earphones tucked into my ears and my feet up on the table, trying to zone out and focus on the evening ahead and not think about the nuclear bomb in the basement, when Gina's beaming face appeared in front of me.

She plucked one of my earphones out and stage-whispered, "He's here."

"Who?"

"Hollywood. He's in the shop. Looking at books."

"That is what people do in book shops." I sounded blasé and moved from my chair like there was no urgency. Dropping everything and dashing down the stairs might give my racing heart away.

"He's here because of the auction, you know that right?" I asked. "He's feeling us out."

"He can feel me out any time." She grinned.

He was taking a risk showing up in the shop in broad daylight and browsing books like a tourist, assuming the Met were actually searching for Gareth Clarke's killer and hadn't filed his case in the bin. Or maybe his being here was genius? Kempthorne & Co was the last place anyone would look for the American assassin.

In the shop, a few customers chatted beside the floor-to-ceiling shelves. Sunlight poured through the front bay windows and dust motes sparkled in the air. People milled about outside in Cecil Court too, enjoying the rarity of London on a sunny day. The scene was so idyllic, I almost missed Hollywood standing by the window display. He'd propped sunglasses on his head, holding back his dark fringe, and had a book spread in one hand, appearing to be engrossed in its pages. Black jeans and a purple V-neck T-shirt had him blending in. Without his dramatic coat, he was just a guy browsing books who happened to be ridiculously gorgeous. With the sunny window behind him, the picture he painted was a perfect ad for Booksellers Row.

He glanced over, straight down the narrow space between bookshelves and right at me, spurring me into motion.

"What are you reading?" I asked, leaning against a shelf. He lifted the book. Harry Potter. Signed second edition. Typical. "You don't look the sort."

Humor glittered in his eyes. "Not a fan?"

"I'm English so I kinda have to be. Honestly, I'm more into McNab thrillers."

"Maybe we can work on that." His perfect teeth flashed behind his award-winning smile and it was difficult to believe he'd had me in an arm-lock with his hand down my pants not so long ago.

His reply implied we'd have time to work on it, which was definitely not on the cards. Hollywood was a job.

Besides, his cold apartment made it clear he wasn't sticking around London. Once whatever had brought him here was done, he'd vanish. His sort always did.

"Are you buying books or do you have another reason for prettying up our window?" I asked, keeping my voice low.

He scanned the shop behind me. "Is Kempthorne around?"

"You'll see him tonight," I hedged.

His stare returned to me. "Will I see *you* tonight?"

Despite all his smiles and his easy manner, he stood still and kept checking the window, the street outside, and the meandering customers. Nervous or something else?

"You wanna get that coffee?" I asked. Maybe he wanted off my turf and back on more neutral ground. He wanted to talk.

He dropped his sunglasses over his eyes and unleashed his Oscar-winning smile again. "Sure."

Gina, who'd been pretending to tidy the shelves, gave me the thumbs up when I passed her by. Laughing silently, I followed Hollywood outside and stepped into the sunshine. The air was warm and the sky blue above Cecil Court's pitched slate roofs. People ambled and chatted. Gaggles of tourists bumbled from shop window to shop window.

We strolled for a little while until I gestured for Hollywood to step into one of my favorite less-fancy coffee shops. We took a seat in the comfy armchairs at the window and ordered coffee and cake like normal people and not two men on opposite sides of a case that needed solving before more latents died.

A thousand questions sat on the tip of my tongue. Why was he really there, why did he kill Gareth Clarke, who was pulling his strings, and was it M? Hollywood smiled at me over sipping his coffee and I smiled back, reading him the way he read me. He was agency-trained, not military, but our skills were similar. Agency wasn't far from military, especially in the US.

"Shall we skip the small talk and go right to the real reason you're here?" I used my fork to cut off the corner of my piece of cake, then popped it into my mouth, playing at casual until I noticed Hollywood's stillness. He still had his shades on, hiding his eyes, but he was watching my mouth. Caught staring, he cleared his throat and fiddled with the packets of sugar, lining three up between his finger and thumb and tearing their tops off in one clean swipe. So efficient.

"Don't go to the auction," he said, pouring the sugar in, then picking up his spoon to stir.

"Hm. Why not?"

"The artifacts there will be dirty."

All right, so he'd seen me lose my shit over the pen and didn't want me going nuclear at the auction, which was fair enough. But he didn't know me, and no amount of background checks and Googling would be enough to figure me out. He knew I was Psy Ops though, albeit *retired*. I wasn't just any twitchy latent. "You're the second person to warn me off the auction. It must be good."

"And you're not going to listen to me either, are you?"

"I can look after myself. I've been doing it for years."

He laughed without humor and raised his coffee to his lips, and now I was staring. Watching him sweep his tongue across his top lip, I had no trouble imaging how that tongue would feel on other parts of me. Parts that were becoming uncomfortably stiff. I shifted in my seat and chuckled to myself, then dug into my cake to give me something else to think on instead of Sex-on-Legs seated opposite.

"How did you get caught up in the London artifact-dealing scene?"

He took off his sunglasses and slipped them over the V of his T-shirt, drawing my eye to the curve of his neck, where I'd kissed. "A job came up. Here I am."

"Right." I smiled around taking a sip of coffee, then sat back. "And just happened to meet Annie, a prominent TV presenter, the second you stepped off the plane at Heathrow?"

His grin tilted, turning sly. "Annie and I go way back."

"So how does an FBI dropout meet a British TV presenter?"

Hollywood cut his slice of fruit cake in half, right down the middle, and then cut each half into tiny equal bites, and all before he'd tasted it. If there was a weird way to eat cake, that was it. Instead of answering my question, he scooped cake onto his fork and slipped it between his lips.

Christ, he was triggering all my bad boy urges.

After licking his lips, he said, "This is beginning to feel like an interrogation."

I shrugged. "We could skip to the windowless room and beating, if you'd prefer."

"Why skip the fun when I can bring my own cuffs?"

Bloody hell. It was a good thing we were in a public place or I'd have been all over that like icing on his cake. Leaning forward, I planted an elbow on the table and wiped all the smiles off my face. "Just tell me one thing straight. Whoever has hired you, are they trying to eliminate anyone at Kempthorne's? Is my team in danger?"

He lifted those long lashes. "Nobody hired me, English."

"Bollocks." I might have upped and left then if I'd had a way of hiding the semi propping up my trousers. Bloody inconvenient, that. "You just here cruising the artifact auctions for your girlfriend? Or maybe you're on a one-man mission to kill unstable latents like Gary Clarke?"

"If I was killing latents, there would have been two dead in that alley."

Which wasn't helping his case. "Who's paying you?"

His cheek twitched. "Maybe you should look closer at Kempthorne?"

"Don't throw shade at Kempthorne when you're the one holding the smoking gun." This wasn't getting us anywhere. I paid for the coffee and cake via the café's app as he leaned back, watching me fume. "See you at the auction, *Hollywood*."

"Dom, wait." His voice stopped me at the door.

Half the other customers perked up, listening to our drama while trying not to make it obvious.

Hollywood still sat in the chair, leaning back, chilled as you like, but all the fake smiles and charm had vanished. He pinched his lips and tiny worry lines appeared at the corners of his mouth. "This isn't Syria. If the op goes wrong here, civilians die, not soldiers."

He knew I'd lost my team and he dared hang that over me? I took the few strides back to the table, standing over him. He blinked up, tensing for a fight. The urge to lay into him almost overrode common sense. But this was not the place to discuss what had happened in Syria. Besides, he was just fishing for a rise out of me, and he'd found the right bait. Screw him. "If Kempthorne or any of my team get hurt and you're part of it, then this"—I circled a finger between us—"whatever this is, is over. You killed Clarke like he was a dog. Don't think I won't do the same to you."

He lifted his chin, putting on a mask that tried to convince me he didn't care. "I've warned you—"

"That vague back-off crap? C'mon. If you know more, tell me."

He thought about it, but whatever secrets he was keeping, they had him shaking his head. "See you tonight, English."

"Yeah, whatever." I left him there to stew and marched back to Cecil Court. Hollywood wasn't ever going to talk. He was too tight for that. But I'd seen the worry on his face. This wasn't just a job for him. He was in deep, and if I found out why, we'd probably have our mysterious top man.

11

C ovent Garden is a hub for all things shopping with indoor market stalls and cafés. At night, clubs and bars keep its heart beating. A strange place to hold an illegal artifact auction, unless you're so far up your own arse and you own half of London, so you believe you can do whatever the hell you want. Like property developer, Devi Ahuja. His club was all cool blue lights, thumping music, sexy waiting staff, and a shit-ton of ex-military security. Subtle.

Although, this was more my scene than a posh dinner party in a Chelsea mansion. Perhaps unsurprisingly, given how Kempthorne could blend into any scene, he looked at ease striding through the crowd. Gone was the stiff, standoffish persona from the dinner party. Colorful lights caught in his blue eyes, turning them electric. More than a few women noticed him, prompting his polite smile. Men too. Not that he'd have cared. His mind was on the job. Anything unrelated to our mission didn't feature on his radar.

We didn't have long to wait with the masses when a woman in a grey suit sporting an earpiece whispered in Kempthorne's ear and guided us through a back door into a thick-carpeted hallway. A heavy security guy grunted at Kempthorne to lift his arms and patted him down. I got similar treatment. My guy predictably missed the deck of cards, assuming they and me were harmless. Rookie mistake.

We descended to a swish basement bar area populated by a handful of guests. Heads turned our way and the whispers grew, probably gossiping about Kempthorne. He rarely went anywhere without being recognized.

I took a seat at the bar and ordered a lightweight whisky and coke. I needed my head clear for later. "Aren't you worried word might get out that the boss of Kempthorne and Co is selling artifacts?"

Kempthorne ordered straight whiskey with an ancient-sounding name and took the stool beside mine. We were the only two at the bar. The rest of the guests had gathered in cliques around the room. No sign of Hollywood.

"People love to talk," Kempthorne said, accepting his drink from the barman.

He'd know. When I'd researched the Kempthorne name before starting to work for him, Google had provided hundreds of results, most from trashy websites speculating on what one of London's most eligible bachelors did in his spare time, what tailor he used, what car he was seen in. Any serious articles were hard to find among the gossip, and those I did find revealed nothing alarming about Kempthorne & Co.

"Is this the usual crowd?" I asked, nodding at our fellow bidders.

Kempthorne glanced over my shoulder, reading the groups in a few seconds before dancing his gaze back to me. "Proxies, mostly. They'll be in contact with their buyers by phone. Devi offers the service to anyone who wants to remain anonymous."

"Any latents?"

"Difficult to tell."

"You think M might be buying tonight?"

"We'll see." He grinned and it was genuine, more like the Kempthorne I'd seen in the moments between jobs, more relaxed. He was enjoying this secret get-together for illegal purposes, which said a lot about Alexander Kempthorne. Most people with his wealth would've been playing golf or schmoozing with the elite, but he liked to get his boots on the ground and his hands dirty. I could respect that. Too many officers in the military were soldiers in title only.

"What made you get into artifact retrieval?" I asked.

Gina was right: talking about our private lives was usually off the table, but I got the sense that this relaxed Kempthorne might open up.

"My parents, mostly." He cupped his glass loosely, fixed wristwatch glinting. "Before artifacts and latents were heavily regulated, the Kempthornes founded the first company dedicated to studying both. My mother was an authenticator, actually. Like you."

Was. I'd read about the accident before accepting the job. His mother had discovered the link between psychic trauma and the creation of artifacts at a time when so little was known about either. Both his parents had died when their private jet had gone down in the English Chanel, leaving their sixteen-year-old son, Alex, as the heir to the Kempthorne fortune. Six months later, his older sister, Charlotte, had vanished on a trip to Scotland, presumed dead. Her case remained unsolved. All of that made Alex Kempthorne perfect tabloid bait. Billionaire family struck by tragedy twice. The press had lapped it up. He'd been London's favorite representative of the artifact world for the last sixteen years.

"You ever want to do anything else?"

He laughed, like the idea was absurd. "Like?"

"What do you like to do, besides collecting artifacts?" He had a whole life outside of the office that nobody ever talked about. "Hobbies? Horses? Hunting? *Books*? C'mon, I know you like books."

"There's only the agency," he said, still chuckling at the ludicrous idea of a hobby.

I wasn't sure I believed that.

"Ladies and gentlemen, welcome to the Night Auction," a tall, middle-aged man of Indian heritage announced. Dressed impeccably in a blue suit, he had to be Devi, the auctioneer. "Please, follow me." He turned on his polished heels and led the crowd from the room.

Kempthorne threw back the rest of his whiskey and arched an inquisitive eyebrow. "Let the fun begin."

We joined the crowd at the back and were all led deeper into the bowels of the building. I caught sight of the two security guards closing the doors behind us. Seconds later, the locks clunked into place.

Nobody was leaving until the auction was over.

12

Hollywood's absence was an itch at the back of my mind. When we'd spoken earlier in the day, he'd indicated he was coming. So what had stopped him? Did he know something we didn't? He'd warned me off, citing dirty artifacts, and the last time we'd all been together around similar items, it hadn't ended well. Maybe he'd gotten cold feet?

Nervous laughter tittered through the small crowd as we made our way down the corridor, while others—the proxies—strode ahead, having done this before.

A deep, thumping background beat began to roll over me the deeper we went, the sensation as though I'd spent too long underwater and needed to *breathe*. We rounded a corner and entered a narrow room with a curtained stage area. On the stage, five podiums supported five artifacts, including the innocuous-looking pen that had almost seduced me to the dark side.

All the artifacts crooned and teased the latent part of

me, trying to reach out and have me scoop up all the pretties, then unleash them all on London. I leveled my thoughts and guarded against the psychic assault. Even so, deep in concentration, I missed the auctioneer's opening statement.

Kempthorne's surprise hand on my shoulder jolted me back into the moment.

"Let's begin with Lot Number One, a charming necklace authenticated as belonging to Queen Victoria herself." Devi continued his sales-pitch, spilling the artifact's gruesome past.

Maintaining my guard against the siren song of multiple powerful artifacts while also staying alert wasn't easy, but years of military training were paying off. With half a mind on protection and the other half aware of my surroundings, I almost missed the woman standing behind Devi, tucked into the shadows at the back of the room. Cropped blonde hair, straight fringe, startling blue eyes scanning the crowd. She stood on alert, like security, or ex-military. A professional.

"The woman?" I whispered, tilting my head toward Kempthorne but keeping my eyes on her.

"Devi's authenticator," Kempthorne whispered back.

Huh. Her sharp-eyed glare narrowed on me and lingered, authenticator to authenticator. Was she registered and competent? London's artifact world was a small one, and I hadn't seen her before.

"Bidding begins at one-point-five," Devi announced with flair. "Do I hear one-point-six?"

A proxy lifted her hand, taking instructions from the phone pressed to her ear.

"One-point-six," Devi beamed. "Do I hear seven?"

Fuck. I knew the artifacts sold for big numbers, but seeing it in action was something else.

"Two million," Kempthorne said.

"Christ," I muttered. I was asking for a pay rise on my two-year anniversary. Despite my internal alarm at the numbers being thrown around, there was nothing here that wasn't unexpected. Bored rich people with too much money buying illegal artifacts had been happening for years. So why the warnings? Besides the obvious risk of having a latent near all that temptation it was all pretty routine.

'Two-point-five," Kempthorne said, his voice drawing me back into the moment, reminding me to focus.

The door rattled, locks turning over. Heads turned at the interruption. And in walked Hollywood with his hair disheveled and coat slightly askew. He swept his locks back and straightened his long coat, spotted us all staring, and flashed a grin.

Hollywood's gaze skated over me and Kempthorne to find the authenticator at the back of the stage. A look of familiarity passed between them that I might have been able to decipher if my concentration hadn't slipped, making the artifacts suddenly damned *loud.*

*Touch me. Pick me. Play with me. **Burn with me.***

I squeezed my eyes closed.

"Three million." Kempthorne's voice pierced my concentration. Then the proxy to our right, the one who he'd been bidding against, upped her bid.

My heart had begun to beat halfway up my throat, which was a bad sign. Sweat moistened my palms.

Kempthorne and the bidder battled it out, the numbers racking up as I tried to get a better grip on my rocky control. *Flooding*, the military called it. They locked a latent trainee in a bunker and with every hour they increased the number of dirty artifacts locked inside with them. Half failed the test. Some died, taking the bunkers with them. I'd made it to nine. Five was a walk in the park, usually.

And I wasn't the only latent here.

Opening my eyes, I found Devi's authenticator watching me. Fine crow's feet lined the corners of her eyes and sweat glistened in her hairline. She wasn't immune either.

She shifted an inch on her feet and discreetly sank her hand into her back pocket. A subtle change, but I knew it well. I made the same move when I went for my cards.

I dropped my hand to my pocket, cradling the deck in my fingers, my thumb poised to let a card fly.

She had an artifact *on her*. I had one on me. That made seven in the small room with two latents. Things were beginning to get interesting.

I took stock of the scene:

Hollywood stood at ease to my left, lurking at the back.

Kempthorne was still engaged in a bidding war and those in the crowd who weren't proxies all simmered with anticipation and typical British restraint.

An armed, probably ex-military authenticator on the stage.

The throb of seven dangerous artifacts cloyed the air. The original five artifacts would have been kept off-site, in separate, secure locations, like Kempthorne's safe. Until now.

Now they were all here. All together. With no security in the room. If I was going to pull something to get my hands on all those artifacts, this would be a great time and place to do it.

"We may have a problem," I whispered.

Tease me. Twist me. Take me, all the artifacts urged. But the pen, that one *knew* me, I'd had it in my hands. Had it so close. It wanted me to listen, to *hear*.

The blonde authenticator stepped forward, emerging from the shadows. A knife glowed in her hand. *Artifact*, my latent senses twitched. She reached for Devi.

I freed my cards and felt the hard press of cool, blunt metal against the back of my neck. The nozzle of a gun. "Your deck stays in your pocket," Hollywood's voice rumbled in my ear.

The authenticator yanked Devi against her chest and pressed her glowing knife to his throat. "Put the artifacts in the bag," she barked, European-accented. With her free hand, she tugged a plastic bag from her pocket and tossed it at Devi's feet.

Kempthorne *moved*. I only saw the blur in the corner of my eye but heard Hollywood's grunt of pain. The gun vanished and so did Hollywood, tackled by Kempthorne.

The blonde shoved Devi forward off the stage, raised her knife, and flung it—right toward Kempthorne and Hollywood in the throes of wrestling for the gun. I flung a charged card. It struck the knife, knocking it out of its trajectory, sending it spinning. It hit a wall and clattered to the floor. The blonde made a dash for her artifact.

Kempthorne and Hollywood threw messy punches. The crowd surged toward the door.

In the noise and the chaos, nobody noticed me clamber onto the stage.

And nobody saw me snatch the pen.

13

Power. Christ, it was like the best sex and chocolate and sunshine all rolled into one mind-numbing, body-tingling blast. Sweet-fucking-power lit up my body and brain, making everything sing. The easiest thing in the world would've been to let it wash over me, to drown in it. I'd take half of London with me, and maybe I didn't care.

But I'd been trained for this—exposed to artifacts over and over, like a rat in a maze, buzzed every time it took a wrong turn. Control had been drilled into me, until every breath and every heartbeat and every thought were weighed and measured. Until I could damn well hold a dirty artifact in my hand without leveling all of central London.

"Nobody. Fucking. Move!"

The crowd, Hollywood, Kempthorne, the *other* authenticator, the auctioneer—everyone froze. Their lives were all balanced in my hands. I could wipe them and myself off the map if I just *stopped fighting*. But I wasn't thinking about that. Couldn't. Think. About. That.

"Devi," I snarled, "put all the other artifacts in the fucking bag."

He blinked dimly at me. Sweet-fuck, if he didn't hurry it up we would all be dead. *"Hurry!"*

The auctioneer scrabbled into action, collecting the artifacts and dumping them into the plastic bag.

Hollywood—his fight with Kempthorne forgotten—stepped forward.

"Don't," I warned, raising my free hand. I couldn't handle his distraction and *the* pen.

Power throbbed down my arm, soothing, like a lover's touch. Like we both knew all I really wanted was complete surrender.

"Dom." Kempthorne had approached the stage and stood almost within reaching distance. He held out his hand, fingers unfurling. "Hand it over." His hair had flopped over his eye. He'd lost a button from the collar of his skewed shirt. Those things were easier to focus on. *He* was easier to focus on, as if his being here meant every-thing was going to be fine.

Hand it over. Right. I could do that.

But I wasn't moving.

The pen was *mine*!

Fuck.

He climbed onto the stage, got to his feet, and held out his hand again. And this time he was so close the subtle scent of his expensive cologne tugged on a thread of thought in the same way his presence tugged on bits of my mind, soothing the desire to lose my shit.

"Dom, it's all right." His deep voice promised it would

be. I'd rarely heard a tone like it. Nobody ever talked to me like that, like they *cared*, and it struck at the part of me I kept hidden—the vulnerable, scared part. The latent boy who'd had to make sure he was the hardest, most savage kid in the estate so he didn't get knifed in the back for being a latent.

Was it all right? Not much had been all right since I'd been forced out of the military. I had nothing and nobody. But I had the pen, and the pen was *everything*.

Recognizing the thoughts as a slippery slope, I shook them from my head. Why wasn't I giving Kempthorne the pen? I really needed to do that, but... I also really didn't want to. The artifact made me powerful. It made me a fucking god. "*Shit*," I gasped.

"Dom, okay? Look at me."

I looked into his calm blue eyes. So cold, but fierce too. Like ancient glaciers. Like nothing could stop Alexander Kempthorne when he put his mind to it.

"I'm going to take it... All right?" he said. "I'm going to take it out of your hand. Like this." His fingers touched mine and a jolt of cool, calm clarity spilled over me, washing away the artifact's beating, cloying heat. It all became clear: handing the pen to Kempthorne was the only option. I opened my fingers. He snatched the pen, turning away, putting his body between me and it.

Relief washed over me, almost dropping me to my knees. Christ, that had been close.

A gunshot barked.

Kempthorne jolted, rocking back a step—toward me. Blood bloomed through his shirt, at his right shoulder.

My slow, sticky thoughts dragged, struggling to keep up. Kempthorne had been shot. Fucking Hollywood! But his startled face was the same as those around him. He didn't have his gun. The blonde authenticator was the one with the weapon cradled in her hands. And she smiled.

Kempthorne tossed the pen at Devi and barked, "Get the artifacts out of here! Go!" He dropped to his knees and slumped forward with a hand clasped to his shoulder.

Devi bolted for the door, flung it open, and was gone.

The authenticator dashed after him. The crowd suddenly realized they'd come within inches of being blasted all over London and surged as one heaving mass toward the exit.

Seconds... all of this had taken seconds. My training finally kicked in, revving my thoughts. Kempthorne was down. The artifacts were on the move. Prioritize.

That many artifacts, all in one place. Shit, if there was a latent in the club, or outside, anywhere near Devi, we'd have more to worry about than the psycho authenticator chasing them.

I caught Hollywood's distinctive figure in the corner of my eye, running for the door, coat flaring. "Hey!" Was he going after the authenticator to stop her, or help her? Didn't matter. I knelt by Kempthorne, grabbed his hand, and pushed it against the bloody patch in his shirt, over his shoulder. "Hold it there. Stay upright."

"Yes, yes," he said, annoyed. He fumbled with his phone in his right hand, dialing for an ambulance. "I'm fine. Stop her."

"You goin' to be okay, boss?"

"Fine. Go."

I didn't need to be told twice and was up and fighting my way through the crowd in the next second.

"Don't touch the artifacts!"

"Move!" I tore through the fleeing auction guests. The guards that had patted us down earlier weren't in the hallway, or anywhere, and when I burst into the club, people reeled from being shoved aside.

"Outta the way!" I shoved out of the club into Covent Garden's glazed atrium. It was still early and the nightlife was warming up, making the place buzz with activity. The authenticator's blonde hair marked her out like a neon sign. She raced between café tables. I spotted Devi behind her, slinking out from behind an advertising board, plastic bag clutched to his chest. Wide-eyed, he looked like a deer in headlights. Probably because he knew he had an armful of potential bombs and latent-bait for any latents among the crowd.

With the blonde disappearing outside, having missed her target, I quickly headed toward Devi. A young man from the crowd sprang at him before I could. Devi squealed and jerked back, running blindly toward me.

He saw me and his face screwed up, in despair and alarm.

I grabbed my badge and thrust it out. "I'm Agency!"

His shoulders sagged and the latent who'd tried to take Devi down slunk away, thinking better of it.

With all the bluster drained out of him, he lifted his gaze to me. I bundled him into the nearest doorway, out of sight from the crowd. "Oh god, what do we do?" he sniveled. "I'm never going to make it back with all these—"

Don't think about the artifacts. Focus. Calm. Control.

The pen...

Don't think about it. Control. Breathe. Control. Breathe. I chanted them in my head to the rhythm of my beating heart.

The latent who had lunged at Devi came plowing through the crowd from a different angle. My fast and efficient right hook had him promptly meeting the floor. He went down hard, crashing through a chair and table. And now the rest of the people were spooked. Some lifted their phones, trying to film whatever drama was unfolding around them. That was all we needed, videos on Facebook.

There were too many people here for the artifacts and Devi to be safe. The authenticator would soon realize she'd missed Devi. She'd be back soon.

"We need to get you out of here." Grabbing his arm, I tugged him through an old pedestrian alley, out onto the quieter back-street of St Martin's Lane, and called Gina.

"Dom, how's it going?"

"I have custody of five artifacts. How quickly can you get a team to St Martin's near the Pret, on the corner?"

"Oh shit. Let me check... There's a cleanup team near you —five minutes out."

"Do it." I hung up and checked the street. It was quiet for now. Just Devi and me, and one random bystander walking away, oblivious to the drama a street-over in Covent Garden.

"What now?" Devi jittered on his feet, checking up and down the street.

"We wait for the disposal team to come and take those artifacts off your hands."

"What? No! These are precious." He clutched the bag tighter to his chest. "My clients need them—"

I had a hand at his throat and the man against the wall before he could say another fucking word. "Nobody fucking *needs* an artifact. Each one of those artifacts puts lives at risk. Your rich friends can find something else to turn them on. Those are going to disposal."

The presence of the artifacts, just a flimsy plastic bag away, beat like a drum inside my head. I shoved off him, putting distance between us, and checked the street again. No movement. Good. We might get away with a clean extraction. "The man bidding against Kempthorne, who was he?" I asked.

"I c-can't tell you that." He eyed me like he might bolt at any second. I couldn't blame him. "My auctions are strictly anonymous."

Christ, I was going to punch him. I thrust my fingers into my hair instead and paced to keep from getting too close to the bag again. "You must have some way of knowing who's buying? How do you deliver the lots to the winners?"

"Mules." Devi shrugged.

"'Mules'?"

"Yeah, they have the end address. I don't see it."

"Like Gareth Clarke?" Who was working for the top man and knew his delivery address. Who Hollywood conveniently executed.

"Gary? Yeah, but he's gone quiet, so I was looking for a new guy. You know? The new guy, he was there. Showed up late though."

I narrowed my eyes. "Tall, long black coat? That guy? American?"

Devi grinned. "Yeah, him. He came highly recommended."

"Yeah, I bet he did." I snorted. "He's not a mule, but he did want into your little circle of elite buyers." Funny how every turn I made, there was Hollywood.

The street was still quiet. I checked my phone. Two minutes to go. "So what happened back there? At the auction? Your buyer didn't want Kempthorne outbidding him so he decided to steal the batch instead?"

"What? You think my buyer did this? No, no... I don't see it. The price was getting good. My highest lot." His eyes glazed over some. "Man, the commission on that would have gotten me out of some tight spots, ya know?"

"The woman, your authenticator, who was she?"

"What woman?"

"Fucking stall one more time and I'll take one of those artifacts and turn you into a human firework. Start talking, Devi."

"Anca something. She's Swedish, I think. I hired her a year ago to authenticate my lots, when I first started out —she's expensive, but worth it—until, yeah, until this happened. Fuck, nobody will ever buy from me again."

"Good."

"You don't get it! I need this. Property prices are falling. The bloody artifacts keep stopping builds. So I thought, if artifacts are going to price me out, I needed in on that action, right? Anca was good at finding them—"

"Anca was just about to steal every last artifact you're clutching right now."

Headlights swept over us as a car pulled into the street. It could be cleanup. I checked my phone. No messages. The timing was right. The car cruised closer, headlights on low beam.

"Back up," I told Devi, stepping between him and the car.

"What? Why? Don't you know these people? What kind of amateur hour is this?!"

"You're holding a bag of tricks worth more than your life to some people, so back the fuck up and do as I say."

The car—a black Audi—pulled to a stop at the curb. The driver lifted his hand off the steering wheel in a friendly wave. The passenger window hummed down. "Cleanup," the passenger said. Average-looking guy, maybe my age. The driver was older. I couldn't see into the back to know if there were more.

"Where's the rest of you?"

"On the way."

Cleanup did have undercover crews, pros at securing artifacts without alerting the public, but something about these two had my instincts twitching. "You got ID?"

"Oh yeah." The passenger grinned. "Right here." He reached down, out of sight.

I dropped my hand into my pocket and skimmed my fingertips along the edge of my cards, sparking them to life.

The passenger brought up a blocky, yellow device with two sharp prongs sparking at its end. *Fuck.* I jerked a card out.

The Taser's twin prongs struck. I didn't see it, or feel it, not to begin with. The first I knew I'd been hit, I found myself facedown on the pavement, gasping for air with my whole body tingling, like I'd rolled in electric ants. Ants with pins for legs. Survival instincts levered me up onto an arm. The street tipped. My body wasn't playing the same game as my head. I knew I needed to be standing, but the messages weren't getting through.

The car door flung open, struck me, and down I went again like a bag of bricks. Devi's scream registered in a tiny part of my brain that hadn't turned to Jell-O.

I blinked at London's black night sky, caught sight of my glowing cards still clutched in my hand, and tried to pry one free.

A kick punted the deck from my grip, scattering the glowing cards across the pavement. They fizzled, spluttered, and died.

"Stay down, latent prick." A second kick landed in my guts. Fiery pain curled my spine. Gasping, I rolled onto my front and reached for my cards scattered nearby.

"Boss wants him done," the driver said. To me or Devi?

"You can't do this!" Devi screamed. "Get off! He's Agency! Hey—those are mine!"

"Stop fighting."

"Get him in the car—quick! Shit, the fuzz is here."

Car doors slammed. Thumps sounded from inside the car—Devi trying to kick his way out—then stopped. Tires squealed nearby. All the sounds and voices spiraled around my groggy head. I touched a spilled card, lighting it up, and dragged it under my fingers.

"What about the latent?"

"Leave 'im. Boss ain't ready yet."

Hands landed on my shoulders. I twisted, flung my card,—blinding the prick—and kicked out, sending him sprawling backward into the passenger seat.

"Fuck this!" With his eyes streaming, he slammed the

door closed. "Go! Go!" The Audi roared away seconds before a marked cop car raced by, blue lights flashing.

Another cop car anchored to a stop as I picked up each of my scattered cards and tucked them home inside their pack. Maybe if I moved slowly I wouldn't throw up. Christ, my ribs ached. I'd be feeling that kick for a while.

"You all right, mate?" A uniform cop climbed from the car. "Dom, isn't it? Mister Kempthorne has us looking for you."

"I'm peachy." My legs somehow held me up until I fell against the wall. "You need to track that car. They have dirty artifacts."

"We're on it. You need an ambulance?" the young cop asked.

"Nah." I waved him off. Getting Tasered, kicked in the ribs, and losing the artifacts was not how this night was supposed to go down. "Kempthorne sent you? Is he all right?"

"Dunno. We just got radioed to find you." He raised his radio and reported doing exactly that to his colleagues.

My phone rang. I answered and listened to Gina tell me how Kempthorne had been taken to A&E. Apparently, he'd been coherent enough to call the DI he was friendly with and dispatch the Met to find me.

"You sure you're all right?" the copper asked. "You don't look so good."

"I'm good. Thanks for the save." Even though they were about twenty seconds too bloody late. Wobbly, I reached for the wall again. "Maybe you could drop me at the hospital after all?"

I helped myself to a plastic cup of awful hospital coffee while waiting for the doctors to give Kempthorne the all clear. Gina showed up in the morning with her no-nonsense face on. "God, you look like shit."

"You're so kind. Remind me why we're friends again?"

She threw me a plastic-wrapped sausage roll. "Get that in you and go home. I'll wait for him."

"It's fine." I'd been waiting hours on the hard plastic chairs, stewing on the mission failure, so what was a few more hours? After devouring the sausage roll in a few bites, I frowned at Gina's worried face. "What?"

"Did Kage set this up?" She paced, chewing on her painted nails, then screwed up her face after getting a taste of polish.

"No. Maybe. He was Devi's new mule. He didn't shoot Kempthorne though. There was a woman—Anca someone—an authenticator. She got her hands on Hollywood's gun. She shot Kempthorne and would have grabbed the artifacts if Devi hadn't legged it. She probably has them anyway after the fake cleanup crew jumped me."

"Oh man, that's one shitty night."

"Tell me about it. You ever been Tasered? Hurts like a bitch. I still can't feel my balls."

Her laugh lightened my dire mood. "Wasn't security supposed to be tight?" She stopped pacing.

"My guess is someone paid them to look the other way during the auction. Someone with deep pockets who really wanted one of those dirty artifacts."

"Hi," Kempthorne croaked, stopping in the waiting room door. If I looked like shit, he looked like death warmed up. A sling supported his right arm, half hidden by the jacket draped over his shoulder. Whiskers shadowed his jaw, making me scratch at my own developing bristle in sympathy.

"Hey, boss." Gina winced at the sling. "You okay?"

He waved her concern away. "Bullet went straight through. It'll be fine in a few weeks. Dom? Are you all right? Gina told me about the ambush."

"Sore, but I'll live." With a Herculean effort not to wince or groan, I got to my feet and breathed around the bruises in my chest. "They're professionals. No way a couple of chancers can organize all that. They knew I'd call in a crew. Probably had multiple exits covered, watching for a runner. Has Devi been found?"

"Not yet. We'll talk about this some more on the ride home, shall we?"

"Yeah, about that." Gina's concerned expression turned to worry. "Word got out you were shot, and the press are flashing pictures of the missing artifacts all over the news. You should also know there's a crowd of journalists outside, including Rebecca."

"Yes, I know. I invited them, and Rebecca," he said, making his way down the corridor toward the main entrance.

"Oh." Gina hurried alongside. "Er... why?"

Who was Rebecca?

"We need those artifacts off the street," Kempthorne said. "And the best way to do that now is to make them too hot to handle, in the financial sense. I've offered a reward for their safe return."

I trailed behind. The fact the artifacts were on the street at all was my fault. I kept my hands buried in my pockets, reassuringly on my cards. Whoever had taken Devi and the artifacts knew what they were doing, and they knew enough about me to know that my cards were my weapons. It was starting to feel like whoever we were after knew a whole lot more about us than we did about them.

Kempthorne could have died. If my control hadn't been so damn good, we *all* could have died. Whoever was playing these games either didn't care about lives, or they wanted the carnage. But why?

"Dom, are you sure you're all right?" Kempthorne asked again, shoving through a pair of hospital doors while looking back at me. "The artifact you held—"

A camera flashed in front, startling all of us. Then another flash to the right.

"Mister Kempthorne!? Alexander Kempthorne!?" a gaggle of voices squawked. "A few questions?"

"Are Kempthorne & Co investigating the artifact dealers in London?"

"Is this case related to the explosion in Chelsea?"

"What's the value of the artifacts?"

Kempthorne found some energy from somewhere and pinned a charming smile to his lips. "Please, let's move out of the way of the doors shall we, and I'll answer your questions." He proceeded to charm them all by answering their questions with cool clarity. Their eyes lit up when he revealed Kempthorne & Co were dealing with an extraordinarily sensitive and dangerous case in an effort to bring down one of the most prolific dealers in London. He also said we had a number of promising leads, and he regretted the unfortunate accidents at Chelsea and Covent Garden but assured everyone we had it under control. By the time he was done, even I believed him.

"Now, if that's all, I'd like to head home. A night in A&E just isn't the same as a bed in Kensington."

The reporters tittered and we began to move off when a stocky late-fifty-something woman in a flower-print blouse said, "Alexander, Rebecca Stevens, *London Today*—"

Kempthorne turned and gave her his warmest smile. "It's good to see you, Becky."

The others jostled and quietened, now it was clear one of their own had all of Kempthorne's attention. Becky lifted her phone, recording. "Alex, are you and John in a relationship?"

The Taser hadn't stopped my heart, but her question almost did. I froze. The crowd's collective stares turned on me, each one a spotlight. Kempthorne glanced behind him, and for a brief, electric second, his gaze caught mine, saying *something,* then he laughed his smooth, high society laugh and waved a hand. "If I were seeing anyone, Becky, you'd all be the first to know. Now, please excuse me."

The reporters erupted in a wave of questions, demanding to know everything about his sex life. How he didn't tell them to keep their fucking noses out of his business, I've no idea, which was probably why I was never allowed to talk to the press.

A black Lexus pulled up, the driver jumping out and opening the back door. Kempthorne politely gestured for Gina and me to climb in first. He settled into the back seat after us and closed the door. Only when we were behind the privacy glass and the car pulled away did the cracks show. He slumped in the seat, propped his good arm on the door, and rubbed the bridge of his nose.

The urge to apologize sat on the tip of my tongue. The last thing either of us needed were rumors swirling about a gay office relationship. Personally, they could write all the shit they wanted about me, but Kempthorne had his reputation and his good name to uphold. It shouldn't have mattered who he or I liked to fuck, but in the real world, it did.

We rode in an awkward silence all the way back to Cecil Court.

Gina climbed out, leaving the door open for me to follow. I shimmied across the rear seat, escape so close.

"Dom?"

"I'm sorry," I blurted, dropping back into the soft leather, wishing it would swallow me whole.

"What for?" he asked, like he genuinely didn't know what the problem was.

"Dragging my personal shit into all this. You don't need that on top of everything else."

"Like I said, people talk. It really doesn't bother me. Does it bother you?"

"No." Which was a lie. Now wasn't the time to tell him how my CO Sawyer had royally screwed me over, using our relationship as a reason to kick me out of Psy Ops. It also wasn't the time to tell him how the struggle with my sexuality had dominated my life as a kid growing up in the East End.

Our office rule meant we didn't discuss personal stuff. He'd never shown any interest and genuinely didn't seem to care about anything outside Kempthorne & Co. But it was one thing having a gay staff member and something else to be asked if you were in a relationship with him.

A strange, soft quiet settled over us. The back of his car was comfortable after the wretched hospital waiting room. I sorely needed a shower and to catch up on some sleep but didn't feel much like leaving the quiet bubble inside the Lexus. After the adrenaline hit of the previous few hours, I was crashing fast.

"I'm er..." Kempthorne rubbed the bridge of his nose again and closed his eyes. He shrugged the sling off, tired of it, but the motion had him gritting his teeth. "I'm going to retire to Kensington."

"Yeah." I took that as a sign to leave and quickly climbed out, then ducked my head back inside. He still rubbed his forehead. "First time getting shot?" I asked, hoping to see his smile again—the real one, not the fake one.

"Yes," he admitted, and there was that little upward tilt of the lips. I often forgot we were the same age behind all the flashy cars and classy suits, but his smile was real and reminded me we weren't so very different.

"If it makes you feel any better, that was my first time getting Tasered," I added.

"Oh, I've been Tasered before," he said.

"What? When?"

"In the theatre, actually." His smile grew. "Get some rest. We'll debrief later."

I closed the door, sealing Kempthorne behind black privacy glass. The car pulled away, and I thrust my hands into my pockets. He'd be all right. His Kensington house was probably full of people hired to pamper him. Also, who got Tasered at the theatre? How did that happen?

Chuckling to myself at the thought of Kempthorne causing enough of a scene in public to get himself Tasered, I turned and walked down Cecil Court, making it to the door just as my phone blipped a text alert.

Unknown number: You okay?

Who is this? I tapped out.

The ellipsis danced ... *Kage.*

It was still early, and the people striding up Cecil Court were shop employees. Faces I knew. None were Hollywood. He just happened to time his message the second I got home? Or was he still watching me?

U stalking me, Hollywood? ...

I waited a while, but when the ellipses stopped moving and no text came through, I had Robin buzz me into the house.

My phone blipped while I climbed the stairs.

Unknown number: ... Devi is dead. It wasn't me.

Shit. I slumped against the wall. Devi was a selfish prick, but he didn't deserve to die.

Why should I believe you? I texted back.

... I want to stop them.

Stop who?

"Dom, you okay out there?" Robin called.

"Fine!"

Unknown number: ... M

Who is M?

... I don't know

I chewed on my lip. I wanted to believe him, but every bad thing that had happened during the last few days, he'd been there. He was either the cause of all the shit or miraculously ready to pull me out of it. Maybe because he was working against the same person we were, or maybe because he worked *for* them.

I can help you, but you gotta be straight with me, I sent.

...

"Dom?" Robin opened the door leading off the stairs. In an emerald-green top, with her auburn hair pinned up, she was as relaxed as I'd ever seen her. "Oh. There you are, lurking on the stairs. Is Kempthorne with you?"

"Nah, he ditched us for his rich pad."

Unknown number: ... I'm definitely not straight

I laughed. The sly bastard. "No shit."

Robin frowned. "He has an appointment with the DI in an hour."

"Christ, he was just shot," I snapped. "He's been in hospital all night. The DI can wait." Her eyebrows furrowed. "Shit, sorry Robin."

"It's all right. You've had a rough time too." The frown eased, turning sympathetic. "Get cleaned up. I'll put the kettle on," she said.

That sounded more than fair. "Thanks."

She disappeared back inside the apartment while I lingered in the stairwell.

Unknown number: ... meet me in the park, under the tree

You got me TASERED and K shot. No

... I'll give you Anca

Bollocks, now I had to go.

Fine. Give me 20 mins

... it's a date

"Robin, I'm heading out!"

"Get custard creams," she called. "*Someone* ate the last packet."

15

Showered and in fresh black jeans and an old green T-shirt, I briefed Gina on my way out the door, who immediately said no to my meeting Hollywood, citing various personal safety concerns. Ignoring all that, I waved my phone at her—implying it could protect me from a known-latent killer, said I'd text every ten minutes so she knew I was safe, grabbed my coat, and left before she set Robin on me.

Halfway to St James's Park, I spotted a guy on my tail. He wasn't dawdling like a tourist or power walking from A to B like the rest of the commuters. Thick sweater, dark trousers. Bulky muscles.

picked up a tail—I messaged Gina.

G: Told you bad idea! I'm coming.

It wouldn't hurt to have another pair of eyes on my back. Hollywood wasn't going to shoot me, despite his threats, but I was still feeling the bruises from the kick to the middle put there by his likely associates.

This could, of course, have been a trap. Hollywood

had held a gun to my head, enabling Anca to bag the artifacts. Maybe whoever was paying him figured I was too much of a pest and wanted me out of the way.

Taking a long route toward the park, I crossed a few busy roads, slipping between traffic, marching with purpose.

G: Where r u?

Iron railings. Near Admiralty Arch.

A few minutes later. G: *I see u*

See my tail?

G: No

I'd either given him the slip, or he'd realized I was on to him and broken off. He wouldn't have gone far though.

Stay close.

G: OK

Strolling into the park, I spotted Hollywood leaning against the same tree we'd met under a few days ago and strode toward him. He straightened, stepping out from under the shade to join me on the path.

"I'm being followed," I said.

"Yeah. Me too."

The concern in his eyes suggested he wasn't screwing with me. "You couldn't have mentioned that in your text?"

"I wasn't sure—until now." His gaze snagged over my shoulder. "You know a quick exit route?"

I followed his line of sight and spotted two big bruisers crossing the park's manicured grass toward us. I wasn't a small guy, but these two clearly worked out when they weren't beating the shit out of their victims.

"Yeah, okay..." I started toward the opposite side of the park. Sure enough the gorillas followed. "You wanna tell me who your new fan club is?" I asked while texting for Gina to stay back.

Hollywood frowned, sharpening all his model-like angles. "Looks like I've worn out my welcome. Figured this would happen—when I didn't shoot you at the auction."

He'd had orders to shoot me?

"In the leg," he added. "I tried to warn you."

I shoved through an iron gate onto the pavement running alongside a busy road. Cars rumbled by, but it was still early—still time to make a quick getaway without getting stuck in the rush. I spotted a taxi and waved, giving Hollywood the side-eye as I stepped off the curb. "You and I really need to talk."

He grunted an acknowledgement. The cab pulled up and he yanked the door open.

"Where to?" the cockney cabbie asked.

"Paddington." I slid in, and Hollywood slammed the door behind us as the two brutes made it to the gate in time to see us peel away from the curb.

"What's at Paddington?" Hollywood asked.

"A whole lot of exits." Twisting in the seat, I watched the two guys hail a cab. "Shit." Leaning forward, I gave our cabbie a friendly grin. "You couldn't step on it, mate? We've got a train to catch."

The cabbie's salt and pepper brows pinched. We didn't have any bags and didn't look like commuters, but London cabbies were pros, they didn't ask questions. "Do my best," he said, threading the black cab through slower traffic, keeping his eye on the mirrors.

Hollywood watched out of the back window. "They're following."

"Course they are," I muttered and typed out a quick message to Gina to return to the shop while I took the long way 'round. "Who are *they*?"

"Anca's men," Hollywood replied, surprising me with an actual answer.

All his pretty had etched into an intense frown. He wasn't enjoying this any more than I was.

"You two have a falling out?" I asked.

"Something like that." Unamused, he slid his gaze back out of the rear window.

"She works for M?" I pushed, while he was chatty.

"She works for Devi, but that stunt she pulled at the auction—that was for someone else. Someone at the top, probably M but I don't know for sure."

Now we were getting somewhere. "And who is M?"

His eyebrows furrowed. "I don't know."

"Yeah, except, I don't believe you."

"You can trust me, Dom," he rumbled in his sexy American voice, sounding so reasonable that he couldn't possibly have been lying. "I'm trying to help."

Luckily, I hadn't been born yesterday, and despite my libido finding Kage Mitchell to be the perfect antidote to my dry spell, the desire to jump into bed with him hadn't overridden my common sense. Yet. "Trust you? *Right*."

The other cab was a few cars behind. Once we hit the Paddington drop-off, the heavies would be on us. I checked my phone—8.05 a.m. Right on peak travel time. Paddington Station would be the perfect circus.

"Anca probably has artifacts from the auction," I told Hollywood.

"She'll be getting twitchy after Kempthorne offered a two million reward."

"Two mill is a lot of cash. You grassing her up for the reward, Hollywood? Or did your conscience get the better of you?"

His lips twitched. "Not gonna lie, it's tempting. But two million won't help if I'm dead."

"True, that. So whose side are you on?"

He took a while to think on his answer as the cab rumbled and bumped along uneven roads. "Mine."

That was probably the most honest thing he'd said since we'd met. "If I'm going to help you, you have to tell me everything."

The packed roads outside Paddington slowed the traffic to a crawl. Traffic lights turned red and we were dead in the water. Hollywood twitched between looking behind and ahead. "I'll tell you what I can—*they're bailing.*"

"We'll get out here," I told the cabbie, then swiped my card to pay and bolted out of the door. Hollywood followed me down Paddington's side-ramp, hot on my heels.

I shoved through a gaggle of tourists outside Paddington's open concourse, ignoring their muffled barks of surprise. "I'm going to teach you how to get where you wanna go in London, but if I lose you on the Underground, you'll be halfway to Luton. So stay on me."

He stayed glued to my back. "English, I got no idea what you're saying."

I tossed him a smile, which loosened him up some and teased his own smile onto his lips. I lived for this shit. The hunt, the chase. "Just stay on my arse."

Hollywood's gaze dropped. "Copy that."

The two heavies had barged into Paddington behind

us, but the crowd was refilling between us and them, hiding us from view.

A newly arrived train dumped its cargo of commuters onto the platforms. Suit-clad men and women spilled from trains in waves, flowing like an army in pinstripe. We were heading for the Tube, down the escalators right by the main concourse, but the heavies didn't know that. Diesel engines grumbled. Arrivals and departures were announced over the speakers. Loud and busy and chaotic was exactly what we needed, and within a few steps, we'd merged with it all. The perfect hiding place.

I steered us behind a sandwich hut, one of several operating in the middle of the station, and joined another stream of people, heading toward the waiting areas. The ticket gates lay wide open to ease the flow, enabling Hollywood and me to slip right through.

"You see 'em?" I asked. His height gave him a better view than me.

He checked around us and spotted them. "Yeah—talking to security by the entrance. They haven't seen us."

With any luck, whatever story they were spinning wouldn't matter. We just had to make it down the escalators to the Underground unnoticed—

A pair of high-vis yellow jackets flashed among the commuter sea of grey and blues. Transport Police—train cops. They hadn't seen us yet, but they were clearly looking for someone.

We just had another few meters until we made our escape down into the Tube.

A second pair of transport coppers rode the escalators up from the sub-station levels, both their gazes locked on Hollywood and me.

"Shit," I muttered.

"All right, you two. Let's have a quick word over here, eh?" The copper on the right brought out his all-purpose keep-calm smile. Hollywood stiffened. If we made a dash for it, we might make it down to the underground tunnels, but if we didn't, we'd both get nicked. Better to play along while everyone was being friendly. They couldn't arrest us for just being here. Well, not Hollywood anyway. If they figured out I was a latent, things might go differently.

I dropped my hand, ready to flick my jacket back and show them my badge, but apparently that was the wrong thing to do. The coppers dashed in, grabbing us both in armlocks, and frog-marched us away from the startled commuters.

"Hey." The copper bent my arm awkward against my back. "I was reaching for my badge. I'm Agency."

"We have a report of two latents matching your description. We're just doing our jobs by checking you out. Understand? Stand still and don't resist." The cop gripped my wrists behind me while patting me down with his free hand.

"Check my belt, I'm Agency." Nodding at Hollywood, also getting the rough-treatment, I added, "He's not a latent."

"But you are?" My friendly copper sneered into my ear.

Great. One of *those* cops. "Registered," I growled, warning him not to fuck with me.

"That just means you're stable until you aren't," he muttered. The transport police, like the Met, didn't have a lot of love for latents, not helped by the IRL posters all over the station declaring that passengers be alert for suspicious behavior or potential unregistered latents, suggesting we all liked nothing better than lurking in shadows and ambushing unsuspecting normal people with our sparkly tricks.

"Get any closer and you're gonna have to pay me by the hour," Hollywood quipped, then got his legs kicked apart and frisked for his snark.

I shot him a warning glare not to run his mouth off. He tossed back one of his sly little grins. He was beginning to enjoy this way too much. His grin grew, his thoughts headed south. I rolled my eyes.

"Got a badge," my Happy Cop announced. Finally, they'd let us go. "Could be fake."

"Oh for fuck's sake, really?"

"Watch it or I'll book you for resisting." He spoke into his radio, asking for an ID check on my badge number.

The two heavies broke from the crowd, heading right for us. Hollywood's smile died on his lips. He'd seen them. He wasn't worried, he was *scared*.

Screw this. I jerked my head back, slamming my skull into the copper's nose. He grunted and reeled, finally letting go. Hollywood doubled over, throwing his cop into a heap on the floor.

"Go!" We dashed down the escalator, leaving the cops barking into their radios.

"Oi!" Shouts echoed around the Underground hall. "Hey!"

I barreled through loitering groups and sprinted through the ticket gates, toward the Circle line. Any train would do, just as long as it took us *away*. But if we didn't hit the platforms at the right time, we'd be stuck with nowhere to go until the next train showed up. Those few minutes between trains would be the difference between getting away and getting caught. We just needed a little bit of luck.

Sinking my hand into my pocket, I lit up my cards. "Outta the way!" People sprang aside. Hot air blasted down the tunnel, carrying the squeal of brakes and clattering carriages. Either a train had just left or arrived. It had better be the latter.

Hollywood's shout echoed from behind. I whirled. One of the heavies wrapped their thick arms around his waist and flung him face-first into the tunnel's shiny tiles. The brute landed a hard punch deep into Hollywood's back that ripped a silent cry from his lips.

Fuck, that was brutal.

I launched my card straight and true, striking the bastard in the side. It burst into sparks, jolting the prick from Hollywood. Blinded, the brute groped for the wall to steady himself. Hollywood planted a quick-as-a-whip right hook into Heavy's jaw with the same lethal efficiency he'd tried to take me out. His attacker teetered and went down hard.

Hollywood staggered, and I swooped in, looping an arm around him. I half carried, half dragged him onto the platform where a packed train waited to depart. There was *always* room for more on a London tube. The trains were never full unless someone had an arm stuck in a door.

"MIND THE GAP."

Oh shit. I shoved Hollywood into the carriage, earning the fiercest snarl of contempt from the passengers already wedged in like sardines in a can, and forced my way on board, making my own space, just as the doors hissed closed. The train clanked and groaned into motion. Between sweaty arms, bored faces, and through the grubby window, I spotted the remaining heavy sprinting onto the platform, spitting a curse I couldn't hear.

The lights flickered and the train plunged into London's spaghetti-like underground rail network. Hollywood clutched the pole like his life depended on it. Blood dribbled from his split lip and his hair was all mussed, but he still found a battered smile. "You all right?" I asked.

"Think so." He brushed his lip clean with the back of his hand. "Thanks to you."

The thrill of the chase pulled my lips into a grin. "It was time I saved your arse."

16

We hopped off the Tube at Baker Street, then back on another few routes to muddy anyone thinking of trying to tail us, and ended up being spat out at Mile End. Then, at Hollywood's idea, we took a cab to the park and strolled along the canal. He walked off his aches while I just walked, wondering where we were headed, until Hollywood jumped aboard a moored narrowboat like he owned the thing, leaving me standing on the canal side, with my hands in my pockets and what must have been a dumb expression on my face.

"You coming, English?" Hollywood descended the boat's little wooden steps, then ducked inside.

He has a boat. I hadn't seen that coming. He didn't seem the boating type. A posh docklands apartment? Yes. A manky old river boat?

Color me curious.

The inside was fitted-out like a caravan, but narrower... and on water. A floating caravan, then. Grey and white kitchen units and furnishings brightened the tiny space. Pink cushions scattered here and there. It was nothing like I'd imagined a narrowboat to be. Someone had spent a lot of money making the floating caravan look posh on the inside and like it might sink at any second on the outside. Had he hired it? Was hiring a narrowboat a thing?

A framed photo caught my eye. A young man, mid-teens, too-long hair tucked behind his ears next to a girl in cropped leggings, full of bright smiles somewhere with pine trees as high as houses. Probably the US. He wasn't wrong when he'd said he and Annie went way back.

A pang of guilt and maybe a touch of jealousy did complicated things to my head. Kage and Annie were clearly an item. I'd had my hands on Hollywood and my tongue down his throat. Did that make me an accessory to cheating?

"Turn off your phone," Hollywood said from farther down the boat, where he collected a first aid kit and dumped its contents across a table. "Just a precaution."

Fair enough. I switched off my phone and drifted toward him, soaking up the twee surroundings. The boat had warmth and personal touches. A creased kid's drawing of a house was stuck to the front of a mini fridge. Reminders to get bread and pay the bills had been pinned to a corkboard. This was a *real* home. And he'd brought me here.

He wet a wad of cotton wool, and using a shaving mirror he'd grabbed from the bathroom at the back of the boat, he dabbed at his lip, cleaning off the dried blood.

Giving him space to work, I leaned against the little

kitchen units, dying to ask if this place was his, but that would make me interested, which I wasn't. We had more important things to discuss. "Why were they after you?"

"Why do you think?" he grumbled, wringing out the cotton and dabbing again.

"What were they planning on doing with you... and me?"

"I reckon I'd be getting real personal with the dead auctioneer by the morning."

"Devi's really dead, huh?"

"Yeah." Setting the bloody cotton swab down, he rolled his shoulders, and carefully removed his coat. "Anca killed him. She hired me a few months ago to root out artifacts for her employer. Mostly high-end pieces. I was doing okay until a stubborn English artifact agent got in my way."

"And Gary Clarke?"

"Anca wanted the artifacts intercepted before they got to auction. She had me track him down. The man was fast coming undone. He knew he was being watched. I confronted him the day before you and I met, tried to warn him. Reckon I made it worse. The bar in Leicester Square—that was supposed to be a grab job—get in, get the artifact—but when he ran, Anca ordered the hit." He slumped back in the booth-seat around the table, his lip all fixed but his face still pale. "My guess, he knew too much. More than me."

Now I was grateful for the space between us. "She ordered you to kill a man and you pulled the trigger? Do you get off on it or does she have something over you?"

Holding my gaze, he lost all his smiles and there was the real man, hiding behind all the Hollywood bullshit.

I'd seen that man when he'd last kissed me, right before he'd left me in his fake apartment. That man had seen a whole lot of shit, and half of it was still on his hands. Like me. Sometimes, life made soldiers out of people, even if they weren't in the military. Kage had that look about him.

He finally sighed. "If we're doing this, I need coffee." After sliding out from behind the table, he grabbed two mugs from the compact cupboards and filled them under the kitchen tap.

"Got tea?"

"No, I'm American."

Then—to my horror—he put the mugs in his *microwave.* "What are you doing?"

"Heating the water." He raised an eyebrow at me like I was the idiot.

"No." Rolling my eyes, I stepped up and elbowed him out of the way. "Just no. Where's the kettle?"

"What's wrong with—?"

"Stop." Rummaging through the cupboards, I found a tiny, dusty kettle shoved at the back behind a toast rack nobody would ever use, filled it with water, plugged it in, and flicked it on. "You can't microwave water. You'll get cancer."

"I'm pretty sure that's not a thing." He chuckled and retreated to his side of the table, wincing with each new movement.

He slouched at the end of the built-in sofa, tucking himself into the cushioned corner and resting his head back against the wall. Amber eyes under long lashes watched me make the coffee. It was all very domestic and surprisingly comfortable. Seeing him in genuine surroundings made the man more real, and it was screwing with my ability to keep my distance.

Coffee made, I shoved his across the table and sat opposite with mine. "You were about to tell my why you're murdering latents."

He wrapped his fingers around the mug but left it on the table and stared at his steaming drink. "I didn't plan it that way."

"You just sorta fell into the murder gig?"

Frowning, he leaned forward. "You can be a real prick you know that?"

"It has been suggested."

After dragging a hand down his face, he sighed. "I left the US because of the way latents are treated there. I didn't mean for it to follow me here."

"Uh huh." I sipped my coffee. "Still not hearing the reason *why*."

"I'm telling you all of this in confidence. I'm trusting you. This can't get back to Kempthorne."

Now I was frowning. "Kempthorne is the last thing you should be worried about. He's only interested in the truth."

Hollywood shook his head and stared out of the small windows at the greenery of the park beyond the canal.

"Kempthorne comes across as a hard-arse, but he's not. He wants artifacts off the street and people safe. That's all any of us want. We're good people. Well, they are. I'm working on it—which counts for something."

"Why did you get kicked off Psy Ops?" He asked it fast, like a slap across the face.

Clearing my throat, I looked him in the eyes. "Is this

like a tit for tat thing? I tell you a secret and you tell me why you're killing-on-command?"

"It'll help."

Breathing in, I mentally dug up all the old crap I'd worked so hard at burying. "I joined the military to get off the streets. A latent in the East End... They say East London is all cleaned up, but it's not. Organized crime just got smarter. It was military, or I'd end up on the wrong side of the law, in prison, or dead. I fucking loved Psy Ops, honestly—at least, in the beginning. Found my calling. Until Syria. An op went wrong, my team got caught in the crossfire. Only me and Hardhat—his tag— got out. I was booted right after, to cover the CO's fuck up."

Hollywood narrowed his eyes. "That's the official line. You gonna tell me what *really* happened?"

"I was fucking my CO and when the op went bad, I threatened to expose his negligence. I shouldn't have, but he got my team slaughtered. He figured I might also tell everyone how he likes to suck dick, and the easiest way to bury all of that, and me, was to crush my career. He gave me the choice of getting signed off for PTSD or fired for misconduct."

"Wow."

Punching Sawyer's—my CO's—teeth through his face probably hadn't helped my defense. "Your turn."

"Annie and I met years ago in summer camp. We've been friends ever since she kicked a guy in the nuts for telling everyone I kissed him."

"I like her. *Did* you kiss him?"

His grin returned, on full beam. "We did more than that. Guess he didn't know he was gay, until I showed him. Annie and I kept in touch over the years. We'd get together every time her folks flew over from the UK, dragging her with them. Then, a few months ago, she called me up... What I tell you now does not leave this room, Dom."

"All right."

"Your word."

"You've got it."

He hesitated, still weighing if I was trustworthy. "Annie is an unregistered latent. Nobody knows—nobody was *supposed* to know. And you don't tell anyone, you hear?"

I raised my hands. "Totally off the record." Also, bloody hell, one of the best known daytime TV hosts was an unregistered latent?! She'd done well to hide it for so long.

"She was being blackmailed. I got on a plane, came right over, and organized a meet with the woman black-mailing her, the authenticator, Anca."

"And offered to work for Anca if she stopped black-mailing Annie?"

"It was supposed to be a few artifact retrieval jobs and we'd be done."

"Naïve."

He huffed a dry laugh. "Didn't have a choice. But once I was around Anca, I saw things, heard things too. Like the figure known as M in the background pulling Anca's strings, collecting powerful artifacts, eliminating latents who know too much. I've never seen them. They operate through burner phones and Pay-as-you-go SIM cards. Anca is the only one who speaks with them and she's never trusted me, especially once I started asking questions. Whoever they are, they're building up to something. Something big, here in London, with a whole lotta artifacts. Now I'm neck-deep and as we saw earlier, no longer required."

It wasn't the whole story, but it was a lot more than I'd started out with, and some of it was true. Working out what bits were the truth would be more difficult. Still, hearing there was an organized force behind all this, who was collecting artifacts for a potentially malicious purpose, had my skin crawling. One dirty artifact was bad, but if the anonymous M had several, they could level all of London, or worse.

"Is Annie at risk?"

"She doesn't know anything and she's a celebrity, high-profile." He swallowed. "I think they'll leave her alone, for now. It's me they want, especially now I'm close to Kempthorne and his agents."

"You could have come to us with this. Kempthorne has resources."

"Resources like you?" he asked in a knowing tone.

"Meaning?"

"You and him—"

"We're not *together*. Christ, why does everyone think we are? Kempthorne and Co is a professional agency and we're damn good. He doesn't fuck around with his employees. The man's as focused as a missile."

"And operating from the back of a bookstore?"

"Don't knock it. Besides, you like books. I saw you fondling that Harry Potter second edition."

His soft, deep laugh was almost contagious. "I wasn't fondling it. I was appreciating it."

"Huh." I wasn't going to say it, but he'd definitely

been appreciating my cock with the same kind of heated desire in his eyes.

The clock on the wall caught my eye. I'd been gone two hours. Gina would be freaking out. I had to get back and debrief the team.

"I should—"

His hand covered mine on the table, sending a startled jolt through me. "I can't believe I'm asking this. Will you... maybe stay?"

There was a lot said in that one little word. Need widened his eyes, but not the "let's fuck" kind. He didn't want to be alone. The thought of leaving him didn't sit easy with me either, but staying wasn't a good idea. Hollywood and his little narrowboat with its pink cushions were beginning to chip away at the barriers keeping emotions out of this, and now I knew he was a victim, the old soldiering part of me couldn't drop it—or him. He'd just wanted to help a friend and instead he'd gotten sucked into London's criminal underworld of artifact dealing. He was lucky to still be breathing.

I pulled my hand from under his. "I have to check in with the team. While I do that, I'll walk the park and make sure you're floating shoebox isn't being watched." I left him at the little table, his gaze on all the bandages and plasters he'd stripped from the first aid kit. And bloody hell, he looked like a lost dog, all beat up and exhausted.

Dammit. I couldn't fall for Hollywood. He was a job. Nothing more. "I'll be right back."

His bruised face was full of honesty. "Thanks, Dom."

"Just for a few hours." I opened the little door and climbed out.

I'd stay a little while and use the time to try to convince him to have Kempthorne help him. Staying was all for the job. Which was exactly what I texted Gina, even as my treacherous heart fluttered at the thought of heading back to the boat.

ll safe. *I'm working on Hollywood.*

G: Ok.

Had trouble with transport cops. Can u get K on it?

G: Kempthorne already on it.

Awesome. Have more info on M. I'll debrief tomorrow. Don't wait up. I added some emojis of an eggplant, a donut, and a laughing face that had me chuckling to myself on my walk around Mile End's pretty green park.

If I was trying to convince Hollywood we were a professional team, he'd better not see my texts. Or he might find them amusing? He had a sense of humor; I'd seen it sparkle in his eyes when the cop was frisking him. Maybe I could coax that side of him out some more now we had some time together without an imminent threat breathing down our necks.

There was no sign of anyone staking out the narrowboat, but I'd have to be careful heading back into central

London later. The Tube was probably a no-go area for a while, at least until the transport police forgot my face.

I mulled over the information Hollywood had shared, turning it over in my mind, like a pebble found on a beach. Anca worked for this M figure. Gareth Clarke was their mule. And M was the mysterious artifact bidder? Something still didn't feel right with it all. The pieces only loosely fit together. Hollywood had been honest, to a point, but there was no doubt he knew more. Talking with Annie to get the other side of the story would help. Gina would jump at the chance, and she was a lot less conspicuous than Kempthorne or me. Maybe she could organize a subtle meet with Annie?

Climbing back onto the narrowboat, I was greeted with the sight of a freshly showered Hollywood. He'd changed into jeans and a T-shirt that was a deliberate size too small and hugged his chest like body paint. "The park's all clear," I said, trying not to admire how his jeans hugged his arse too.

Once out of his favorite coat, all his lean self was on display. I already knew there was strength in that body. I'd felt his right hook and had him wrestled against a kitchen island. If he tried those moves again, I wouldn't be putting up much of a fight.

"Did you speak with Alex Kempthorne?" he asked. He'd collected a handful of potatoes and prepped them for peeling. With him turned away, I unashamedly roamed my gaze down the man's back, over his hip, and around the curve of his arse. There was no way he didn't know he was attractive. His dark, wet hair artfully finished the fine picture.

"No. I said I wouldn't." I propped myself against a

cupboard and tore my gaze away. "I did text Gina though or she'd come looking for me. Don't worry, I turned my phone off." His quick hands chopped a potato like a pro. "You cook?"

"Sometimes. It's pointless when I'm alone but..." He glanced over his shoulder, flashing me a charming smile. "I don't mind with company."

Must stay professional. Which was easier said than done when my thoughts were ragged from lack of sleep and my body hungry for all the things Hollywood's body was broadcasting.

I watched his quick hands work with that knife, grateful all that lethal precision wasn't aimed at me.

"You can sit down, yah know," he said. "Instead of hovering. You must be exhausted."

I'd been on my feet since leaving for the club with Kempthorne, and now the danger had passed, I was beginning to lag. "Thanks. Can I use your bathroom?"

"Have at it."

The tiny bathroom had plenty of places to hide personal affects. I had a quick rummage around, still trying to get a read on the man, but didn't find anything unusual. My reflection was rough though. My stubble grated my fingers, and my hair was a tousled mess, and not in the fashionable way. I ran my wet hands through it, trying to shape some control into it, and splashed water onto my face, clearing my head.

Don't get involved.

I tried to avoid peering into my own eyes for too long. They always seemed to call me a liar.

Returning to the kitchen and Hollywood prepping soup, I tucked myself into the little booth-style seats around the table. "So how'd you end up with a houseboat?"

"It's Annie's. She uses it for breaks away. Or did, until I showed up."

It wasn't his pad, it was hers. That explained the photos on the mini-fridge and maybe the pink cushions, although I kinda liked the aesthetic. "It's cute."

"Yeah, it's nice, and it moves, which keeps my paranoid ass happy."

He didn't like to stay in one place for too long? Hollywood was a riddle, one I was finding myself more and more intrigued by. I watched him cook up a vegetable soup for lunch and let my thoughts drift. Everything on paper said Hollywood dropped out of every career he'd tried, but records lied. I was the perfect example of that. "Why'd you leave the FBI?" I asked quietly, easing the question in now we were both comfortable.

"I knew a latent in middle school." He served up the soup in two bowls as he talked. "A good kid. Had some issues, you know... He got beat on. I tried to help out but made it worse, and then one day he was gone. Just didn't show up for school. Nobody said a thing. Nobody cared. He vanished like I'd dreamed him up."

I felt my lips pinch. Everything he described was routine in the East End. Latent kids slipped through the cracks all the time and nobody batted an eye.

"About a year later, a report in a newspaper said remains had been found, dumped in a firepit. I knew then. He didn't just die, someone killed him, and nobody gave a damn about that kid."

Hollywood's gaze met mine and a knowing passed between us, the kind of knowing two people have when they've seen a lot of shit and know how it all ends. "I finished high school, did all the right things, got selected for training, but it's different in the US. I thought I was going to do good, but it turns out nobody really gives a shit about what's good." He placed my bowl of soup in front of me and sat opposite with his. "I think of that kid often. I couldn't be the person the FBI wanted me to be. The state marshals, the agencies, they're all the same, just with different names. More coffee?"

"Got anything stronger?"

"It's a bit early for wine."

"I haven't slept in over thirty hours. Early is relative."

"Wine it is." He found a bottle in one of the many tiny cupboards, popped the cork, and poured two glasses.

I took mine with a smile of thanks, then asked, "For a latent sympathizer, you had no problem shooting Gary Clarke."

He smiled and swirled the wine in his glass. "You like to ambush with questions."

Shrugging, I tucked into my soup, surprised by the explosion of taste on my tongue. "This is good," I mumbled around a mouthful.

His smile grew and he took a few bites before replying. "Clarke knew Anca was on to him. He kept that artifact with intent. He was about to blow."

"I know people. Know latents—as I am one. Gary was scared, but he wasn't stupid. It seems to me like you killed him because Anca was worried he was about to talk."

Hollywood shook his head. "He was going to blow, and you would have died with him."

"We'll just have to agree to disagree."

We talked some more about Annie, and it was clear

they were close childhood friends, but not lovers. The relationship angle was a lie to keep the press at bay. Annie didn't do relationships, and having Hollywood on her arm kept people from asking when she was going to marry. The press never bought the *just friends* line anyway, which I was fast discovering from their infatuation with Alexander Kempthorne.

Hollywood was a good listener. A few hours went by like no time at all, but as comfortable as this all was, I couldn't ignore my responsibilities and the threat looming over London. "I have to get back." I slid from the table seats and retrieved my jacket, my thoughts turning toward Anca and what Kempthorne might be able to find out about her.

The moment I turned toward the door, Hollywood's hand landed on my shoulder and stroked down my arm. My heart leaped into my throat, freezing me rigid, giving Hollywood time to step around me and block my exit. "Or..." His single step brought him close. "We could find something else to do," he said in that slick, sultry American voice.

"I can't—" The denial stalled the second he pressed all of his delicious self against me. His fingers slipped into my hair and his mouth nudged mine open. All my efforts to *not* think about how fine his naked body would be writhing under my hands collapsed. Dropping my hands to his hips, I pulled him in when I should have pushed him away. I was lost from there. Lost in the feel of his mouth opening mine, his tongue dancing, his grip on my hair, and lost in the feel of his steely body. I barely registered him walking me backward against a cupboard, just moaned when he sandwiched me tight against it. The hard press of his cock dug into my hip and there was no doubting if Hollywood was invested in this. I vaguely recalled Robin saying something about no fraternizing on the job, but this *was* the job. So what was a man to do if not go with it?

He tasted of wine. I nipped at his bottom lip, wanting more of him. He hissed and jerked away, dabbing at the re-opened cut. "Oh shit, sorry—" His next kiss swallowed all my apologies and me. His hand dropped to my arse, his knee had me pinned, and his cock was damned insistent that I get in the game.

Gasping, I dropped my head back, reeling from the whirlwind that was Hollywood's hands and mouth and body suddenly *everywhere*. And it still wasn't enough. Christ, the wine combined with lack of sleep had my head spinning. There were a hundred reasons why screwing Hollywood was a bad idea, but in that moment, I couldn't think of a single one.

He pulled back and dragged his thumb across my bottom lip. "I've been wanting this mouth since you snarled at me in that alleyway."

I could have said something clever in reply but grabbed the back of his neck instead and kissed him as though I could carve out his soul with my tongue. We were doing this, and it was fucking happening now before common sense crept back in. We danced back toward the table. He stumbled, put a hand down to steady himself, and now I had him pinned against that little table, right where I wanted him. His physique was a feast, just waiting to be devoured. Running my hands under his T-shirt, I danced my fingers over his abs and imagined teasing my tongue over those hard ridges soon.

I needed to sink my teeth into a whole lot of Hollywood's stunning angles, like his curved shoulders that demanded to be sucked and nipped.

He shoved me back, crossed his arms, and yanked his too-tight T-shirt off, exposing the striking planes of his chest. Christ, I didn't know where to start. Lick him up the middle or nip at one of those tight abs. I ducked and flicked my tongue over a nipple, making him hiss. He shifted, propping his arse on the tabletop and spreading his knees, inviting me in.

I caught him gazing at me with heat in his eyes, his mouth crooked and face lit by cocky delight. Bloody hell, when he looked like sin walking, I was helpless to resist. Gently grabbing his chin, I tilted his face up and came in for a ghost of a kiss, not quite meeting his lips. "No interruptions this time?"

"Just us."

Kissing Hollywood slowly was a whole other game of temptation-laden seduction. His tongue teased, his teeth nipped, and if I hadn't been lost in the feel of him before, I was now. This gentle kiss was more dangerous than the rest. The others were fucking with our mouths. This undemanding kiss was something else, something that triggered a touch of fear in my fluttering heart. Breaking off revealed Hollywood watching me. He rolled his lips together, tasting. His throat moved as he swallowed, and I absorbed all the little tells, drinking him in.

Okay, this was... a lot. What was happening here? Were we just fucking around or had we somehow stumbled into something more?

"It's probably best not to think," he said, dragging his voice over gravel. His fingertips skimmed my rough jaw, scratching bristle, then danced across my lips. His gaze followed their path, committing everything to memory, as though he feared—no, he *knew*—none of this would last.

He seemed pained somehow, afraid all over again. And that hidden, vulnerable part of me broke open. I had to get this back before we both fell in too deep.

I caught his hand, stopped its roaming, and with a wild grin, lowered it to the ridge upsetting the line of my jeans. "So stop thinking."

His smile flashed across his lips and his hand found the right way to grip my cock, pulling me in. I skimmed his mouth and dipped to kiss his neck, breathing in his clean soapy smell. After our dash through the Tube, fuck knew what I smelt like. Diesel and sweat? Definitely not soap. Next to his smooth handsomeness, I was the scruffy one—the hopeless one who always missed a shirt button. The bastard who would punch a fucker down for glancing at his sexy boyfriend. Although, Hollywood was capable of doing his own punching.

The crazy thought of us as a pair had me smiling into his neck. I sucked and nipped at his ear, making him jerk and chuckle. His free hand pressed against my chest, over my heart. And when Robin had hinted that maybe I had a soft spot for Hollywood, she might have been on to something.

Hollywood shoved me gently, levering some space between us. "Bed?" Dark eyebrows lifted.

"There's a bed in this hobbit house?"

He slipped out from under me, took my hand, and led me through the middle of the boat to a tiny narrow door at the back. The bed was a double and tucked into an impossible space. That was all I noticed because Hollywood crawled onto the sheets and propped his head on a hand. He crooked a finger. Fuck, this man was trouble, and I was here for every inch of him. I tugged off my shirt and began undoing my belt but stopped when he shook his head. "Come here," he said. A bottom that liked to issue orders?

Oh fine. Like I was going to argue.

I inched onto the bed, and when he dropped onto his back, propping himself up on both elbows, I prowled up the length of him until we were eye to eye. Having Hollywood beneath me was hot as fuck and messed with my usual desires. His soft expression told me he didn't get onto his back for just anyone, or maybe that was my ego talking.

After laying himself flat, his fingers sank into my waistband. He flipped off the agency badge and tossed it away, then those quick fingers had my belt undone, freeing the pressure on my cock enough for his touch to find my straining length and wrap tight.

"Ah, fuck,"

"Love your accent," he drawled, using his encircled fingers to meet my short, rolling thrusts.

I might have been the one on top, but he was in control. With half my mind on the ripples of pleasure, the other half was focused on getting my hand around *his* dick. I tugged roughly at his jean's fly, my efforts so sloppy that he knocked my hand away, deftly undid the button and zip, and shifted his hips, shucking the jeans down. No pants. He went commando.

I wasted no time in getting his cock in my grip.

He sucked in a breath, sending more wicked shivers through me. There weren't enough hours in the day for me to do everything I wanted to do to him. Make him cry out, make him moan, make him issue more orders and grip the sheets in his fists while he came. The options were limitless. But my time wasn't.

I had my hand on his cock, his on mine, my mouth hovering over his, and said, "I'm so going to rock your boat."

He laughed a rich, carefree laugh that choked off the second I scooted down the bed and took his cock between my lips.

18

I revved Hollywood up with my mouth and tongue until he clutched at my hair, half holding me down as he fought to breathe while controlling our pace. I'd have happily tipped him over the edge. He seemed as though he needed it. But then he grabbed my face in both hands and hauled me up off his cock and pulled me into a salty kiss. I wasn't sure which of us was the more desperate. I'd figured it was me, but Hollywood was so bloody hot that his raw need left me breathless.

He tore from the kiss, still held me trapped in his hands, and growled, "I want you."

He already had me, so he was asking for more. And I didn't usually top guys until I was sure they weren't trying to kill me. Lately, it had just been a few rushed hand-jobs with guys I'd met in the bars. Nothing like this.

His brows ticked inward and his grip eased. "You don't want to?"

"Fuck," I puffed out, burying my face in his neck. "It's not that." He dropped his hands, withdrawing. Christ, I didn't want to lose him for some stupid hang up. Sliding my tongue along his jaw, I teased a kiss. He turned his head. He was all amber eyes with specks of green, so beautiful it was a crime. And this was where the don't-think part came in, because I was thinking too hard about all of this, about him. I'd figured this would just be some meaningless, hot sex but with every glance, Hollywood was chipping away at my heart. Or maybe I didn't want meaningless. Maybe I'd stumbled into feeling this with my eyes closed.

His thumb caressed my cheek. "Kiss me."

I did, soft and slow and filled with too much heart. Fuck it, I was already beyond the point of no return, so the only option was to dig myself deeper, right?

His fingers worked at my shirt, unbuttoning it until he could get his hands in and dance his fingertips down my back. I smirked, almost laughed, more than a little tick-lish way down low, and he chuckled into the kiss. Christ, this was too good, too honest. Suddenly, in this moment, it felt real. *He* felt real. All the fake smiles, charming words, the gun, the coat. It was all a show, and now I was beginning to see the real Kage Mitchell—the vulnerable guy who kept trying to do the right thing and fucking up —and I kinda liked the prick. Like, *really* liked.

"Lube?"

He flung a hand out, twisted, and rummaged around under the bed. Seeing as he'd exposed a shoulder, I went to work on teasing its firm, warm skin between my teeth, making him twitch.

Hollywood straightened, coming up with his prize of lube and condoms, with a crooked smile that said he was game. So practical.

It had been a while since I'd had to tool-up, and Hollywood had already sensed my hesitation. Whether knowingly or unwittingly, he did the only thing that would get me invested. He stretched his arms above his head and surrendered. "I'm all yours, English."

Fuck.

Naked, he was a vision. Like forbidden fruit, and not for rough East End latent boys like me. So of course I was going to fucking take him. He spread his knees and I lunged, smothering him. "You're pushing all my buttons."

"I figured you're a control freak."

Two control freaks because he damn well knew who was pulling the strings here, and it wasn't all me.

"Tell me if it gets too much."

He bit his lip and nodded, and right around then, I stopped thinking and fell into the feel of Kage writhing, his slick cock in my hand, his hard body beneath me, and later, the tight, sheathing warmth of him rippling pleasure all the way through me.

Maybe it was an epic mistake, or maybe it was nothing. But as I later dozed with Kage in my arms, I didn't regret it.

I woke with a start in an unfamiliar bed and sat bolt upright, almost hitting my head on the low ceiling. Oh right, the narrowboat and exploring Hollywood in all the right ways. Hollywood's side of the bed was empty, the sheets wrinkled. I listened but heard only the gentle lap of water against the boat's hull. If Hollywood was aboard, he was dead quiet.

What was the time? Where was my phone? Gina would be losing her shit if I didn't check in.

Tugging my clothes back on, I spilled from the tiny room, spotted my phone on the table, and snatched it up. The dark windows told me it was late. The kitchen clock said past nine. "Shit." I'd slept the rest of the day away. And there was no sign of Hollywood.

I grabbed my jacket and headed toward the door, then spotted a note on the mini-fridge.

Getting groceries.

Back soon.

X

Freeing the slip of paper from its magnet, I dropped it onto the countertop and rummaged around the drawers for a pen. The *x* was a good thing, right? A kiss. Or was it too much too soon? Did an *x* mean the same thing in American as it did in English? Shit, I was overthinking this.

Finding a pen, I stalled with the nib poised over the paper. Dammit, what to write? Opting to keep it simple, I scrawled *TEXT ME* under his neat, blocky writing, and returned the note to the mini-fridge. Then added—*STAY SAFE*—with the words almost running off the paper.

It was too late to chance finding a cab, so I hit the Tube and hoped the transport police weren't nearby. My phone pinged with various messages from Gina, each one getting more irate until she threatened to file a missing person report. I quickly tapped out a reply, telling her I was on my way, and then sent a message to Kempthorne, asking him to meet me in the office ASAP regarding Anca.

Gina buzzed back: *Where are you?*

Back in 20mins.

G: OK. Are you alone?

Yeah, Kage wouldn't come in.

G: Where is he?

I typed out *Canal boat Mile End Park* but hesitated with my thumb hovering over *send*. Hollywood's paranoia had me holding off. He'd trusted me. That meant something.

Deleting the message, I sent instead: *Debrief when I'm back.*

Cecil Court outside the shops buzzed with fancily clad people all holding wine glasses and chatting over tiny sandwiches. One of the other bookstores was having a party. I nodded at a few familiar faces and hurried to 16a. The door didn't budge, and I still hadn't picked up a spare key.

Hitting the buzzer, I tapped a foot, and when no signs of movement came from inside, I called Gina. It rang through to her answerphone. "Hey, G, I'm outside…" Nothing. Okay, that was weird. Leaning on the buzzer didn't rouse anyone either. The shop's window blinds were all drawn and no lights were on. Nobody was home. Someone was *always* home.

Something wasn't right here.

With the background sounds of party laughter and chinking glasses, I dialed Kempthorne's number and lifted the phone to my ear. "C'mon, boss. Answer the phone. Where is everyone?"

A reflected shimmer in the shop's bay window caught my eye too late. A hand slammed into the back of my head, smacking me face-first against the glass. I gasped, more shocked than hurt. A thick arm looped around my waist and something cold and hard punched into my back.

"Easy now, mate. Don't make a fuss and we won't 'av any problems, all right?" a cockney voice said, a voice I recognized.

"Fucker—"

The knife dug in harder, beginning to burn, cutting off the rest of my insult.

"Oi, what did I say?" the cockney growled. "These nice people don't wanna see your guts all over the shiny cobbles. So don't be a prick and come along all friendly-like." This guy, I got a look at his square jaw and recognized him as one of the heavies who had chased us through Paddington. Big guy, lots of muscle. He could probably have shoved me through the shop window, so this was him being nice.

"How's your friend?" I asked. "Got his vision back yet?" The knife dug in, twisting, sending a rush of prickling heat up my side.

"Smart-arse, aren't you."

Warm, wet liquid ran down my leg. Blood. Gritting my teeth, I stumbled along, locked in my new friend's hug like he was just helping a drunk find his way home. All these people, smiling and laughing, and not one of them cared to look over.

"Just do as we say, all right, an' your agency mates will be safe."

They had Gina? Robin? Kempthorne? No way. Not all of them. They couldn't have got to them all. Thoughts racing back to Gina's texts, I remembered their wording.

Something had felt off about them since leaving St James's Park.

Fuck. They'd grabbed her in the morning. I'd been texting her updates. Christ, what had I said in those messages? Had Kage been exposed? Did they have him too? "What have you done with them?"

"Like I said, mate. Relax, eh? An' you'll find out."

A black Audi idled at the end of Cecil Court. Party-goers drifted back and forth, too wrapped up in their world to notice anything outside their little bubbles.

The Audi's rear door flung open and the cockney shoved me inside, following close behind me. The knife was gone but the throbbing heat in my side wasn't. I twisted, about to kick out—cold steel touched my neck.

"Don't fucking think it, Prick," the cockney growled, slamming the door closed.

The car lurched into motion, throwing me back into the seat. Devi had been in the back of this car. That journey hadn't ended well for him.

My new cockney friend dug my cards from my pocket and tucked them into his, muttering, "Fucking hate latents."

"We're not that fond of arseholes like you either."

His first landed right where his blade had stabbed, setting my left side ablaze all over again. Doubled up, I coughed around brittle agony, fighting to fill my lungs and stay conscious. Shit, shit, shit....

"If he throws up like the last one, you're cleaning it," a voice piped up from the front.

Keeping my head down, I focused on filling my lungs. A few punches and a shallow knife wound weren't going to kill me, but wherever we were going wasn't going to be fun. I scanned the back of the car. The Audi had auto-matic locking. I wasn't leaping out any time soon. I couldn't see much of the driver in the seat in front of me, but a third passenger was the bastard who had Tased me.

He caught my eye and grinned. "Remember me?"

"Where are we goin'?

"Anca wants a word."

Straightening, I fell back in the seat and winced around the leaking stab wound in my side. "Yeah well, I'm bleeding, and if you don't stop it, I'll be dead before we get there."

"You stabbed him?" the driver snarled.

"He's ex-forces," Cockney whined. "He nearly set Jonesy on fire. Of course I fuckin' stabbed him."

I slumped against the door and peeled back my jacket, revealing a very wet, sticky dark patch.

"Oh shit," Taser said.

Yeah, okay. My head spun. It was deeper than I'd thought. Blood had spread down my leg, soaking into my jeans. A lot of it. Not good.

"Pull over," Taser snapped.

"What?" the driver grunted.

"Pull over. He's gonna bleed all over the back seat and die. For fuck's sake! Do I have to do everything?"

The Audi bumped against a curb. I got a look at tall, terraced houses and leafy trees and figured we were near the multimillion-pound houses of Hyde Park. If they opened the doors, I could try and make a run for it.

Cockney grumbled at my side and leaned over to grab my arm. Taser left the front seat, making his way around the back of the car. If I was going to make a run for it, it had to be now. I slammed my hand over Cockney's face and sent a pulse of power through my fingers, giving the bastard a sudden, blinding head-splitting ache, and manually flicked the door lock over—now we were stopped, it opened. I was out and running in the next second. A car horn honked, and a black cab skidded to a stop, its front fender nudging my legs enough to spin me around.

Something struck me hard in the side. Blinding head-lights spilled into my vision and the cold, hard pavement slapped me in the back, then darkness chased me into unconsciousness.

19

The pillowcase over my head allowed a blur of shapes to leak through, but nothing that helped identify where I'd woken up, cuffed to a bloody chair. A radio chattered in another room, but I didn't hear movement nearby, or other voices.

A thick bandage clung to my side where the wound throbbed hot, which wasn't good, but I had more pressing problems. Like how to get away from what was fast becoming a shit situation.

I twisted my hands, bound by the wrists to each chair leg behind me, testing the cuffs. They rattled but didn't give. The chair was bolted or fixed to the floor too. This wasn't someone's cozy living room. The set-up was professional. I wasn't the first guy to be chained to the chair. There was a high chance Devi had been cuffed here too.

Stuck listening to Radio 2, and with my side on fire, I focused on what I knew, not what I couldn't control. I had a date with Anca the authenticator, the woman who had applied screws to a man like Hollywood, had Gareth Clarke terrified enough to contemplate blowing himself and a London alleyway to tiny pieces, and had murdered the auctioneer she'd been working for and probably others in her pursuit to buy up or steal all the dirty artifacts she could get her hands on. Anca was bad news.

I also knew nobody had been at the office, which suggested Anca and her heavies had Gina, and possibly Robin and Kempthorne too—they'd taken them while I'd been fucking about with Hollywood.

Guilt soured my tongue. At least Kage was safe—as long as he stayed on his boat and didn't do something stupid like text me—like I'd asked him to in the fucking note I'd left.

Anca was a latent. An authenticator. Same as me. I'd only met one other, and he'd been on the wrong side of sanity. We weren't known for our stability. Something about authenticators and how the psychic energy reacted to us made us notoriously twitchy. Anca hadn't looked unhinged but sociopaths never did. Maybe I could talk my way out of this. Authenticator to authenticator.

I tugged some more on my cuffs and breathed into the pillowcase.

They'd taken my phone. It was locked, but it wouldn't be hard to get my thumbprint seeing as my hands were tied. Once unlocked, it would be easy to lure Hollywood out of hiding. Shit. I really didn't control much of anything. And I didn't have my cards. Just my wits, which were lacking.

Boots thumped the floorboards somewhere in the house. New voices rumbled behind walls. Someone turned the radio up—to hide my screams? Great.

I steeled myself, calling on old Psy Ops training. Whatever it was they wanted, they weren't getting anything from me. A door groaned open and the thumping boots paraded inside the room. Outlines took shape through the pillowcase. Three—no, four people.

The pillowcase lifted and I blinked into the light from a single, filthy lightbulb hanging from the ceiling. Taser was here, with his idiot friend Cockney and the driver. Anca stood in front of me, her expression unimpressed. Tight trousers disappeared into laced-up leather ankle boots. Her fitted jacket had a few dark stains that looked suspiciously like blood. Black leather gloves stood out stark against the pale skin of her arms. She had the look of someone who had seen a lot of shit and was tired of it all. The look of an authenticator.

"John Domenici," she said.

Devi had said she was Swedish, but her accent, now I heard it clearly, was eastern European. Criminal gangs out of the eastern block often employed latents as sleepers, inserting them deep into UK organizations. Was that what she was? Someone else's tool or her own?

"I see your mind is working, yes? You think you know me?" Her smile was a cold, hard thing. "Know why we are here?"

"I have no idea, honestly. This is all a misunderstanding. You've got the wrong guy."

She snorted and folded her arms crossed. She didn't look like much, but neither did I until you put an artifact in my hands.

Moving in closer, she tried to touch my face. I turned my head away, but her slim, gloved fingers caught my chin, yanking me back. Psychic energy tingled beneath her fingertips. So familiar I could have called it my own.

"You do not look like much, *John*."

"If we're going to be friendly, it's Dom," I growled out. "Not John."

She pinched my chin hard enough to sting, then let go. "You join Kempthorne two years ago. Yes?"

"Two years Wednesday. I'm hoping for cake and a pay rise. Mostly a pay rise. I figure if Kempthorne can offer a cool *two million* reward for all those artifacts you stole, he can pay me a decent wage. Am I right, fellas?" A few nervous glances bounced around the room. Two million was a lot of money. Two million could change a life. How loyal were these men to Anca?

Anca's pale pink lips thinned. She crouched in front of me, putting herself at my level. "You like to talk."

"Sometimes." Here it came. The questions about Kage's location and what he knew of her operation. When I didn't tell her what she wanted to hear, she'd set her heavies on me. None of this was surprising.

"Then let's talk..." Blue eyes, as cold as ice, peered through me. "Tell me about Alexander Kempthorne."

I frowned, mentally stumbling. Glancing at Taser and his friends bought me a few seconds to realign my thoughts around protecting Kempthorne and not Kage. Why did she want to know about Kempthorne? "Like what?" I asked, then added, "Google him. You'll probably find as much as I know."

"I did." She pulled a slim phone from her back pocket and showed me an open browser with an image of Kempthorne and me heading into Devi's club. The photographer had caught us at ease, with Kempthorne's rare smile on display and his blue eyes alight with the thrill of the chase. The headline read: *London's Most Eligible Bachelor Taken?* Admittedly, we did make a sexy couple. I was the shorter, heavier, rougher one, while he was the sophisticated, taller, skinnier one. But it wasn't as though I was holding his hand. If I wasn't out as gay, the press would have written us off as two mates going for a drink. They just loved the gay angle, even when there wasn't one.

I chuckled humorlessly. "What do you want me to say?"

"You are close, yes? To Alexander?"

"I work for him." I shrugged. "What is this? You his superfans or something? There are easier ways to get him to notice you instead of tying me up."

"How did you get job with agency?" Anca pushed on.

I huffed and rolled my eyes. "A friend on Facebook hit me up about a vacancy. Is this really all you want? Untie me and we'll chat over coffee, authenticator to authenticator. We don't need the cuffs. You and me? We're the same."

She smiled, and it was like looking at a crocodile's smile, knowing the creature could eat you the second you turned your back. "The cuffs are for *your* protection."

Why the fuck would I need to be restrained for my own protection? I glared back at her. "We could be friends, but you're making it really difficult to like you." Christ, my side hurt. I shifted in the chair, trying to find a more comfortable position.

"What do you know about experiments?" she asked.

"The what?" What bollocks was this now? "Where're my friends?"

Her eyes narrowed.

"I really don't know what the fuck you want, lady."

"I do not believe you, John."

"I work for Kempthorne. He pays my wages. That's it. I don't know anything about experiments. What experiments is he supposed to be doing? He's just some rich guy playing at saving the world from artifacts. There's nothing else going on."

"Have you ever seen Alexander with a coin?" she asked.

I snorted. "The man's a billionaire. He has a lot of them."

Anca nodded at Cockney and the big man moved his bulk behind me. She straightened from her crouch and left the room, leaving the door wide open, revealing a corridor with exposed floorboards and peeling wallpaper.

When she returned, the heavy, thumping beat of power followed her back into the room. I knew what she had in her gloved hand before she crouched and set the pen on the floor between us. That fucking pen just kept coming back to haunt me. She'd just put a massive red button in front of us that read *DO NOT PRESS*, and both our mammalian brains were clamoring to get at it.

Anca stepped back, giving herself room too. The gloves had helped her resist its pull, but she wasn't immune.

"What fucking game is this?" I snarled. "Get that out of here."

"Beautiful, do you not agree, John?"

My shrill laugh came out panicked. "No." I'd had that pen in my hand twice, and each time the horrid thing had sung me a siren song. How many more times did I have to deny it purchase in my head? How many more times did I have to fight the bloody thing off?

Cockney's big overly familiar hands got hold of the middle finger on my right hand. I bucked, startled at the touch and trapped between whatever he was about to do and the ticking bomb in front of me. The pen lay innocently thrumming its seduction on the floor. At least I was restrained... Ah, that was what the cuffs were for.

"You have special connection to this one," Anca was saying somewhere far away, somewhere behind the pen's lullaby. "It likes you."

Pick me up. Take me. Twist me. Use me. Ruin the world with me.

"Do you know how it is so powerful? When you held it before, did you see its past?"

She needed to shut the fuck up and get the bloody thing out of the room. Words didn't come easy as I panted through my gritted teeth. I hadn't read its past, knowing that if I did, the pen would get its claws deeper into me. I didn't need to know its story to know it was off-the-charts dangerous for a latent like me.

Anca picked up the pen. Her eyes turned glassy as she gazed at the thing, and a pang of jealousy almost pulled a groan from my lips. I wanted to hold it, I needed it.

"Boss?" Taser stepped in from looming at the edges of the room.

Anca startled herself from the pen's thrall and stepped forward, handing the pen over my shoulder to Cockney.

Wait... what...

"Ready yourself—"

Oh Christ, no. They were going to put it in my hands. "No, wait." Panic spilled through my veins. I yanked on the cuffs. "Stop. I can't…" I wasn't ready, I wasn't prepared. "Do that and we're all dead!"

Anca's smile turned reptilian again. "I think you can handle it, John."

The cool casing of the pen touched my fingers. I locked up, as though Taser had zapped me again. The pen crooned and whispered, sang its song, demanding to be known, tugging me down and down into its story.

"Read it, Mister Domenici. And learn all about your Alexander Kempthorne."

Oh god, no. I couldn't stop it. I wasn't prepared. I wasn't strong enough and the pen's magic was sweet and tempting, and I wanted to know its secrets. It told me I needed to know them. Squeezing my eyes closed, I fell hopelessly into the artifact's memory.

20

I mages came like lightning strikes. Fast and bright, but bitterly cold, and I was powerless to stop them. *A boy on a metal table. Straps at his wrists and ankles. A mother's touch—achingly soft. A whisper in his ear. Tears falling. Lies. Hollow screams.*

I snapped my eyes open, gasping and dizzy, my face cold and wet—screams still ringing in my ears.

Fuck.

Kempthorne.

I was still cuffed to the damn chair, but the room was empty and the pen gone. Spent, I slumped over and breathed around the trembling, trying to anchor myself in my own body, in this time, abandoning memories that weren't mine. Kempthorne... his parents. No, not both. Just his mother. She'd experimented on their boy. *Tortured him.* Christ. I could hear him sobbing in the room with me now. I'd felt what he'd felt, and the horror of it had me wanting to crawl out of my own skin and hide somewhere nobody would see me.

The pen was Kempthorne's, made dirty by his trauma.

The people who were supposed to love and protect him—the people he trusted, people that were his whole world—had abused him in the worst way.

My insides roiled. Acid burned my throat.

This was... a nightmare. I had to get a grip on myself, on my own mind, get back my control. Whatever happened, whatever Anca said, whatever she did, if I lost control, it'd be more than Anca and her heavies who paid with their lives.

Breathing hard, I lifted my head and stared at the door. Emotions would be my undoing. They always were. If I was going to survive this, I had to shut down, like I had in Syria.

Shut it all down.

Be cold. Be hard. Unfeeling.

Anca later returned with a bottle of water. Without a word, she unscrewed the lid and tipped it up at my lips as a show of camaraderie from a fellow authenticator or more likely as a little kindness to get me to talk.

"Thanks," I rasped.

"I am not animal. I just want answers."

"What do you want with Kempthorne?" Just saying his name had the vulnerable part of me shying away.

Screwing the lid back on the bottle, she set it down beside my chair. "I ask questions."

"I don't know the things you think I do," I said softly. It was just the two of us. Just two latents in a world that hated us, when it wasn't using us. We didn't have to be enemies. *Don't make me read it again.*

"Where is he?" she asked.

Then she didn't already have him. That left Gina and Robin at risk. "I honestly don't know."

"Where would he go, John?"

"I don't know."

"Answer or your friend will be hurt."

I stared back at her. *Friend*, singular. I kept my face blank. "If he's not at the shop or Kensington, I don't know. He has houses all over London. He could be in any one of them."

"No. He is not."

I shrugged, rattling my cuffs. "Like I said, I'm just a grunt. I don't know anything about Kempthorne outside of work."

"You know more, John Domenici. You live with man for two years. You must know more."

"Yeah, except he's Kempthorne. So, I really don't."

She had her phone out again, with the same article on the screen. "You are in relationship. You *fuck* Alexander Kempthorne."

"Believe everything you read in the papers, do you? Look, sure, I'd tap that, I mean, he's hot, right? But he's not into guys. Like I said, you're barking up the wrong tree."

She huffed and left the room. The sound of her boots clipping the floorboards faded away until the chatter from the radio drowned them out. Some muffled voices travelled through the walls, but nothing I could decipher. Were Gina or Robin here too? In another room? Robin knew a lot more about Kempthorne than I did, but despite looking like the cliché secretary, she was as hard as fucking nails and wouldn't talk. Gina was softer, but still mighty. Anca wouldn't find any of us easy to break. Of course, it helped that I didn't know anything.

She knew more about Kempthorne than I did.

If Kempthorne knew these people were onto him, he'd have gone to ground. He was always a step ahead. Although, a head's up would have been nice, but that was Kempthorne—always with the secrets. And now I'd been forced to witnesses a horrible glimpse into his past, I wasn't surprised the man was the way he was. His crusade to get artifacts off London's streets was beginning to make a lot more sense. Secretive, intense, driven, distracted. Not in the same world as the rest of us. He'd suffered a shit-ton of psychic trauma, enough to create at least one dirty artifact. It was a wonder he functioned at all.

The pen had confirmed other things too. Like the fact his mother had been an authenticator and she'd been the one administering his torture. Was there something in the authenticator angle? Mrs Kempthorne, Anca, and me? We were rare, but if there was a reason authenticators were in any way special to this case, I couldn't see it. Unless it was something to do with what we'd seen *in* artifacts, like the pen? Anca had mentioned a coin... The coin Kempthorne kept in his safe? That was the only damn thing Anca had said that I might know something about.

If I got out of this, Kempthorne and me were due a long, hard chat.

Anca was back, and this time in her gloved hands she held my deck of cards. "Tell me about these."

I shifted in the chair. "What do you want to know?"

I'd had them so long, the cards were a part of me. Constant companions through all the shit, they'd been with me in the East end, in the military in Syria, and during my time at the agency when cases had gone pear shaped. They'd saved my arse countless times.

She pulled a card free of the deck. Without a latent trick running through them, they were just an artifact. Dirty, but not the worst out there. The card she held up now was the three of hearts. Over the years, I'd replaced missing cards with others from new packs. The psychic energy that made my deck an artifact leaked into new cards, replenishing the pack. But it meant the deck was made up of mismatched cards—51 cards. A complete deck, minus one. One card was always absent. One card I never replaced.

Fluttering her pale lashes, she dropped the deck into her pocket, took the three of hearts between her fingers, and tore it in two.

I filled my lungs and locked my lips together to keep from losing my shit.

The two pieces fluttered to the floor and laid at her feet.

When I was sure I wouldn't scream, I carefully said, "D'yah like pulling the wings off flies too?"

"It is uncomfortable?"

"What do you think?"

"I understand. This artifact is precious to you."

"Are you going to ask me any questions or just fuck around?"

Her teeth flashed in a brilliant smile. "Now you are

paying attention. Yes?" Stopping close, she peered down her nose. "Where is Alexander Kempthorne?"

"I told you already. I don't fucking know."

She plucked another card from her pocket, tore it in two, and tossed the pieces at me. They hit me in the chest and landed in my lap. I looked at them, feeling my heart pound, its beats filling my head, trying to leak out of my ears.

"Try again, John."

"I'm not his fucking PA." Another card appeared in her fingers. The sound of it tearing had my spine trying to curl up. "Bitch."

"Now we are getting somewhere, yes, John?"

"Fuck you." I bucked in the chair. "Where's Gina? Are you keeping her here too? You're not going to get anything from us because *we don't know anything.*"

"Hm." She pulled a lighter from her pocket and lifted my deck in her other hand.

Oh hell no. "You're a real piece of work, woman."

She flicked the lighter and a flame sparked to life, dancing and swaying. "If you burn my deck I will light up this fucking room with the both of us in it. Let's see who fucking walks out then." Power tingled down my arms— the kind of power that shouldn't be able to do much without an artifact to boost it. But I wasn't just some random latent. Unlike Anca, I was *Psy Ops.* My trick was trained to dance at my command.

Taser appeared in the doorway and didn't hesitate to fire the electrically charged prongs. I checked out of my own body for a few seconds—snuffing out the trick too— and swam back into my buzzing body, limp and light-headed. Fucking Tasers. How many times could I get hit with that thing before I was broken forever?

Anca's thin fingers grabbed my hair and jerked my chin up and off my chest. "Now we are doing business." She flicked off the flame and tucked the lighter away again. "We know what you are, John Domenici. We know why you work for Alexander Kempthorne. Plans are in motion. He is just one man. He cannot stop us. Tell us where he is or your friend dies."

Through my swimming vision, I watched the tall, blurry figure drag a gagged Gina into the room and drop her to the floor. She blinked wide-eyed at me and then back at the man standing over her.

A man I knew intimately. Long coat, amber eyes. How was he here? "Kage, what..." The rest of the words stuck to my thick tongue.

"Just tell her, Dom," he grumbled, resigned.

"Shoot the woman," Anca barked at Kage.

Hollywood flicked back his coat and freed the gun from its holster. Gina's muffled cries leaked into the part of my head left fuzzy from the Taser, sharpening my thoughts. Kage wouldn't shoot her. He was being coerced. Anca had found him, got to him, applied pressure on Annie—but he wouldn't go so far as to shoot Gina. Would he?

He pointed the gun at Gina's head.

"No!" I bucked, jolting forward, hung up on my cuffs. "Kage, don't—Anca, shit. The coin! I know where the coin is!"

Hollywood's gun fired and Gina yelped, but it was Anca's face that buckled, pirouetting her around. She twirled and flopped to the floor.

Fuck.

Taser lunged for Kage.

"Look out!"

Kage whirled, punching Taser out cold. I expected it to end there, but Kage casually emptied two rounds into Taser. One in the chest and one between the eyes. Execution style. Our eyes met, and for a gut-wrenching second, I was sure he was about to turn the gun on me.

He'd just killed a man like he was nothing.

He knelt, untied Gina's wrists, and said, "The keys."

Boots thundered up the stairs.

Gina scrabbled into action, tearing off her gag. She pilfered Anca's pockets and found the keys to my cuffs along with my deck of cards. Scooting behind me, she unlocked my cuffs and handed me my cards with a sorry frown and a hint of guilt. As if she was somehow to blame for all this.

The cuffs clattered and my aching arms protested as I slumped forward. "You don't look surprised?" I mumbled, bringing my lead-filled arms around to rub at my wrists.

Gina's big eyes widened. "Dom, I—"

"Can you stand?" Kage butted in, offering a hand.

I slapped his hand away. "I'm fine." How did everyone seem to know what was happening but me?

Shouts sounded in the hallway outside the room. Hollywood dashed out. A few more muffled double-taps sounded, followed by the distinctive *thump* of falling bodies.

Gina grabbed my arm and hauled me to my feet. "Sorry, Dom. Here." She thrust a phone at me. "Kempthorne."

Taking the phone, we stumbled out of the room

behind Hollywood and around the two bodies of Cockney and the driver. Shit. There would be hell to pay with the Met for this.

"Dom?" Kempthorne's crisp voice of reason spilled down the phone into my ear.

"Uh huh."

"You need to come out of the building slowly, with your hands up and palms open. I'll explain everything once you're outside."

"What?"

"Straight down the stairs, Dom," he said. "Come right out the front door. Do you understand?"

"You've got some fucking explaining to do, boss."

"In good time." He hung up.

Kage led the way, and with Gina on my arm, I hobbled down the stairs and outside, onto a set of stone steps. Faced with a row of armed response officers and flashing blue lights from a street full of cop cars, we all lifted our hands.

"The artifacts are inside," Gina announced. "All of them. Be careful."

"Well done." DI Barnes in her smart pantsuit and flat heels stepped of the glare of the headlights and smiled up at us. "Search him."

A pair of FOs made a beeline for me and did the usual frisking. "No offense, John," Barnes said. "Just routine."

Right, because nobody trusted a latent not to pocket the artifacts. Whatever. I was used to it. The FOs backed off, grunting about me being *clean*.

"Any casualties?" Barnes asked.

"Three dead," Hollywood said. "They resisted."

The fuck they did. About to challenge him on that, my eye caught a silhouetted figure emerging from between the cop cars. Kempthorne wore a striking dark blue suit, as though he'd arrived straight from the opera. The flashing lights glinted in his cufflinks and stroked over his polished Oxford shoes. The corner of a red handkerchief peeked out from his jacket pocket. How did he do that? How did he always look so fucking pristine while I could barely keep a shirt clean?

He nodded a tight greeting.

"The Met has the scene," Barnes told Kempthorne. "Take your people. We'll want statements first thing tomorrow." She smiled again, dismissing us. "Well done agents. You've removed a high-ranking terrorist threat. You've earned some downtime."

Her armed coppers hustled into the building, barking orders and reports. I would have glared at Hollywood if Kempthorne's presence hadn't kept drawing my eye.

"You can lower your hands now," he said. "We had to be sure you weren't carrying any artifacts."

I'd just seen Hollywood waltz into an interrogation, threaten to kill Gina, and then execute a bunch of people, and now he stood next to me and nobody seemed to care. Gina smiled at Kempthorne like she hadn't just come close to being another body among those we'd left inside. None of them were surprised. What the fuck was going on?

"You'll naturally have some questions," Kempthorne said, addressing me. "Kage, perhaps you could accompany Dom home while I see to things here."

Kage? The two of them were friends now? Fuck this. "If it's all right with you, boss, I'm going to make my own way back." I started walking, not entirely sure where I was heading but needing to get *away*. Nerves and the adrenaline come down had my trick eager to spark free, and control was the last thing on my mind. I was beginning to feel like Gareth Clarke might have felt when cornered in that alley. The only difference being, I had a way out.

Kempthorne caught my arm. "Dom, just—" The trick snapped from me to him, making him recoil with a hiss. He shook the burst of energy out of his hand and for a second, something dark and dangerous shimmered in his eyes. Then his gaze softened again. "I'm sorry," he said. "It was necessary. I'll explain everything later."

"Whatever. I'm done with this circus."

"It was last minute." Hollywood came forward. "I got a bunch of weird messages from your cell number, asking me to come to this address. Obviously a setup. With you compromised, I called Kempthorne. He told me Gina was also missing. Alex suggested we use the opportunity to track Anca's gang here. I talked my way back in—said I could get you to tell them everything about Kempthorne..." He saw my back-the-fuck-off glare and stopped talking.

"They *resisted*?" I asked, with enough venom in my tone to make him go quiet. He'd just executed people back there.

Showing Kempthorne a tiny gap between my finger and thumb, I added, "That bollocks in there? Me going in blind—*again*? That's how ops go wrong and people fucking die."

"I couldn't have done any more to get you out," he said.

"Talk to me again when you're ready to tell me the truth." I couldn't stay a second longer or I'd have done something stupid like hit him.

As I walked away, I heard Gina say I'd cool down by the morning. But by the morning, I'd be gone. I was finished at Kempthorne & Co. It was over.

21

"I saw the bags by your door." Kempthorne removed his sunglasses and loitered by the café table. I'd been sulking in The Rouge, in my favorite spot in the window, since my quick visit to the A&Eto fix the shallow stab wound. It still throbbed, but I'd swallowed enough painkillers that I'd rattle when I walked.

Kempthorne looked around him like he had somewhere more important to be. Whiskers shadowed his jaw and creases crinkled his shirt. He'd been up all night. Good.

Finally deciding I was worthy of his attention, he peered down his nose. "You never struck me as a quitter."

Wow. He just had to get that dig in. My laugh sounded hollow. "You've got some nerve, Kempthorne."

He placed a hand on the back of the vacant chair beside me and breathed in, steadying himself, building up to something. Maybe it was an apology. Maybe he was firing me. Whatever it was, I didn't care. "Before you leave us," he said, "I'd like to show you something, if you'll humor me?"

He leaned on that chair, knuckles going white from gripping it a little too tightly. The pinch around his mouth was new, either put there by anger or frustration. I knew he'd been through terrible things and people didn't just walk that off. His past made him who he was. And his past was fucked up. "Who are you really, Kempthorne?"

He swallowed and offered his hand. "Let me show you?"

I had a feeling that if I took that hand, a lot of things would change. If I took that hand, he would show me those secrets that hid in his eyes, and did I really want to know?

When too many seconds passed, he took his hand back and gripped the chair again, making it creak. "Something is moving in the shadows of London. Something unseen. I need your help to stop it."

And what if that something was him? Alexander Kempthorne was dangerous; he was reckless and excellent at subtle deception. Despite all that, for two years I'd believed him to be good. Now I wasn't sure. In the military, I'd been a pawn in someone else's game. Used. Sacrificed. It was always the way with latents, but I didn't want that again. And I *was* good, or trying to be. If I left Kempthorne & Co, and something happened to Gina or Robin, or anyone, for that matter—could I live with myself knowing I'd been close enough to do something?

Leaning back, I folded my arms. "Tell me one thing now, and answer me truthfully. Did you order Hollywood to execute Anca because she was getting too close to you?"

He held my stare. "To me?" He blinked, surprised. "No."

Anca had known a lot about Alexander Kempthorne. She'd wanted to know more and now she was dead. Dead like his parents. Probably like his sister. And like the agent he'd lost. Strange how the people close to him kept disappearing or dying.

Was I going to walk away from this? From him? Was I going to quit?

Standing, I left cash on the table for the barista and collected my jacket. "Where are we going?" I stepped outside the café behind him to find his glossy silver Aston parked on the curb, straddling double yellow lines. Sharp lines, smooth curves and impeccable styling. The car didn't shout to be seen, it quietly commanded.

Kempthorne slipped his shades on and slid behind the wheel.

I gingerly climbed in, careful not to tug on the stitches in my back, and recalled the last time I'd bled all over this car's soft leather. Seemed like a lifetime ago.

"We're going to Surrey." He pressed the button to start the engine. The Aston roared to life, then burbled as Kempthorne rolled the car off the curb. "Trust me?"

Arching an eyebrow, I sat back in the seat. As a billionaire, he had a lot of things, but my trust wasn't one of them.

Twenty minutes into our journey and with the heavy London traffic beginning to ease, Kempthorne broke the suffocating silence. "So... Kage Mitchell. What did you discover about him?"

I told him what I knew, leaving out where he lived. If Hollywood hadn't told him, then it wasn't my business to either.

Gina texted: *Are you leaving?* And added a sad face.

I ignored it.

"He was worried about you... when he called," Kempthorne said.

"Hm."

Kempthorne eased the Aston into lighter traffic. We began to make progress out of the city and into twisting, leafy lanes.

"He asked for my help reluctantly," Kempthorne added. "If he didn't care, he wouldn't have called."

"It's more that he doesn't trust you. There's a lot of that going around."

That shut him up for a few more miles before he said, "What does your gut say about him?"

"Kage has his own agenda. There was a moment, back in that room, when..." When he'd thought about killing me too. "He didn't need to kill them all."

"I agree."

"Anca could have been useful. She was a bitch, but she knew things." Now she was another dead latent. She probably wouldn't even get a funeral. The IRL cremated latents without families and brushed their ashes under their rugs—or so the rumors went.

"Things like?" he asked carefully.

"She wasn't acting alone. She didn't want those artifacts for herself. Maybe she was a terrorist, but that wasn't why she was there."

"So what was she?"

"Someone's lackey. I might have been able to get more out of her but Hollywood permanently stopped her talking. He could have shot her in the knee."

The gentle hum and motion of the car was beginning to smooth out my irritation, but a ride in the country wasn't going to be enough to lure me back into whatever shit Kempthorne was involved with. Not when I couldn't trust him.

The horrible things I'd seen in the pen were a flicker of a thought away from climbing inside my head again. Now Anca was dead, maybe I was the only one who had witnessed Kempthorne's past. Did that make me a target too?

"Did er... something happen... between you and Kage?" he asked, staring dead ahead.

"Define 'something.'"

"I er." He cleared his throat. "Well, you know. Did you and him...?"

I smiled and stared out of the window. Christ, watching him squirm was painful but also amusing. I wasn't sure if it was the gay thing, the sex thing, or just me, but he was clearly uncomfortable with the subject. "Yes."

"Ah. I suspected. He was quite passionate about finding you."

"Yeah, well. He shot Anca's men like they were target practice. That's not how I do things."

"That's not how *we* do things."

I made some noncommittal noise. There wasn't a *we*. Not anymore.

Rolling green fields, iron gates, and long driveways

broke up the high hedges lining the road. We were out in the sticks now. "So where in Surrey *are* we going?"

He stared ahead, which meant I couldn't miss the frustrated little flicker in his cheek. "I gather this *Anca* had some things to say about me," he said, ignoring my question. "Things that perhaps made you see me differently. Things you weren't expecting?"

I snorted. "No shit. She had a lot of questions too. You owe me some playing cards, by the way. She tore up mine."

"Yes, well. We're going to address some of those issues and the things she undoubtedly said. At least, as much as I can."

"You could just tell me instead of dragging me out to the countryside."

"I could, but it's easier if you see it. And I'm sorry." He looked over, all honest eyes and Mr Charming, but I wasn't falling for it. "I should have done this a year ago. If I had, you'd have gone into that situation far better equipped to deal with it."

Hm. A real apology. That was worth something. "Thanks for the rescue."

"You and Gina should never have been taken. That's on me too. I..." He rippled his fingers on the steering wheel. "I become so consumed by work that I miss what's happening around me."

He flicked the car's indicator on and prowled the Aston between two red stone gryphons. A stone sign under one of them read: *Ravenscourt*. Okay, this was new. A long track with grass growing in the middle snaked down a hill and through fields, leading to a multi-pitched red stone house. Ravenscourt wasn't as pretentious as I'd expected. Ivy grew up much of the front, trying to creep in the leaded windows. Quaint, compared to the Surrey mansions that sold around those neck of the woods. The house was old, wonky, and crooked, but full of charm. Most people in his financial situation would have bull-dozed the house and built a McMansion in its place.

I climbed from the Aston and soaked in the Surrey ambiance. Warm breezes, tweeting birds, and not a rumble of tires or an angry horn for miles. Christ, for a city boy like me, it really was like stepping onto another planet. I breathed, filling my lungs with clean air. Nice. Isolated, kinda creepy, but nice.

A camera over the porch clocked our arrival. Nestled in the middle of a few hundred acres of green fields and woodlands, with no neighbors for miles, Ravenscourt was a great place to hide away from the world. What the hell did Kempthorne do all the way out here?

"Come in, Dom." He turned the key in the lock and shoved open the thick oak door. "Make yourself at home. Housekeeping should have left milk in the fridge. I'll be right down." He hurried up the sweeping staircase, prob-ably to hide whatever incriminating items he had on display up there. Maybe this was where he brought all the kinky friends Gina had hinted at.

I wandered from room to room, avoiding the low beams and navigating sloped floors and creaking boards. The house wasn't so large that it felt daunting, or so small that it was dark. There was a warmth to it that came with hundreds of years of history. It had a good soul; I liked it.

In the kitchen—one of the few rooms with glossy modern fittings—I flicked on the kettle and rustled up two steaming mugs of tea. Kempthorne reappeared without his jacket and his sleeves rolled up in his typical harried fashion.

"Thank you," he beamed, scooping up his tea. "So, here we are."

"Here we are." I sipped from my mug while watching him squirm some more. The anxiety from the car had intensified instead of easing off. This wasn't easy for him. I'd never seen him so jittery. How he was right now, all movement and hand gestures, his gaze bouncing all over the place, this was another side to Kempthorne. The uncertain side that few of the team saw. His anxiety was rubbing off on me, making me twitch.

"This is... nice. I don't usually have people here." A little nervous laugh escaped him, unexpected from a man as confident as Kempthorne. "Just the housekeepers, of course." Another nervous laugh tittered free.

Okay, now he was making me uncomfortable. "Maybe you should show me what you brought me all the way out here for?"

"All right. Er... yes. Follow me."

He led me out into the hallway and jogged up the curved staircase to a second-floor landing with multiple doors. All were closed. He marched to the farthest door, turned an old skeleton-style key in the lock, and pushed inside with purpose. I drifted in behind and stopped in the center of the room, unsure what I was seeing.

Photographs of all colors, shapes, and sizes papered the walls. People and places. Newspaper headlines and articles had been pinned among them. Colorful sticky notes peppered here and there, like polka dots.

"I know." He said with a wince, tossing a hand gesture at it. "It's a lot."

"Er... it's not what I was expecting."

"What were you expecting?"

"Maybe a bat cave? Not a murder wall." His face fell and some inexplicable hitch caught in my throat. "It's fine," I croaked. "Murder wall is fine, just a surprise, and... I'm not a big fan of surprises, as you know."

"A bat cave?"

"Bruce Wayne?" I was getting a whole lot of blank. "Gotham's billionaire who fights crime... Never mind." I'd forgotten who I was talking to. And now he just looked more lost than he had when we'd arrived. Christ, he'd shown me his soul pinned to the wall and I'd recoiled. "I mean..." I swallowed more tea, wishing it was whiskey. "It's thorough." Venturing a step closer, the sheer scale of it all was hard enough to take in, let alone its actual contents.

"It is." He puffed out a sigh. "A life's work."

Setting my cup down on a table, I ventured closer and scanned the most obvious headlines and photos. The common theme seemed to be latents, but the articles varied from achievements to murders. Some were in Russian, some in Chinese, some were so old and faded their contents were almost lost. "What is all this?"

"My mother began collating the earliest instances of latents, back in the seventies, looking for a connection, a source. Where they come from. Why the psychic energy collects more in a latent than anyone else. Why isn't everyone a latent? She was always so full of questions." He approached the wall and stared up at it. "I just... continued her work."

Was this the same mother who had tied him to a table? If it was, he didn't talk like he despised her. It sounded more as though he *admired* her. I approached the wall and stopped beside him. Floor to ceiling, wall to wall, some five meters across, it looked like an obsession. "You know there are scientists who get paid to figure this out?"

"Yes." He tucked his hands into his pressed trouser pockets. "But paid by who?"

"Governments?"

"Exactly. Someone always has an interest, an angle. This is pure. It's the truth."

Okay. I glanced at him, side-on. Recalling what I'd seen from the pen, I understood the man standing next to me wanted answers. But the extent of the hours that had gone into this display was verging on crazy. Was this where he went when he disappeared from Cecil Court? Was this his life outside the office?

Then I remembered Anca's words about Kempthorne not stopping *them*. "Did you find something in all this? Something connected to the case? Is this what Anca wanted? What M wants?"

"I think so." But he didn't sound pleased. Or convinced.

"You think so?"

"I don't know exactly... There's a lot here. I've always asked questions, collected information. Once dirty artifacts started showing up at auctions, I began to see a pattern of bidding. Someone in the background was asking questions too. Someone whose questions led them to me. The answer is probably in all of this, yes. But I'm too close to see it. Which is why I need you."

I backed up to get a wider view of the wall and Kempthorne standing in front of it. But for all the information, all the photos and articles and colored dots, screaming for attention—I couldn't keep my eye off the man. He seemed smaller in front of his wall, like the boy I'd seen from the pen's psychic burn. He was just trying to figure all this shit out like the rest of us. In my head, I'd put him on a rich man's pedestal as though he was a different breed to me, but when it came down to the basics, we were just two men trying to find our way in a world that had kicked us in the nuts.

"I understand if you want to leave." He looked over his shoulder, and that curl of hair flopped near his eye. "You didn't agree to any of this."

"What?"

"After the military, you've been trying to keep your head down. *This research* won't allow that. My life… there's nowhere to hide in it, Dom. And with your past, well… it seems likely there will be strife ahead for us."

Had I been trying to keep my head down? Maybe. I'd also been searching for an escape. He was warning me off his life, when in reality, I should be warning him away from mine. "There are some things you should know about my time in the military, and what was done. And some things from my past—"

He lifted a hand, his attention already drifting back to the wall. "It's not necessary."

"Well"—now it was my turn to squirm—"you might feel differently about me once you hear—"

"The experiments they ran on you? The flooding, the control?" he asked, eyes narrowing. "Making you handle more power than you should. I already know. It changes nothing, other than you really shouldn't be tripping over artifacts in pubs."

What? He knew the military had used me as their latent guinea pig? I laughed, surprising myself. How? How could he know? My record was so classified it was buried in a bunker somewhere, a hundred feet down. But more than that, he'd known all this time that I was potentially highly unstable and he'd still hired me?

"I had to pull some strings, but the military was happy to let me have you on my team, just so long as I kept you managed."

I blinked. "'Managed'?"

"Your commanding officer—Sean Sawyer, a detestable man—wouldn't have signed off on your dismissal otherwise. Really, it was Kempthorne & Co or a maximum-security facility on the isolated, barren hills of Dartmoor. I do hope Cecil Court is better than that, at least." He said all this like it was perfectly reasonable.

It was a good thing there was an armchair behind me because I stumbled back into it. Kempthorne knew Sawyer, my ex, the dick of a commanding officer who'd gotten my team killed and kicked me out of Psy Ops. Wait... He'd organized my current employment *with* Sawyer?

"Dom?" Kempthorne started to make his way over, then stopped, unsure, and loitered by the long table instead. "This is a lot. I'm sorry I kept it from you. You can perhaps see why I did. I thought everything was working rather well until recently. I suppose it was all going to come out eventually—"

"Just give me a second. My CO, Sawyer, signed off on you employing me?"

"The Ministry of Defense did, yes. That tiresome man was just their mouthpiece."

"He's a mouthpiece, all right," I muttered, then rubbed at the building ache across my forehead. Okay, so my ex, a man who I'd slept with and who really didn't like me, had signed the order, giving me to Kempthorne? "So what, you took me on as a favor to the Ministry of Defence? To keep me from what?"

"As far as they were concerned, to protect you from outside influences, to keep you on British soil. You're a multimillion-pound asset."

"It's a wonder they let me go at all."

"I can be very persuasive, and a substantial check helped." He seemed pleased with himself—with saving the military's latent experiment.

But I was still trying to catch up with what this meant. "Whoa, wait. Back up there a second... You *bought* me?"

His smile stuttered, flaking away. "When you say it like that it sounds—"

"Fucking messed up, is how it sounds. Can I even walk away from you? From any of this?"

"In theory, yes. In reality, I suspect not."

"Hold on. Let me get this straight so we're all on the same level... So it's what, Kempthorne & Co or some hell-hole on Dartmoor where the MOD bury all their secrets?"

Kempthorne at least looked sympathetic. "The world is full of people who control others."

"Son of a bitch," I snarled, at nobody in particular. I'd been the one to sign up and I'd been the one to volunteer for latent testing. But what happened after, I had no control over that. No control over anything, not even myself. I'd thought joining Kempthorne had been my choice. But even that had been manufactured by someone else. "Fuck, Kempthorne, I'm not some artifact to be traded at one of your posh auctions."

"I understand that," he said, "and if you've read the pen, as I suspect you have, then you know why you and I are more alike than appearances suggest. We've both been used."

Ugh, the pen. Slumping in the seat, I blinked at the ceiling. *We'd both been used.* But Kempthorne had *bought* me from the military. "Fuck." Did Hollywood know all this? Was that why he was asking about my military career? Where did he fit in all this?

"For what it's worth, the circumstances of your arrival change nothing," Kempthorne said. "I value you as a member of the team, as I always have. Gina would be heartbroken if you left and Robin... Honestly, I think Robin tolerates you."

I laughed and I only sounded slightly unhinged. "I suppose I should be grateful I'm not in a hole on Dartmoor?"

"For now." His lips toyed with the idea of a smile. "I don't trust the military not to take you back, honestly." And that smile vanished. "They're watching you and I closely."

"Great. That's just fucking great."

Staring again at the wall and Kempthorne, who now looked more troubled than ever, I swallowed hard. Nothing had changed. I knew more, which was what I'd wanted. And now the genie was out of the bottle, the damn thing wasn't going back in. So the military had sold me to Kempthorne. Like he said, nothing about that changed what was happening now, and we had a case to solve. "All right... so what do we have? Anca was not a lone terrorist as the Met seem to believe. She was probably working for forces unknown, according to Kage—this M person—and we're assuming M the puppet master is not finished with us, or London's artifacts. The Met have the artifacts Devi took from the auction but this M already has a large collection. They have to be found."

"Agreed." The smile was back, but softer and warmer. "I need your help, Dom. You're uniquely qualified for this case and have already proven yourself invaluable."

"'Invaluable'? Huh." Yet he'd bought me, so by definition, I had a monetary value.

"Will you stay?" he asked, poised at the table's edge.

"You ask like I have a choice."

"If you truly want to leave, you could not only make it happen, I'd also help. A new identity wouldn't be a problem, but your biometric thumb print, iris scanners at airports—those are much harder to fake—"

Wait, Kempthorne knew how to fake a new identity? Somehow, I wasn't surprised. I lifted a hand and shoved to my feet. "I'm staying. The way I figure it, if I run, they'll catch me. At least, right here, they'll leave me alone, right?"

He nodded. "Will you tell Gina you're staying? I've had to turn my phone off to stop her harassing me. I'll find the whiskey. We're going to need it."

I watched him leave and dragged my gaze back to the murder wall. The questions it raised had merit. Why did latents exist, and how? If there was a source, could it be reversed? Governments all over the world were funding research to answer these questions, but Kempthorne was right. Governments were biased.

Was this what Anca wanted?

Kempthorne would figure it out, while also doing everything he could to keep London's artifacts and latents safe. I trusted *that* even if I had a hard time trusting the man himself. He had told me his secrets—some of them. But he'd already proven he liked to keep things to himself at the expense of others. And apparently I was already up to my neck in all of this, I just hadn't known how deep I'd been.

I texted Gina: *K is a dick*

She sent back a kissing face and cocktails, then: *Never doubted u wud stay.*

Now the initial shock had worn off, the extent of Kempthorne's work was impressive. He'd listed latents from all over the world, with a clear concentration in the UK, most notably London, going back as far as when the first latents had appeared, in the nineteen seventies. It had been noted before that London was the epicenter, the site of the first known latent, but nobody knew why. What made London so hot in terms of artifacts and latents?

Kempthorne returned with a crystal decanter of golden whiskey that was probably older than me, and we got to work. He collected items from the wall and spread them over the long dining table under the watchful gaze of a portrait of an older man who bore the same high cheekbones and impressive profile as Kempthorne. The more items Kempthorne took down from his wall, and the more he talked, the more animated he became. He talked about exotic countries, experiments from all over the world, about latents who turned out to have more extraordinary abilities—like those I'd faced in the military. Latents who could do much more than go off on various levels of meltdown. Latents like authenticators, latents who caught glimpses of the future, absorbers who nullified other latents, absorbing their tricks; some latents were so damn classified nobody truly knew what they did.

We talked into the night, forgetting to eat until the morning hours, when I offered to throw some sandwiches together. By then, we'd talked ourselves around in circles and had covered every inch of the table in articles and notes and pictures. It looked chaotic, but Kempthorne didn't even need to source the information. It was all in his head.

We'd emptied all the whiskey, and the both of us had begun to wilt, losing track of time. Luckily, it was the weekend. I didn't need to be back in the office until Monday, and Gina would have already returned my prematurely packed bags to my room.

"I'm sorry... we've veered off-topic," Kempthorne said, slumping into one of the chairs by the table. "I've kept you here all night. That wasn't my intention. I just... I've never shown anyone all this before. Having you listen made it feel less insane, honestly." He laughed softly at himself.

"It's fine, really." I'd enjoyed it, enjoyed bouncing ideas around, seeing the connections and how his mind worked. Enjoyed watching him come alive like he never had before. The Alexander Kempthorne I'd known these past two years had been a cold, distant man, a figure in the background—a shadow. The Alex Kempthorne in this room, with his sleeves rolled up and his eyes glassy, his lips flirting with a smile and some warmth in his face, was yet another new facet to the man—one free of London and all its responsibilities.

"There's a force at work in London." He poured the last dregs of whiskey into his glass. The drink hadn't done much to slow him down, just softened him around the edges. "Spreading outward." He stood, grabbed a map of the city, and unfolded its huge spread, covering all the documents. Sweeping his hand over the great map, he revealed a web of connections. "I'm not even sure it's a person. But it's there, pulling threads."

Standing, I studied the map and the parts of London the lines intersected. There was something here. Something right in front of us but invisible at the same time. As an authenticator, touch was a key to doors others couldn't see. I reached out to touch the map now, almost expecting to hear voices whisper back, but the map stayed silent. It wasn't an artifact, but the contents, the connection, they felt important in the latent part of me that Kempthorne wouldn't understand.

"Latent numbers are increasing," he said, after watching me closely. "Tensions in the city have never been greater. I fear more people will die... Not just latents, but anyone who crosses *this*." He frowned at the map. "That is not acceptable."

This was deeper than a simple mission for Kempthorne; it was personal. And it stemmed back to everything I'd seen in the pen. The reason for his doing all this came from agony, from his time on an examination table and a latent mother who sought to hurt him to find these very answers, even though he wasn't like her. He should hate latents. But, every day, him and his agency tried to save them.

It didn't have to be all bad. Perhaps I could give him something good back?

"What if everyone has looked at it all wrong since the beginning?" I asked. "All the scientists and doctors, trying to pick it all apart, trying to give it a reason and equations. They named it *resonance friction*, trying to organize our tricks, like they understand it. But what if it's all just magic?"

He frowned like I'd lost my mind.

"Here." Before I could think, I'd scooped his hand into mine and pulsed a small amount of trick through my fingers, into his. He froze and stared wide-eyed at our hands. "See? It's not bad. It just wants to be felt. To be known. You can't science the shit out of magic. It won't be studied in a petri dish or simmered to dust in a test tube. Science and magic are two negatives repelling each other. Magic can't be quantified. It doesn't work like that. Latents don't work like that—"

He yanked his hand from mine and stumbled against the table. Rage tightened his face and my heart leapt, readying for defense. I already had the trick at my fingertips. Maybe he saw some of it glow in my eyes and that was the final blow that snapped him into action because he marched for the door.

"Wait—"

"You can take my car back to Cecil Court, if you wish," he said—not quite running, but close. "Or use a guest room. Whatever." He slammed the door behind him hard enough to rattle the window.

I slumped against the table and willed myself back under control. New rule: Do not touch Kempthorne.

My phone buzzed. Tired, whiskey-addled, and hungry, I scowled at the message:

Unknown number: ...We need to talk

I couldn't deal with Hollywood at 3 a.m. on top of everything else.

We will, but not now, I sent back.

I turned off my phone and hunted for a guest room to crash in.

22

After sleeping the morning hours away, I woke to find an overnight bag outside the guest room door. If Kempthorne had gone to the trouble of having his people bring me a change of clothes, then I figured it was okay to stick around. I showered, dressed in fresh clothes, and took myself on a tour of the sprawling house. Old places like this told their own stories, and for a latent like me, running my hands along the walls generated a familiar tingling. Every room had a voice, if I cared to stop and listen, but unless there had been any substantial trauma the voices were soft and easily ignored. But listening to old houses was a fast way to lose a grip on reality. I already had enough voices in my head keeping me from sleeping. I didn't need to add Kempthorne's mansion to all that.

The quaint frontage was a ruse. The place was huge. It contained wood-paneled walls, tiny spiraling staircases with barely enough room to pass, thick curtains, wonky floors, and multiple spooky portraits of stiff Victorians. I wandered, climbing and descending multiple staircases. Peeling back a heavy curtain, I discovered a thick door, hung on huge iron hinges and fixed with chunky bolts.

I tried the latch, shrugged when it didn't open, and was about to wander back down the hall when an icy power leaked from beneath the door like a draught—the same icy leak I got from potent artifacts. Pressing my hand against the door's ancient wood, I spread my fingers and leaned in, listening. *Damn.* A powerful, ear-thudding throb sounded from behind the wood. Whatever was behind there, it was hot.

"Looking for something?" Kempthorne said.

I jumped and yanked my hands back. "Sorry. I was just...er... "

"It's fine." Turning on his heel, he marched back, waving for me to follow. "We have much to go over."

I trotted along behind him and glanced back at the locked door. The thick curtain had fallen back into place, muffling the energy.

"Ask," Kempthorne said.

I found him looking over his shoulder and jogged to his side. He didn't seem pissed off, but his neutral expression was almost impossible to read. "It's hard not to notice you've got something going on back there."

"Knowing everything you do, I suspect it wouldn't take much to guess the source of what I assume you're feeling."

The pen. The psychic burn. The boy strapped to a metal table. That had happened behind that door? I plunged my hands into my pockets. "Sorry."

"Like I said, it's fine." His fake smile told a different story. "But you understand why I keep the door locked."

As we were skirting around the subject of the pen and his past, it seemed a good time to try and get some more answers out of him. "The pen..." A twitch tugged at his right eyebrow. "How did they get it?"

"I don't know. Not from me. Breakfast?"

"Er, yeah." The change of subject made it clear the conversation was over.

Kempthorne waffled about having sent the house-keeping staff away for the weekend, so we wouldn't be getting a breakfast spread, and would cereal be fine? I threw him a look as though he was crazy for asking a lad from a council estate if he was all right with Corn Flakes for breakfast?

The smell of brewing coffee would have lured me toward the kitchen even without Kempthorne as a guide.

Bright sunshine poured through the windows, and outside, the rolling Surrey hills reminded me I wasn't in London anymore.

"Hm..." Kempthorne stared at the cupboards. He opened one, frowned, then opened another next to it, then another.

"You okay?"

"Hm, yes. Where would you expect to find cereal?" He rummaged through another cupboard.

"I can help?"

"No, sit, it's fine..."

I took a seat at the breakfast bar and watched him open and close all the cupboards until he threw his hands in the air and backed up. "I have no idea."

He didn't make breakfast much then. "Try the cupboard above the drainer, by the window."

He opened it, and there were the cereal boxes, all in a neat row.

"Right, yes." He'd found the bowls during his hunt and grabbed one now.

There was something almost adorable about watching him get flustered over making breakfast. He carried the cereal boxes to the breakfast bar, set down the bowl, then grabbed a French press, mugs, and milk. "There," he said triumphantly. He glanced up with a glimmer of pride in his eyes.

I hid my smile behind a hand. "Thanks." I poured myself some cereal and coffee then noticed he wasn't doing the same. "You're not having any?"

"I don't do breakfast. Just coffee."

So all the faffing about was just for me? "I've been thinking," I said, hurrying back on topic. "The instances of illegal artifacts bubbling to the surface had been increasing in the last six months, which appears to be connected to a rise in artifact retrieval cases and illegal auctions."

"Agreed. I've checked with other agencies and they've all seen a marked increase." Coffee cupped in his hands, he leaned against the kitchen countertop. He wore pressed trousers and an ironed button-down shirt, like he always did, and like always, the shirt sleeves were rolled up, his watch glinting on his wrist. There was something firm about his tanned arms. For a man who didn't do manual labor, he carried strength in the way he moved. Even wounded, although only the occasional wince betrayed his recovering gunshot to the shoulder. His collar gaped and his hair was ruffled. He wore the scruffy casual look so well it made my wrinkled T-shirt and creased jeans look like I'd been sleeping on the street.

"You were saying?" he prompted.

I smiled into my coffee. "Er, yeah..." I'd lost my train of thought sometime while admiring him. I was not about to tell my boss how effortlessly attractive he was. There were workplace laws about that, even if I was in his kitchen, drinking his coffee and eating his cereal. "So..." Clearing my throat and my head, I went on, "Whoever is orchestrating this has upped their game, maybe because they know you're onto them. You've been appearing at auctions, asking questions too, right? They know you're closing in. So... what if it's someone close to you? A friend, maybe? Someone who knows you."

"It would seem likely, if not for the fact I don't have friends."

I laughed, then stopped when he didn't. "C'mon, you must have friends. People you lunch with? Go shooting with or whatever?"

"You assume I hunt?"

"Don't you?" Didn't every rich guy hunt? Wasn't that their thing?

"No," he said coldly. "I abhor hunting."

"Oh."

Christ.

"I have associates," he said. "Business contacts. A financial manager, housekeepers, a driver, multiple business mangers running the estate, but no friends, Dom. Good ones are hard to come by."

He didn't have anyone to confide in, to talk to? Nobody to go down to the pub for a pint with? I hid my face by focusing on devouring my Corn Flakes. The more he talked about his life, the more I realized all my assumptions about him were wrong. The glitzy life he projected was a hundred percent fake. I suspected his real life was here, in this house in the middle of nowhere, staring at his murder wall, and back in Cecil Court, studying artifacts in the basement. Did I even know Alex Kempthorne at all? "Is there anyone in your circle of associates who could be orchestrating this? Anyone with an interest in artifacts?"

"Not that I'm aware of. My work at Cecil Court is not something that's socially discussed."

"Do you personally *know* any latents?"

"Besides you? None. But as we know, latents can be adept at hiding their nature."

"What about latents from past cases?"

"Hundreds, but none who are connected enough to orchestrate an operation to buy up artifacts to this degree. It would require ample finances and an extensive knowledge of the black market. Latents aren't generally wealthy or well-connected."

"That's where you're wrong. There *are* wealthy latents. But they have the means and connections to hide what they are." Like Hollywood's friend, Annie. If enough money changed hands, latent kids could be squirreled away to boarding schools and hidden from the system designed to keep us monitored and controlled.

"You're right," he said, somewhat apologetically. "Wealth can conceal many things."

After shoving my empty cereal bowl away, I nursed my coffee, thinking. Kempthorne had recognized he was too close to the case to see it objectively. This entire circus felt personal. His wall, Anca's questions.

Whoever was behind this had targeted his agency and staff. Was it just because Kempthorne had been stirring up trouble with his investigations or was there more to it?

Meeting his soft gaze, I said, "Anca mentioned a coin." A tiny, almost indiscernible twitch tugged at his right eyebrow. I hadn't been sure if the twitch was a tell, until now. Interesting. "I assume she meant the coin you have in your basement safe?"

"Possibly." He sent his gaze out of the kitchen window at the sun-soaked perfectly mowed lawn. "Likely, even."

"Why would she care about such a small artifact? It's not dirty. Not powerful. It's hot, but nothing remarkable."

"Because of what an authenticator can see in it." He replied so matter-of-factly that his lack of response suggested he was trying very hard not to give anything away.

"Which is?"

"You tell me." His glare came back to me as sharp as a knife.

"I didn't get a good look at it."

"Didn't you, Dom?" Now he sipped his coffee, silently accusing me of *lying*.

"A girl's murder, that's all I saw. I'd have needed more prep to see any deeper." He stared, as though he didn't believe me. "Why would I lie?" I asked.

My phone pinged in my pocket. Kempthorne used the distraction to refill his coffee.

Unknown number: ... The cops are holding me in for questioning. Can K help?

"Shit, the Met have Hollywood."

"They don't like firearms, or Americans killing

Londoners," Kempthorne said coolly. "It was a matter of time."

The Met hadn't cared when he'd killed a latent, but now he'd executed a few thugs, they were suddenly on his back?

I'd told Kempthorne everything I knew about Hollywood, and while I didn't agree with his methods, I couldn't argue with the fact he'd saved my arse a few times. I owed him more than a few saves. "He's asking if you can help him?"

Kempthorne's eyebrows rose. "We don't know his motives, only what he's told you, and frankly, you're perhaps closer to him than you should be." He mumbled that last dig before sipping his coffee.

"You asked me to get close to him."

"Yes, for the case. Look me in the eye and tell me that's all it is."

I looked him in those keen, penetrative blue eyes and Christ, it was like staring into the depths of some mysterious cave that you knew you shouldn't get close to but really couldn't resist. "It's just the job." It was. I just had to keep telling myself that.

He approached the kitchen island and I showed him the text.

His eyes flicked up to me. "Is he worth saving?"

"He has international connections. He knows more about what's going on than he's told us. He's neck-deep in this and he's the best lead we have."

"You think he'll be useful to Kempthorne & Co?"

"'Useful'? Yes. Good for us? Maybe not."

His gaze lingered, his eyes silently asking questions. Sitting in his kitchen, surrounded by his house, his creepy Victorian portraits, his real *life*, he looked at me as though waiting for me to tell him a secret I didn't know.

"All right," he said. "I'll make some calls."

It was almost a relief when he broke eye contact and left the room to presumably make those calls. It was only then I realized I'd been asking about the coin and he'd slithered out of that line of questioning, just like he had with the pen. Was the coin personal too? Dammit, if Anca were still alive, she'd have had the answers.

Hollywood was our next best witness.

My phone rang—Gina.

"Hey—"

"You and K need to get back here ASAP! Some shit is going down."

"Wait, what now? Slow down."

"The phones are ringing off the hook. All of London has gone mad. Seriously, wherever the fuck you two are hiding, you need to turn on the TV."

"Hold on..." I followed Kempthorne's voice through the hallway, into the living room where he stood with his phone to his ear in front of a large TV, watching the news. The news ticker across the bottom of the report read of latents losing control in Dagenham, Stratford, Barking, Ilford. A reporter stood in front of a scene straight out of an action movie, with half a street ripped apart, sirens wailing, and blue lights flashing. A classic latent aftermath scene, where people don't survive. "Shit..."

"Get back here," Gina demanded.

Kempthorne swung a glance toward me and nodded. "Get to the car. I'll be right there."

I grabbed my coat on the way out of the door and hurried across the gravel toward the Aston. "When did

234 | ARIANA NASH

this start?" I asked Gina, switching my phone to the other ear as I fumbled my coat on.

"An hour ago. It suddenly happened, like, all at once, Dom."

"Coordinated? Like an attack?"

"Maybe. Nobody knows yet. I mean, that doesn't happen, right? Latents don't just all lose their shit at once?"

"No." I dropped into the Aston just as Kempthorne threw himself into the driver's seat and roared the Aston to life. "That doesn't happen."

"Seat belt," he said, then swung the car in a U and lurched away from the house, kicking up a fan of gravel.

I fumbled with the seat belt, half listening to Gina while watching Kempthorne grip the gear stick, his wounded arm almost forgotten. "—your way back," Gina was saying.

"What, Gina? I missed that. What did you say?"

"Greenwich!" Robin shouted from somewhere behind Gina. "Get to Greenwich, near Blackwall Tunnel. Dom— latent—dirty artifact—" The signal died.

"We need to get to Greenwich."

Kempthorne dropped a gear and bounced the Aston out of the driveway, between the glaring gryphons and onto the leafy Surrey road. The car whipped around, fighting Kempthorne's control, then hooked up and shot forward, racing us back to London.

23

Kempthorne parked the Aston into a nearby parking lot, and we jumped out, abandoning the car to make a dash through lines of stationary traffic that had been heading toward Blackwall Tunnel until something had snarled all the cars to a stop. Horn honking gave way to a thick crowd blocking the way.

"Agency, move!" Kempthorne shoved though them.

And there she was. Sitting in the middle of the road.

Just a little thing, no more than nineteen. A girl in a grey hooded top and strappy sandals, her pale face streaked with tears. Kempthorne skidded to a sudden halt and flung out a hand, holding me back.

Her arms were bound behind her back and the artifact—what appeared to be some kind of painted stone—had been taped to her hand. She couldn't drop it, even if she'd wanted to.

Her bottom lip trembled.

I stepped forward and Kempthorne's arm stiffened,

holding me back. He turned to me, and for a second, with his eyes wide and hair wild, he looked terrified.

"I've got this," I assured him.

He blinked and the terror faded, leaving him cold. He nodded.

Breaking from the crowd and Kempthorne, I approached the girl and raised my hands. "Hi... All right?"

Her wide eyes locked on me in hope. *"Help me,"* she sobbed.

"I'm Agency, okay? See?" Lowering my left hand, I showed her my badge. "And this guy behind me, he's my boss. We can help you."

Her glances found Kempthorne, and whatever she saw seemed to calm her. She nodded. "I can't—I can't—"

"It's okay." I crouched in front of her, and catching Kempthorne's eye, nodded for him to work on removing the artifact. He circled around, and I left him to it, focusing on the girl. "I'm Dom. What's your name?"

"Penny."

"Penny, how did you get here, like this?"

"They—They did this." Sobs choked her.

"Okay, okay—Just look at me." I caught her shoulder, holding her firmly in my grip. "I'm like you. I feel it too. But you're strong. You know how I know that?" She shook her head, sending tears raining down her face. "You're still with us, you're still talking. You've got this."

Kempthorne made a frustrated sound and backed up, out of my line of sight. I let him work, keeping my eyes on Penny. The artifact would be slowly working its way through her, trying to lever out her control and replace it with its own. It wanted her to let go, to listen to its promises. I felt its thrum, even though I didn't have it in my hands. It was a miracle she'd lasted this long. "You here alone?"

She chewed on her bottom lip and nodded. "The Police—" A wave of power surged through her and tried to climb my arm. Her eyes rolled—the psychic burn consuming her control. She was losing the fight. *Fuck.* The damn thing would chew her up, and unless she could bring it back under control, us, the crowd, and the entire street would go up with her.

"Get back!" I barked at the crowd. The fools weren't moving. Instead, they were filming what could be their final moments on their phones.

"Help me."

"I've got you." I squeezed her shoulder hard. "Feel me. Only me. You've got this, Penny. You and me."

"Can't." She swayed, tipping into me.

Whatever Kempthorne was doing, it was taking too long. The artifact's power was building, surging, sensing freedom through Penny.

"I've got you." I pulled her close, tucked her head under my chin, and grabbed her hand and the artifact in mine. An electric jolt ripped up my spine, filling my head with fireworks. *No, you don't...* the little pebble whispered and crooned and teased and told me all the things I wanted to hear, and maybe grabbing it hadn't been the best idea because now it had two latents to hear it. All the promises it told me, I blocked them, pushed them back. "I've got you," I told Penny again. "You're safe." Those were the only words latents needed to hear. If only someone had said them to me all those years ago. "We control it. We're strong."

238 | ARIANA NASH

Kempthorne's fingers gripped my wrist. A knife flashed. The artifact wailed inside my head and suddenly all the noise and madness cut off, severed.

I spilled backward onto the road, taking Penny with me. The artifact was gone.

Kempthorne knelt on the road with the artifact nestled harmlessly in one hand and someone's penknife in the other.

He looked at it like a man who knew he'd just come within seconds of being blown to bits, then lifted his gaze to me and smiled a soft, genuine smile, made softer by his floppy hair.

Penny sobbed against my chest. "It's over," I told her. "Don't look. It's gone."

Kempthorne nodded and rose. "Out of the way, please," he told the crowd. He'd take it back to the car and lock it in a sealed case in the trunk.

My phone was ringing. It could have been ringing the whole time. I ignored it and helped Penny sit up. "Let's get you off the street." Hobbling to our feet, I tucked her against my side. The crowd had pushed in and maybe grown in number. Phones flashed at our faces. People jostled. "Out of the way people, give us some room."

"Latent bitch!" someone yelled.

The crowd heaved, jostling us some more. I shoved back. "Back off! All right? Give us room!"

"She nearly killed us!"

Someone tried to grab my arm and got a kick to the shin for their trouble. "Back the fuck off!"

"Grab her!"

Oh, this wasn't happening. Not on my watch. I plunged a hand into my pocket and yanked out my cards, instantly making them shine, and lifted them above my head like a beacon. "Any of you bitches comes near us you'd better be ready to throw down." I twisted, letting them all see the sizzling, crackling handful of grenades. They recoiled, losing interest in mob justice now they had to fight. "Thought so. Now get lost. All of you. Show's over."

Penny trembled in my arms as I walked her back down the road toward where the Aston burbled, waiting by the curb. I climbed into the back with her, and Kempthorne got the car underway.

"You okay?" I asked.

"I t-think so." She shivered, small on the back seat.

"This isn't usually how we do things," Kempthorne said, "But I can't get hold of cleanup or processing. Can we drop you somewhere safe? Do you have someone who can care for you?"

"Yeah, my mum," she said, sniffing. She told Kempthorne the address while I shrugged off my coat and handed it to her.

"You did well back there," I said. "Holding on for as long as you did."

"I don't want to think about it."

"Yeah, I get that. But can you tell us what happened? Who did this to you?"

"They took me last night. I was walking home and... I didn't see much. A big van, maybe. They threw me in the back and put something over my head, so I couldn't see." Silent tears skipped down her cheeks. "They had radios, like walkie-talkies? I think there were others... like me."

"How many others?"

"I don't know. I was so scared... I didn't say much or... do much. I wasn't very brave."

"Hey, you were amazing." I smiled at her and hoped she saw how I meant it. A young latent without training, she'd done bloody well. "It's okay, now." I caught Kempthorne's glance in the rearview mirror and felt it sizzle over me. "It's over." It was over for her, but more calls were coming in.

My phone rang again. This time I answered it. "Gina—"

"What's going on out there? Did you get her?"

I told her the brief version as Penny shivered beside me and Kempthorne drove us toward Penny's home address.

"When can you get back? We've got more cases coming in. Robin's out on one now." She told us the address of another possible case nearby and after telling me to be careful, hung up.

After dropping Penny off and briefly explaining the situation to her distraught parents, I had to abandon them with just my mobile number to call if they needed help. Proper procedure would've been to take her in for counseling and to check she was still stable, but the night had gone to hell and there was no time for that.

I hopped back into the front passenger's seat as Kempthorne drove the Aston toward the next address, breaking a few traffic laws. He stewed in uncharacteristic silence.

"Hey, you okay?"

"The girl—Penny—something about that call wasn't right."

"None of it was right." But Kempthorne's tense jaw

and flickering cheek suggested there was more to it. "What are you thinking?"

"She's familiar..." He muttered, his thoughts clearly wandering somewhere far off.

A horn honked, and Kempthorne jolted the drifting Aston back into the right lane. Blinking, he looked over. "I'm sure it's nothing."

We raced to the next address and intervened in a latent getting harassed by a group of guys who'd already gotten the artifact and latent separated, but the crowd was turning vicious. Had we been any later, the latent might have spent the night in a hospital instead of getting a ride in Kempthorne's Aston.

And on it went, case after case, through Sunday night, into Monday and Tuesday, as though latents and artifacts were crawling out of London's foundations. The surge was unique. Nothing like it had happened before, and it didn't show any signs of letting up.

Wednesday came around—probably Wednesday, all the days had blurred into one long waking nightmare—and I jolted awake on the sofa in 16a Cecil Court, where I'd crashed last night. For once, the phones weren't ringing and Robin wasn't barking orders. The building was quiet. Both Kempthorne and Gina were still out on separate cases. I'd passed Robin earlier, on her way to get supplies. Alone, I had a few moments to think... the past few days had been insane. But most cases had not been like Penny's. She'd been set up. The rest were happenstance, latents stumbling on artifacts. The only fact there were so many of them made them unusual. Penny's abduction was deliberate. But why?

The intercom buzzed.

I flopped onto my back and stared at the ceiling. I was still dressed in yesterday's clothes and needed a shower, a shave, and something to eat. Maybe whoever they were would go away?

Another buzz. This one persistent.

Dragging my overtired body off the sofa, I stumbled to Robin's computer and hit the video call button. "Yeah?"

Hollywood peered into the camera. "Hey, you up?"

"I am now." I buzzed the door unlocked and cut the video. I hadn't seen him since he'd saved my arse and hadn't heard from him since Kempthorne had made some calls to get him out of the Met's grabby hands. Clearly, he hadn't been arrested, probably thanks to Kempthorne strong-arming DI Barnes.

Hollywood helped himself into the flat as I boiled the kettle. He scanned the chaos on the countertops and table, a mixture of case files, biscuits, and used mugs. "It's not normally like this." Why I felt the need to explain was beyond me. It was too early in the morning to care. The wall clock showed it was 6.30—a.m.

"No, it's okay... I just thought... I hadn't heard from you since... And I wanted to... drop by and..."

Huh. Look at him, all anxious and out of sorts. He'd ditched the long coat for a grey jacket, trying for casual. But the large sunglasses were too Instagram for casual.

"Coffee?"

"Sure."

I grabbed a mug and set to making us both drinks. "Kempthorne came through huh?"

"I guess so. They let me go a few hours after I messaged you."

"He didn't like the idea of helping you. I vouched for

you. Don't screw me." I handed him his coffee and inhaled the steam rising off mine, hoping it might clear my head.

"Thanks," he said, either for the coffee or the save. "And I won't... screw you, I mean. Unless you want me to."

I couldn't stop my laugh. "Yeah, well, I owe you a few saves."

"Everyone out?" he asked, casually scanning the kitchen.

"All on cases. It's been nonstop. Something crazy is happening all over London. I haven't even seen the team to properly discuss it."

"Can I...er... sit?" He gestured at the table.

"If you can find a space."

Pulling out a chair, he found some space between the files and empty plates and took a seat, then cradled his mug of coffee. "You know, I got to thinking these last few days. I see what's happening out there, latents lighting up all over London, and I can help. I have experience."

"Not to be a dick, but the kind of help you're offering? We don't need it."

"Right. Okay." His smile had broken before it had gotten to his lips and now my wretched heart constricted at the sad look on his face.

"Look, it's not you, it's your methods."

"Which were good enough to save your ass."

"This isn't the Wild West. You can't just shoot people you don't like."

He leaned back and folded his arms, shutting down. "That's not—"

"Anca was our best lead to figure out all this shit, and you shot her between the eyes."

"She was a powerful latent. I saw her kill the auctioneer. I know she's killed others. She didn't trust me, and I wasn't giving her an opportunity to hurt you or Gina."

"Like Gareth Clarke? Kill the latents before they can hurt you? Is that how it works?"

His eyes darkened. "That's not—No. That's why I left the US."

"And brought your bias over here?"

I regretted the words as soon as they were out, but it was too late to take them back now. Hollywood was back on his feet. "I'll just go."

Shaking my head, I set my coffee down and tried to rub away the ache creeping up my neck. I wasn't in the right headspace for this conversation. "Shit, I'm sorry. These last few days—"

He marched across the room and filled all my personal space. I half expected a fist to come at me, but instead he stared, seething. "If I hate latents so much why would I let one fuck me?"

I'd pissed him off. And I kinda liked it. All of him pressed close was waking me up a whole lot quicker than the caffeine. All that fury wrapped up in a body I'd have no trouble losing myself in for a few hours. "Latent kink?"

His dark eyebrows took a dive, then he laughed, molded himself close, and skimmed his mouth over the corner of my mine, down my bristly jaw. "Hm... maybe." When his hot lips and tongue sucked my neck, I clutched at his arm, probably in some effort to shove him off that somehow turned into making sure he didn't leave.

He was so damn gorgeous I struggled to think around him at the best of times. This was not the best of times.

The intercom buzzed.

Hollywood tensed. "Ignore it," I told him, clutching his arse and grinding him close, making him moan. "They'll go away."

His hand came up to caress my neck and his gaze held mine. "Is someone going to walk in on us?" His free hand skimmed my hip and danced across my hardening cock, deliberately teasing.

The shared kitchen was a terrible place to do this, and I was half a second away from not caring.

The intercom buzzed again.

"Bugger. Hang on." Back in Robin's office, I hit the video call and frowned at the live feed of Detective Inspector Barnes standing in 16a's doorway. Her pixie cut had been slicked back, making her look more severe than usual. "DI Barnes, hi. Kempthorne's not here."

"He's on his way," she said with a smile. "I'll wait inside, if that's all right?"

Hollywood leaned against the doorframe, like sin for the taking and knowing it. His left eyebrow arched at the sound of the DI's voice. He wasn't the Met's most popular person but I could tuck him away in my room until Kempthorne showed up.

"Okay, come on up." I buzzed her in and shooed Hollywood from the room. "My room, go." Shutting his laughing face behind my door, I winced at the disarray in the kitchen and scooped the used mugs and plates into the sink and tidied away the case-files.

The DI opened the kitchen door and smiled. "Oh, hello again, John."

"Hi." I didn't bother correcting her on the name. Some people never listened. "Sorry about the mess, it's been a hell of a week."

"Yes, it has." She smiled politely. "Do you mind if I wait? Alexander said he wouldn't be long."

"No problem. I've just boiled the kettle. Tea?"

"Thank you."

"Help yourself to biscuits. Not the custard creams, those are precious for some reason." I kept her in the corner of my eye and watched her browse over the stack of case files I'd dumped on the countertop and the mess in the sink. She wore a simple grey suit under a heavy navy blue coat and slim gloves—as though she'd come straight from a top brass meeting. She had that penetrative stare all coppers had, like everyone was a criminal until proven otherwise. If she knew about me, then she knew where I'd been raised, and probably considered me one tick-box away from criminal.

"So, John, Alexander has been telling me about the events of the last few days. Do you have any theories as to the sudden latent activity?"

"Ugh, I would but I've just woken up, honestly, and I need to er... you know..."

She stared in the same way an owl studies a mouse, trying to decide if it's worth the hassle of getting off its perch. No wonder she got along so well with Kempthorne. "We have some time to kill. Humor me."

It was like being at school again and having the teacher single me out. "The timing isn't coincidence. The case you have us working on, regarding the auctions? My gut tells me this wave is connected. Clearly it's not Anca this time... could potentially be whoever was directing her." The puppet master, M.

"Hm. But where's the connection and what's their motive?"

"If we knew that, we'd probably have our perpetrator."

"I see your point. It's quite the mystery and has certainly kept you and Kempthorne busy these last few days."

"Yeah." My phone pinged and lit up where I'd left it on the counter. I stirred the milk into the DI's coffee and reached for my phone. A message from Penny's mum showed temporarily on the screen. Something about the police. I handed the DI her coffee with a polite smile and scooped up my phone. "I'll be right back..." Hurrying down the hall, I disappeared into my room and found Hollywood at the window, looking down on Cecil Court.

"How much longer do I have to hide in your room like your illicit lover?" he asked, propping his arse on the windowsill and folding his arms. Caught between my job and wanting to go kiss that smile, I hung back. "Just until Kempthorne gets here."

Opening my messages, I read: *Sorry to bother you. The police came and took Penny and we can't get hold of them to find out what's happened to her. You said to contact you if we needed anything. We hope this is okay?*

The Montgomerys were good people. I typed out a quick reply. *I'll look into it and get back to you soon. Will call later.*

"Everything all right?" Hollywood asked, sensing my hesitation.

"Yeah, it's just... A girl we rescued on Sunday, when

this all started. Something about her case doesn't add up. And now the cops have her. Can you er... stay here a little while longer? I need to run this by Barnes."

He shrugged and moved to sit on the end of my messy bed. "While you're gone, I'll snoop through your things like you did with mine."

I played at being shocked. "I did not do that. You can't prove it."

"Uh huh." He leaned back and spread his knees, openly inviting me to swoop in and *take him*. My cock warmed. Christ, Barnes had the worst timing.

"You're killing me here."

He ran a hand up his thigh. "I know."

"Stay."

On the way back to the kitchen, I quickly tapped out a message to Kempthorne asking him when he was due back for his meeting and found Barnes still at the table. "Maybe you can help with something? Sunday, Kempthorne and I picked up a Penny Montgomery. Near the Blackwall Tunnel. Has Kempthorne mentioned her?"

"Nothing, no." She rested her elbow on the table and leaned forward. "Tell me more."

"Penny was kidnapped Saturday night, then dumped on Sunday—hands tied with an artifact—on the road heading into Blackwall Tunnel, left there like a ticking bomb. It was deliberate. Professional. Different to the rest we've seen in this surge. The rest appear to be random, as though someone is deliberately creating chaos, but Penny... she was planted there."

She reached into her coat and pulled out a notepad. "Montgomery, you said? What did she look like?"

"Blonde hair, ponytail. Mid teens."

"Well, that's familiar…"

"I've had a message from her parents. She's been taken into police custody. Maybe you can look her up, make sure she's okay? She was pretty shaken up."

"You didn't take her to processing, John? A dangerous latent like that?"

Dangerous was a matter of perspective and her tone had my skin crawling uncomfortably. "No, we had a shit-ton of other calls coming in and couldn't get through to processing. We took her home."

She scribbled down the name and smiled. "I can certainly check on her for you."

My phone pinged. K: *I'm finishing up in Ilford. I'll be an hour. What meeting?*

In the chaos of the past few days, it had either slipped his mind or the messages from the office were on his answering service. *The DI is here now,* I tapped out, and muttered, "Sorry about this, Detective. Kempthorne's running late."

K: *not for me, she's not.*

Well, this was awkward. I gave her a sheepish smile and shrugged. "It looks like there's been a mix-up—"

"No mix-up, John. I'm actually not here for Alexander." The DI's polite smile sharpened into a hard line and all the warmth in her eyes snuffed out. "Take a seat, please."

We'd gone from friendly chat to threatening in a blink. What did she want me for? I hardly knew this woman. We'd seen each other in passing, but I'd assumed she was close with Kempthorne because of cases and his ability to call her up and have the Met look the other way. So what was this?

I pulled out a chair and perched on the edge. "What's up?"

My phone rang. *Kempthorne.*

"Don't answer that," DI Barnes snapped, then added, "Put the phone on the table, please. Just while we talk."

We could talk and then she was leaving.

I flicked the phone to mute and set it down between us. "You've got three minutes to tell me what's going on."

Barnes's little smiles and polite tone vanished and the woman turned cold and rigid. "Listen to me very carefully. You're one of few authenticators left in London, and due to recent events, your position has much improved. Leave with me now and I will make it worth your while."

I blinked, careful to keep my face neutral as my thoughts raced. Clearly DI Barnes was not the straight arrow I'd thought her to be. Did Kempthorne know his pet Met Detective had an off-the-books interest in latents? "What exactly are you asking?"

"A man of your talents can do a lot more than track and trace latents. You're wasted here, John. This agency? They don't know what they've got in you."

"But you do?"

My phone buzzed again, vibrating the table. *Kempthorne.*

"Military-trained Psy Ops. A capable authenticator, but more than that, you're a capable soldier. I need latents like you for what's to come. Alexander's too wrapped up in his work to see your potential. Work with me, and I'll pay you twice the wage you get here."

She'd always come across as upright and stern, but now she spoke with giddy enthusiasm. The switch reminded me of the way Kempthorne got in front of his murder wall.

"And what would I be doing for you?"

"Tracking down latents, but instead of handing them over to processing, we look after them. Personally."

Leaning forward, I propped an arm on the table. "Look after them *how*?"

She held my gaze, and the shrewdness she'd always carried hardened into a menacing tension. "Aren't you tired of being used, John? Always someone else's dog, never the master? Latents can be and do so much more. Don't you think it's time you had the same freedom as everyone else?"

Her offer was a tempting one. It was a shame I didn't believe a single word of it. If I'd learned anything in the military, it was that people in power rarely told the whole story. I had a good thing going with Kempthorne & Co. Today was my two-year anniversary. I wasn't about to walk way from them because some top brass bird dangled a few tempting offers in front of me. Growing up in the East End had taught me if anything sounded too good to be true, then you were usually about to get your head kicked in. "I think it's time you left, Detective Inspector."

She leaned back and sighed. "Such a shame. I had hoped we could do this the easy way." She pulled off her right glove and reached into her pocket. "What is it you think you have here, John? Certainly not choices. Alexander *owns* you."

I tensed, reflexively dropping my hand to my side, but my cards were in my room with Hollywood. A brief moment of what-the-fuck-do-I-do-if-she-pulls-a-gun had me locked in the chair, until she revealed a phone.

Hollywood's paranoia was rubbing off on me.

She rose to her feet, switched her phone to her gloved left hand, and lifted it to her ear. "This is DI Barnes. I have an active latent situation at 16a Cecil Court. IC-one male unresponsive, send immediate assistance."

"Wait..." I shot to my feet. "Hold on, lady."

Her right hand withdrew a glowing rectangular block that looked remarkably like my deck of cards. With a flick of the wrist, she freed a card between her finger and thumb, with the deck still hugged in her palm, cocked her head, and said, "You should have taken my offer."

Hollywood chose that moment to appear—maybe he'd heard the conversation, maybe he thought he was coming to my rescue—whatever the reason, he stepped into the kitchen, saw me lurch toward Barnes, and swung his gaze toward her too late. She let the card fly. It spun as fast and true as a dagger and exploded against Hollywood's chest. He flew backward, hit the wall, and crumpled to the floor on his side, unmoving. Blood quickly pooled beneath him.

"Well then, John," DI Barnes said, her wicked glare sliding to me, "it looks as though you just killed a man."

24

G rabbing a knife from the block, I flung a surge of trick down my arm, into the carving knife, and spun. Barnes hit me like a truck, grabbed my wrist, wrestling, and thrust my arm high. Her trick blasted through her fingers, into my arm, burning through my veins and skin. My reflexes spasmed, I barked a cry, and the knife clattered to the floor.

"Easy now," she said, sneering, a look of curdled glee on her face. "Don't make this worse by assaulting a police officer."

I got a knee between us and kicked her back. She sprawled against the table, sending it and the chairs screeching across the floor. Papers flew, cups smashed.

"Armed police!" Voices barreled up the stairs along with the sounds of marching boots. How had they arrived so fast? Barnes grinned and tossed her cards to the floor. They fluttered down like butterflies—so like mine, like I'd done this. Like I'd hurt Kage.

I was the active latent situation.

"It's best if you don't resist," she said, sliding her glove back on.

Kage. He wasn't moving. The pool of blood had grown, spreading across the kitchen floor. A card to the chest would kill anyone. He'd come to talk, to help, and now he lay on his side, bleeding out.

I had to fix this. But Barnes's smile said it all. There was no way out.

The door flew in and a wave of black-clad firearms officers spilled in.

Barnes flashed her badge and nodded at me. They swarmed as one, kicked my legs out, dropped me to my knees, and yanked my hands behind my back. "Down! Get down! On your knees!"

"I'm not armed!" It didn't matter. Slammed face-first into the floor, a knee pinned me still and cuffs ratcheted into place, squeezing my wrists together. "Fuck, I'm not armed!"

"John Domenici, you are under arrest for attempted murder," Barnes said. "You do not have to say anything, but it may harm your defense if you do not mention when questioned something you later rely on in court. Anything you do say may be given in evidence. Do you understand? *Get the paramedics in here!*"

Barnes's words were a blur. She couldn't mean me. All of this was insanity. It happened so damn fast. Officers crowded Kage, blocking him from sight. Shiny red blood crept around their boots, across the floor. "Is he alive?"

"Looks bad," Barnes said, wearing a sympathetic face. "Your card found its mark, John. You killed him." Moving closer, she said, "Jilted lovers. Revenge. So many motives. Looks like I'm your only way out of this."

Kage wasn't dead. He couldn't be. But my hasty denials couldn't paint over the obvious. Nobody survived having their chest ripped open. Christ, I was going down for this. I had no defense against a copper. I was falling, with no way of stopping myself. My life here was over.

I tore from the officers' grips and lunged for Barnes. Shouts went up and the cops boiled into action. Three men holding me turned into six, grappling to keep me back. "She did this!" I bucked and kicked and got slammed against a wall for my efforts.

"Oi, calm it down or we'll Tase you!"

Slumping, I glared at Barnes, watching her thin lips crawl into a smile. "She fucking did this," I growled. "She used those cards, they're not mine. She's a latent!"

"Unstable latents like you, dismissed from the military on medical grounds..." she said. "This was inevitable really. I'm sure your commanding officer will agree you're a danger to the public. You just killed a man, John. Just like those old military days. Civilian life not enough for you? Not even Alexander Kempthorne can save you this time. *Get him out of here.*"

Kage wasn't dead. He couldn't be. He'd just been in my room, perfectly fine, flirting up a storm.

The cops hauled me down the stairs and outside, into Cecil Court in full view of the tourists who shoved their phones in my direction, filming London's finest cops taking out the latent trash. I was a tourist attraction, just another London latent who had lost his mind.

Bundled into the back of a waiting van, I slumped on the metal bench opposite my own personal firearms officer. The van doors slammed shut, blocking out the crowd.

"Fuck." I thumped my head back against the van's

panel. I was so screwed. Latents didn't go to court. They didn't get to plead their case. Innocent until proven guilty was a fucking lie for us. We were unstable, and that was as far as it went. The IRL would shove us into a mental institution somewhere for re-education. Or more likely for me, the military would scoop me up and dump me into their Dartmoor facility.

Would Kempthorne believe any of this? My last words to him about Kage hadn't been great, but he knew I wouldn't kill anyone. If the Met let him see the kitchen, he'd figure it out. Him and Robin. Gina would back me all the way. But it might not be enough.

The officer opposite dead-eyed me, keeping his assault rifle resting on his knee.

Someone thumped on the outside of the van. The engine rumbled to life, lurching into motion.

DI Barnes had set me up.

Those cards were replicas of mine, and that wasn't a coincidence. The whole thing was a charade and now Kage was...

I thumped my head against the panel again. He hadn't deserved that.

I was always going to leave 16a with Barnes, either in cuffs or following some bullshit story about a job offer. There was no job. Barnes held all the cards. I'd been Kempthorne's property, and now I was hers.

My gaze roamed over the officer opposite, still staring back at me through the slits in his helmet. Penny had said the men who had kidnapped her had been dressed in black. They'd bundled her into a van. Firearms officers?

What if all this was coordinated? What if Barnes was the top man—*woman*—behind the scenes, buying up artifacts, putting the pressure on latents. Shit, she was on-scene at Anca's. Kempthorne would have handed her the dirty artifacts. Worse than that, she'd had Kempthorne reporting back to her on the case this whole time. DI Barnes was socially connected, and she had the means and the resources to organise all of this.

The person orchestrating everything wasn't someone close to Kempthorne, but someone who had *hired* him. Someone with the power to pull all the strings. She had access to the latent registry database. She could find any registered latent, anywhere. She could confiscate any artifact with the full weight of the law behind her.

Oh fuck.

Was Barnes M?

The firearms officer stared.

His radio crackled and a tinny voice asked, *"Target good?"*

"All good," he replied.

The men who had taken Penny had radios. Gareth Clarke's artifact had been missing since his death in the alley, since the firearms officers had bundled me out of there. Kage hadn't taken it. The FOs had scooped up the artifact for their boss. DI Barnes. *She* was the connection, the link between the missing artifacts, the auctions, and Penny's abduction.

Christ, it had been Barnes's firearms officers all along. But why? What was Barnes's end game?

"Three minutes," the voice through the radio said.

"Three minutes, copy that."

Firearms officers. DI Barnes's officers. Bent coppers. Barnes was collecting latents, collecting artifacts. One thing was clear, this van wasn't going to a police station.

25

"Now," the radio voice said.

The van hit a pothole, rattling us. The officer's gaze locked on mine. "Copy that." He lunged.

I lurched sideways, hit the bulkhead, and sprang back, slamming my shoulder into the officer. The both of us fell to the metal floor in a scramble of limbs with the awkward press of the rifle trapped between us. My hands were still cuffed, so my options for fighting back were limited. I went for the officer's only soft spot I could find —his nuts. My knee crunched home. A strangled, silent scream left his lips, then the butt of his gun cracked across my jaw, knocking my thoughts about my head. I was breathing something sweet and potent through a rag before I could think clearly enough to buck him off, but by then, it was too late. My thoughts lagged, my body checked out, and I was swimming in darkness seconds later.

Pinpricks of light pierced the top of the large, rusted ship-ping container I'd woken in—so at least I had air, if not much else. Still cuffed, pins and needles stabbed my hands while the rest of me ached in protest at being tossed around a police van and dumped on hard corru-gated steel. The knife wound throbbed hot, heavy waves. Hopefully the stiches had held.

Well, this was fun.

I'd been right. This wasn't the cop shop. Which meant Barnes was likely everything I'd suspected, and any attempt Kempthorne made to find me would be stonewalled. I was on my own.

A deep, throaty growl of a motor started up some-where outside the container. Shuffling onto my knees, I got to my feet and shoved at the door, unsurprised when it didn't budge. More clangs sounded outside. Metal ground and scraped. The motor revved—a forklift, maybe. I was probably in one of many containers hidden away in an industrial yard somewhere.

Kage...

My thoughts bounced around my head like I rattled around the shipping container but kept circling back to Kage, to seeing his body and wishing I'd done more, done anything. It had happened so damn fast. The Barnes bitch had cards, she was a latent, and she was in control.

Still, I was fucking trained for that shit. I should have been able to stop her and save him. I'd failed. And a man had died. Again. Just like Syria. Just like my whole fucking life.

I kicked at the container wall, making the metal ring,

bounced back, and kicked at it again, but this time too hard. Pain danced through my ankle, reminding me not to be an idiot and cripple myself. There would be a chance to get out of there, I just had to wait for it.

I *was* still alive. That counted as a win.

I just needed to get free, and to do that, I had to get the cuffs off. I could spill my trick into them, but without an artifact, the trick's spread would be chaotic. I'd be just as likely to burn my wrists as I was to melt the cuffs. I wasn't that desperate, not yet.

I slid down the metal wall, pulled my knees up, and turned all my thoughts over, looking for new information. Hiring Kempthorne & Co to keep an eye on what we knew was a smart move by Barnes. And when we got too close, she put the brakes on, or came in afterward to sweep up the artifacts. She was perfectly placed to undermine the entire latency control operation in London and use it to her advantage. But what was her objective? A latent with access to that much power? She was exactly what the IRL and agencies were designed to prevent. Shit. She could do anything. With a few strategically placed unstable latents and artifacts, each one its own bomb, she could topple governments.

But what did she need an authenticator for? Why was I still alive?

Another engine rumbled outside sometime later, accompanied by slamming doors and boots on gravel. I worked my way back to my feet and waited just inside the door. Metal bolts moaned. Daylight streamed in, blurring two silhouetted figures. A hand grabbed my arm and hauled me from the container into bright sunlight. I didn't see the punch coming but damn well felt it when it exploded in my guts, doubling me up.

I spat into the dirt, fighting bile.

Rough hands yanked me upright and a snarling face filled my vision. I recognized his hard eyes—the firearms officer from the van. He rattled me in his grip and tossed me into the back of a car. Outside the tinted windows, I caught glimpses of countless containers stacked in rows.

We didn't go far. The driver took a few turns through the sprawling industrial estate and pulled the car up outside a Portakabin rooted in place by grass and weeds. The temporary building looked as though it had been dumped here to die, like maybe this shithole was the last thing some people saw before they were buried in the scrubland beyond the yard's chain-link fence.

The guy who'd sucker punched me opened the car door and made a grab for my arm. I scooted away. The big fella dove in, snatching for my ankles. I kicked out, striking his jaw.

"Motherfucker!" he roared.

The second kick he dodged. His thick fingers locked around my leg, and he yanked, unceremoniously dragging me out of the car. I landed arse-first on cracked concrete.

This was my chance. If I could get up, I could run.

I rolled onto my front, wedging a knee under me. The industrial yard was full of cabins and ringed by an eight-foot-high chain-link fence. I was fast. I might make it out a hole in the fence, or a gate.

The kick to my side shattered all my plans. My body locked up, trying to fight my own lungs for air. Yanked to my feet, spluttering, I couldn't do much more than stumble alongside them. They shoved me up the rusted steps into the half-rotted Portakabin. The smell of damp and decay cloyed my throat, mixing with the coppery smell of blood that might have been mine. A single plastic chair waited in the middle of the floor, right over a suspiciously dark stain.

DI Barnes waited for her officers to dump me into the chair. My new friend, the one with the bruised balls, cursed me out and dabbed at his split lip. "Fuckin' prick needs a good kickin'."

"Uncuff me and have at it, handsome." I grinned. The threat sounded more wheezy than I'd intended but it did the trick. Handsome snarled and started forward.

"Thompson, leave it," Barnes said and Thompson ducked his head like a scolded dog.

Barnes smiled her sharp smile and approached. "Now then, John. You don't mind if I call you John? We can finally talk."

I kept the *fuck you* from my lips and glared.

"The inimitable John Domenici. Your father was a mechanic with connections to the London mob. He died like he lived, in a ditch, with a half-burned playing card in his mouth, thought to be a message from the East End's organized crime gangs. Your mother is now retired, in witness protection, and on state benefits. You were trouble in school, when you bothered to show up. At seventeen, after a stint in jail, you joined the military. Without it, the East End gangs would have chewed you up and spat you out like they do with latents."

I laughed dryly. She had no fucking idea what she was talking about. My life was just facts on a screen to her. "What do you want? Someone killed your pet authenticator so now you need someone to read an artifact? You could have just asked."

"No, John. Anca wasn't mine, and you have me all wrong."

"Kempthorne is on to you."

Her sharp smile grew sharper. "Alexander Kempthorne was much aggrieved to discover a member of his team had murdered a man in the kitchen of his much-loved bookstore. It will of course impact on the good name of Kempthorne and Co. What kind of artifact retrieval agency employs an unstable latent, and one with your past?" She tittered a laugh.

Kempthorne could have wiped his hands of me, that would have been the sensible thing to do. And a few weeks ago, I'd have believed Barnes. But I'd seen his murder wall. Kempthorne wasn't going to abandon me. He wasn't the sort. But he was good at lying. He'd tell Barnes one thing and plan another. The man was smart. He'd know something was off, especially when Barnes started blocking him. "A *registered* unstable latent," I said. "Unlike you. So what's your big plan? Revenge? Did someone hurt you so now you're what...? You're going to show them who the real boss of London is by unleashing confused and vulnerable latents? Latents like Penny?"

She snorted. "Well, that would all be very predictable, wouldn't it. However, there's far more at work here than a few unstable individuals who can't control their abilities. Do you truly believe this was all we were meant for? Registered, controlled, observed, and used? Is that truly the latents' fate? No. There is far more happening here than you or I. There are more shadows at work in London than anyone realizes."

Her words rang the same note as Kempthorne's. He'd said something about shadows and other forces at play behind the scenes. "Shadows like who?"

"Not who, John. *What*."

"I don't—"

"You, an authenticator, cannot deny it. You feel it. You hear it, the same as I do, the same as all latents in London hear it. It began in London. It will end here. With us. With you."

Perhaps I'd given her too much credit. I'd assumed she was orchestrating all this for logical reasons. Instead, she was hearing voices. Latents often lost their minds to the sickness—channeling the energy of past trauma, living in fear of losing control—it ate at the soul. But when they crashed and burned, it was normally spectacular. Barnes appeared to be eerily sane.

"You don't believe me." Her eyes narrowed and her lips twisted with scorn. "Years of being told what you can and can't do, years of attending stability tests, registration, and restriction. Of being told you're wrong, and you must hide that wrongness, restrain it, like a dog with its balls cut off. When it is *they* who are wrong. London is tired of having her voice silenced. She will be heard."

I glanced at Handsome by the door and his mate, but neither looked alarmed that their boss was spouting nonsense, trying to convince me London was alive.

"I am saving them," she went on. "Saving *you*, John."

"Honestly"—I rattled my cuffs—"It doesn't feel like it. Uncuff me and we'll talk more about the shadows."

"I don't think so. You've proven yourself to be resourceful, but also entirely blind. A military grunt. A soldier. You will be my proof that we are more than the tools they want us to be, we are born of London's soul."

"Er..." Okay, definitely latent sickness. I was almost disappointed. Everything—the auctions, Anca—it had seemed like so much more than one latent's madness.

With her gloved fingers, she withdrew Kempthorne's pen from deep inside her coat pockets. "And all you have to do is stop fighting."

Flashes of finding Penny in the road came back to me, the artifact taped to her hands, the girl desperately clinging to control. If Barnes did the same to me with that damn pen... "Don't." There was no point hiding the quiver in my voice.

"You've been taught to stay away from artifacts, to push them from you, especially those that are personal. This artifact... This one is special. You already have a connection with it. You feel it, and it feels you."

"Don't do this."

"You just have to listen. That's all any of us has to do."

"That's exactly what I shouldn't do!" She started forward. "Don't... If you put that in my hand, I can't control it. We'll all fucking die."

"That's what you've been told. But there's another way." Now the crazy began to sparkle in her eyes.

No, this wasn't happening. I wanted to live, I wanted to get out of this cabin and go back to Kempthorne & Co and just be there, with them—Gina, Robin, and Alex. I'd steal all the custard creams, go on fake dates to Soho with Gina, paint my fucking nails. I wasn't *done*.

If Barnes put that bloody pen in my hand, I wouldn't win. I couldn't win. It was too powerful and it spoke to me, creeping through all my training and defenses, in a way no other artifact ever had.

Surging the trick down my arms, I lit the cuffs up. Intense heat singed my wrists. Pain crackled and sizzled, but it was almost a relief, if it meant I could escape. The acrid smell of burning flesh laced my throat. Didn't matter. If I could make the cuffs pliable, I could yank them apart.

"You will thank me," she said, circling behind me.

"No—no!"

The pen fell into my hand.

The pen was as seductive as it was vicious. It lured me in, lured me deep, with promises and whispers. It told me all things I wanted to hear, and then it showed me what I didn't want to see.

A boy.

Tied to a table.

His wrists were raw, like mine now. Sweat, and salt, and tears, and piss. Sobs. Begging. A mother's soft voice, telling him she loved him, even as she hurt him.

I couldn't do this. I couldn't be there, but I couldn't stop it, because deep inside, I wanted to *see* and I wanted to *know*. The latent in me needed this connection. It was a part of me. I couldn't hide from myself. And the power knew it.

"*It's a wonder, truly,*" his mother said.

The pen, clasped in her hand, scratched over paper.

"*Please let me go,*" the boy said, sobbing.

"*Do not fight it, Alexander.*"

"*Mother, please.*"

Deeper, the pen dragged me. I followed the swirl of its nib on rough paper, followed the words as they took shape. *Remarkable. Potential. Challenging.*

"Stop, please. Please don't."

"Hush, Alexander, it will be over soon."

Pain, like fire, but so cold. It washed through me—through him—and wrenched silent screams from his lips.

Disappointing. Limited. Failure. The words stained the paper. The pen bled its cold, heartless ink.

"Alexander, tears are for the weak."

He stopped crying then.

He loved her, and feared her. Feared this room. This hard metal table. The scratch of the pen, over and over, judging him, reporting him, reducing him to nothing but words on a line, a study, an *experiment*.

But behind it all, deeper beneath the surface, something else lurked and waited and watched. Something hungry with a heartbeat not belonging to the pen, or the memory, or me. Something that listened, something that fed and grew—not good or bad, but definitely *alive*.

27

"Hey? Hey?"

I woke to the echoes of a voice I knew but couldn't place. The shipping container was familiar too. I'd been here before. If I could just pin down my drifting thoughts... There had been another bumping car ride, Handsome was there—he clearly fancied me but was in denial—Barnes being batshit crazy—*the pen!* I gasped and lurched upright, wishing I hadn't when the container spun and my body tried to eject the last dregs of food in my guts.

At least my hands weren't cuffed anymore. My left shook as I dragged one across my mouth. An angry burn ringed my wrists and now I'd seen it, the pain throbbed back to life.

"Yeah, it's pretty rough the first time," the girl said. "It passes though."

Artifact shock. I'd suffered it before, but this wasn't *my* shock, it was Kempthorne's from years ago. It took me a few more seconds of breathing and thinking and putting all my thoughts back into order before realizing I knew the girl talking—and that she was real. "Penny, are you okay?" I croaked.

She shrugged. "Better now I'm not alone." She wore the same strappy sandals, tight blue jeans, and a tiny top with an anime cat motif. Hugging her knees to her chest, she stared at the container door. "I thought they were going to kill me, but this is maybe worse."

If I could just...get myself together, I could work on getting us out of there. I rubbed at the ache trying to split my forehead open and tried to breathe the trembling back under control. I'd be all right just so long as I didn't think about the hard table and the ice-cold pain, and the pen—*scratch, scratch* with its words.

Fuck.

It would pass. The memories weren't mine. But they were hooked into my head just like they must be in Kempthorne's every day. Christ, how was I going to look him in the eye knowing *all that?*

At least I hadn't succumbed to the artifact's allure and lost my shit. But why hadn't I? Out of control latents went boom, that was how it worked. I'd definitely been out of control. How was I still in one piece?

The next time she put that pen in my hand, things might not go so well. We needed to get the hell out of here before that happened. If I could tackle Handsome and his friend, Penny and me could make our escape... I just had to get a grip on myself, instead of floating somewhere between now and then. "Fuck, what did she do?"

"Overexposure," Penny said. "I heard her guards talking about it. She walks us to the line and holds us there, looking into the abyss. We either fall back or fall over, I guess." She sniffed and wiped her quiet tears away. "I saw it on the Discovery Channel once. A guy was afraid of snakes, so they locked him in a room full of them. After a while, he got used to it. He came out not afraid of snakes anymore."

Not afraid of snakes maybe, but he probably came out with a few more anxieties added to those he went in with. "But why?" It didn't make any sense. What did she *want*?

"I dunno. I just wanna go home."

I shuffled to her side and tucked her under my arm. "Hey, listen okay? We're getting out of here."

More tears came. She sniffled and trembled and all I could do was hold her close and think on how I could get that container door open.

"She has others too," Penny said a while later. "They're kept in other containers, like animals. I hear them calling when they take me out. It's like we're just things to them."

That was why DI Barnes wanted all the artifacts—not for her personal use, or some grand plan to blow up London. The artifacts and us were her experiments. She wanted to *save* latents by breaking us, under some bull-shit excuse about London's voice.

"Did you feel it?" Penny whispered when her sobbing subsided.

"Feel what?"

"When you go deep, the thing there... the thing that watches. She told me about it, and now I can't unsee it. It's like it's in me somehow. Like it's a part of me. She said it's a part of all of us—latents, I mean. She said that's why we don't... you know... go up like fireworks like others do, because it's watching."

I'd felt something, but trying to recall it had me dredging up all of Kempthorne's trauma. I couldn't be sure what it had been. Another presence, the source of a latent's power, or just my own messed up past trying to muscle in on the action. It was getting pretty crowded in my head. The military had drilled control into my bones and subjected me to similar exposure, but those artifacts had never taken me *deeper* like the pen had. I'd never felt a third presence before, one outside the artifact's memory, looking in, in the same way I looked in.

"I'm sorry I got you into this," Penny mumbled.

"You didn't. I was already neck-deep in this shit. I just couldn't see it. I work for the agency Barnes hired to track *herself*. She had us running around in circles for her." Sighing, I rested my head back and blinked at the rusted container roof. "I just realized, yesterday was my two-year anniversary working at Kempthorne & Co. I think it was yesterday."

Penny shifted away slightly, putting some space between us. "Was Kempthorne the posh guy with the fancy car?"

"Yeah." I draped an arm over a drawn-up knee, keeping my scorched wrist from touching anything. "Now he thinks he hired an unstable latent. I should have figured it was all too good to be true. People like me don't land on our feet."

"Sometimes I think it's all just stacked against us. We're latents. We do as we're told or we disappear."

I wanted to tell her it wasn't like that, but couldn't.

"But you seem all right, Dom," she said, adding some

warmth. "You helped me, and lots of other latents, I bet. You're a good guy."

"I'm trying. But it hasn't always been like that."

"Did you get cake?" She brightened and tucked a few lose strands of hair behind her ear. "For your anniversary?"

"Nah. Instead, I was framed for killing a friend and the copper who nicked me turned out to be the psycho doing this to us. Robin probably ate the cake without me. If there was any."

"Sounds like a really shitty anniversary."

I snorted a laugh. "It really was."

"For what it's worth, I'm kinda glad you're here. It was horrible alone."

"Likewise." I offered her my fist, and we bumped.

"So how we gonna get that bitch?" Penny asked. "Two latents, right? We can do this. You taught me that when you saved me on that street. You know how I know that? Because we're here." She'd quoted me. I'd needed to hear it.

Climbing to my feet, I brushed dirt off my clothes, waited for my vision to stop spinning and the dull thud in my back to pass, and approached the container door. It would have a weakness. Everything did. No bolts on the inside—shipping containers weren't designed to contain *people*. Rubbing my hands together, I blew on them for luck and grinned at Penny. "I know an old military trick. Only works with more than one of us. Wanna give it a try?"

She got to her feet and joined me at the door. "What have we gotta do?"

"Take my hand."

She cautiously wrapped her fingers around mine.

"See these hinges? I'm going to borrow some of your power and heat them through. It'll tingle and feel like I'm pulling on your chest. But it won't hurt. It'll just feel kinda weird. Like a tickle inside."

"Um... sure, okay."

Rolling my shoulders, I tightened my grip on hers and centered myself around the part of me that always seemed to be ready to boil over and break free. The trick crawled out of its hiding place and tingled down my arm. When it reached my hand, small sparks jumped from Penny's fingers into mine, no more painful than a static shock. She gasped, but clung on.

Lifting my left hand, I spread my fingers over the upper hinge, closed my eyes, and concentrated the flow through my fingertips and *outward*. The trick liked to be free; the real trouble came when I tried to rein it back in. Metal ticked and groaned, heating under my touch, and my wrists burned with an echo of pain.

"They didn't teach us this in school," Penny whispered.

"They teach us what we can't do, not what we can," I said, keeping my eyes closed and my focus on the hinge. As long as just my fingertips touched it, it wouldn't burn me up, but a slip in concentration and my hand would be bacon. "We used to play latent roulette in the barracks," I said softly. Talking might help relax her, and me. "Sharing power like this until one of us got burned."

"Did *you* ever get burned?"

"Yeah, once. I'm not an absorber—latents who suck power and shape it—so I don't have a lot of control over it." My lips twitched at the memory, until that memory unhelpfully reminded me how the people I'd played that game with had all died in the botched Syria op.

"You do have good control though, right?"

"As long as there's no surprises." Like a crazy DI with a kink for putting dirty artifacts in my bound hands.

The door hinge plinked and the door gave a painful groan, leaning on its two remaining hinges. I dropped my left hand to the middle hinge, focusing the same as before, drawing more of Penny's trick through me, into my touch and *outward*. It twitched, buzzed, and sizzled into the metal, heating it up.

"Still okay?" I asked her, keeping my eyes closed. The more I summoned, the more concentration it would take to control it and stop it from backfiring through us both.

"Uh huh."

The middle hinge gave and the door juddered, wedged in place by the single bottom hinge and the opposite door.

Crouching, I fed more power down my arm, into the final hinge. The power pulsed now, in time with my heart or Penny's—maybe both of us together. This wasn't a science, more of an art. More like the touch of magic that I'd tried to explain to Kempthorne.

"Dom?" Penny asked, voice quivering.

"Just a little more." I still had my eyes closed, my mind focused on the task of directing the power and getting us the hell out of the container. We were close now, but Penny's boost was beginning to twitch, like it sensed one of us losing control and it wanted out. Just a little more... we almost had it.

A violent surge pulsed down my arm. Penny barked a cry and tore free. The severed connection whipped back like an elastic band, landing a sudden lash down my spine. I recoiled with a hiss, but it was over as soon as it had hit, leaving me more stunned than hurt.

"Oh my god! Dom, I'm so sorry."

"It's all right." I blinked rapidly and wobbled on my feet, but I was upright and coherent—not fried.

The container door clunked, groaned, yawned outward, and came to a lopsided halt, hung up on something. The hinge side had come away just enough to squeeze through.

"Yes! Let's go." Penny shimmied through the gap first.

I climbed through after her and spilled out into cold night air. Traffic hummed somewhere far off, peppered by the occasional horn, and a breeze rifled through the long grasses between the containers, but the yard was quiet. No grumbling engines. No slamming container doors. Nobody was nearby.

Penny veered left, heading deeper into the yard.

"Wait..." I loped after her.

"We have to help the others," she hissed.

"We will." I caught her arm, gently tugging her to a halt. "By getting out of here and calling it in."

"To who? The cops? She *is* the cops."

I saw her argument, even agreed with her, but it would take hours to open all the containers, and our clunking container door might have already alerted the guards to our escape. "There's no time. Trust me. We will come back for them. But all of this will be for nothing if we get caught again. Come on—" Letting her go, I started heading down the track that would eventually split off and take us out of the yard, if my glimpses during the Audi ride were correct. Near the rotted cabin the track split, forking toward the exit gates. I hadn't seen any gaps in the fence yet. The front gate might have a weakness. Or not. Shit, what was the best way out now?

Penny jogged up behind me.

"Stay low," I whispered.

She nodded and we scooted close by the rusted containers, keeping to the thick shadows and long grass. There didn't appear to be any movement—yet. A few CCTV cameras observed from high on the gate's posts. It was impossible to tell if they were active. We slunk under their field of vision, just in case. Now I could see more of the yard, it appeared to be an old construction site, with the beginnings of excavations having taken place and foundation rods jutting out of the ground. The weeds had taken over, suggesting construction had stopped some time ago.

The fence was in good condition, no holes. But as we drew closer to the main gates, I caught a whiff of river water on the air and the breeze tossed around the sounds of cars. We weren't far outside a city, maybe still in London.

Searching the skyline, I caught glimpses of blinking lights, the kind used on top of buildings to warn off approaching aircraft, and spotted lights I recognized. The London Eye on the banks of the Thames. We weren't far from Westminster. Half an hour's walk to central London. Barnes had balls, that was for certain. Capturing latents, pushing them to their limits, right under everyone's noses.

"A car," Penny whispered.

We crouched behind some brambles. Lights burst on

over the main gate. The gate clattered open and a car pulled into the yard, wheels splashing through puddles.

I knew those sleek black lines. And the figure behind the wheel.

"Isn't that your friend driving?" Penny trailed off.

"Yeah." Alexander Kempthorne.

28

"It's good he's here, right?" Penny asked, sounding hopeful.

He must have figured out something was amiss with DI Barnes, but my instincts were ringing alarm bells. Where was his backup? Why come alone? *What are you up to?* "Yeah, sure. Just stay down."

The gate rattled closed. We never would have made the dash across the yard out in the open, but we might have a chance at sneaking out when Kempthorne left again.

The car stopped in the middle of the yard, engine running. Waiting.

Barnes and her two-man team approached from the direction of the Portakabins. The driver's door opened and out stepped Kempthorne, buttoning his suit jacket and adjusting his shirt cuffs as though meeting in an industrial yard in the middle of the night was absolutely normal.

Barnes extended her hand and Kempthorne shook it.

282 | ARIANA NASH

They both smiled, just like old friends.

What the hell was this?

"They look pretty comfy," Penny mumbled.

She was right.

But this was Kempthorne. He knew how to put on a mask and play games with others. As far as I could tell, he'd been doing exactly that most of his life. But I'd seen the real Kempthorne standing in front of his murder wall, trying to understand his place in things. He *was* good. I did believe that, even if I sometimes didn't believe *him*.

He'd probably set up this meeting, suspecting Barnes. He was here for the right reasons.

The wind carried snippets of their conversation, but not enough to make any sense of their words.

Kempthorne walked alongside Barnes back toward the Portakabins. The main gate remained shut. Startling white light still flooded the yard. CCTV cameras watched the entrance, but they were angled down on the gate itself. We could make it to the Lexus without being seen. The dash across open ground would be bloody risky though.

"What now?" Penny asked.

"Hide in the car."

She eyed the open expanse of yard between us and the Lexus.

"It'll be fine," I told her. "I'll keep watch. When he leaves, we'll be in it."

"Then come with me?"

"I will, I'm just gonna find out what's going on."

Her eyes sparkled in the dark.

"It's all right." I flashed her a careless smile. "I do this shit for a living." She wasn't convinced. Grinning in the hope she relaxed, I nodded her on. "Go on, I'll be right behind you."

"You better be in that car with me when it leaves."

"Promise."

She narrowed her eyes.

"Go." I chuckled.

Keeping low, she scurried across the open yard, opened the car's back door, and disappeared inside. I waited a few minutes, checking none of the guards were about to ambush either of us. Satisfied she hadn't been seen, I crept back into the shadows and made my way toward the Portakabin.

Voices rumbled from inside. The two guards stood at their stations by the steps. I maneuvered my way around, out of sight behind the cabin, and lingered just below an open window.

"... making progress," Barnes said from inside. "I'm not going to simply hand over the artifacts, Alexander, when you've done little to prove you're fully on board with our initiative."

"I'm here. Isn't that enough?" Kempthorne's words barely registered above a growl. He was there, but he wasn't happy.

"Far from it. You promised me John Domenici. You had two years, Alexander."

"These things are delicate."

Barnes snorted. "John is the opposite of 'delicate.'"

"The military continues to monitor him—"

"Of course they do! They aren't going to relinquish one of their most potent latents no matter the millions you throw at them. Regardless, he's mine now, despite your best efforts to keep him."

"Is he here?" Kempthorne asked.

"He's no longer your concern."

"If you want my assistance going forward, prove he's alive and unharmed."

An awkward silence simmered in the cabin. "There used to be a time you trusted my word, Alexander. A time you believed."

"Things have changed."

"Have *you* changed?"

"Show me John and you'll have your answer."

A rustle of clothing suggested movement and when Barnes next spoke, her voice was pure silk. "Alexander Kempthorne, I've often wondered what makes you *tick*. I thought it was our research, but now I wonder if it's something else." She laughed. The tap of heels moved farther from the window.

Barnes knew about Kempthorne's research?

"*My* research," he corrected.

"Yes, well. Without my resources, you'd still be fishing in the dark—the source just a vague dream. Did you bring the final artifact you promised?"

"Olivia, is there no other way?" Kempthorne asked, voice strained.

Barnes's laugh turned dry and hollow. "You promised me you were on board with the summoning. Back out now and I'll make the provenance of the pen public knowledge and your sordid past becomes front-page news."

Kempthorne's heavy sigh spoke volumes. "The coin is in the car. I'll get it—"

Wait, the coin from his safe? *That* coin?

"No, I'll retrieve it personally. You may decide to leave

without handing it over and I've come too far for you to let me down."

"It's almost as though you don't trust me," Kempthorne said, sounding more like his usual charming self. "It's in the glove box."

Barnes's strides signaled her leaving the cabin. She barked an order for her guards to follow her. Shit, Penny was in the car!

There was no way I could make it back to the Lexus before they reached it without being seen. That left only one option. I stole up the cabin steps and shoved the door open.

Kempthorne looked up from leaning against the table. His brow creased. "Dom?" He crossed the space between us in two strides, then slowed. "You're all right? Are you hurt?"

"Doesn't matter. Penny is hiding in your car. You need to stop Barnes *now*."

"*What!?*" His eyes blew wide. "Dom, no. There's a bomb—" Bolting by, he burst through door and pounded down the steps. "Olivia—*stop!*"

My heart thumped in my ears. *A bomb?!* He'd brought a fucking bomb? Was he insane?!

The coin was bait to lure Barnes out there. He was going to blow the Lexus and take Barnes with it. I flew from the cabin and raced after Kempthorne.

Up ahead, one of the guards reached for the car's front door. Barnes moved in close behind him. I saw it all in perfect clarity, the way the guard's fingers hooked around the door handle, how he stepped closer. How Barnes looked up and her eyes widened on seeing me and Kempthorne running toward her.

Kempthorne yelled something. A deafening blast mangled the sound and punched me in the chest. The devastating roar came next, drowning out everything, even the pounding of my heart. Dirt, glass, and debris plinked against the dirt all around. It seemed to go on forever, then ended in thick, sickening quiet. I staggered, reeling, somehow still on my feet. Flames danced, lighting up the night in shifting orange light. Metal groaned and ticked.

Oh Christ, Penny!

I'd told her she'd be safe. I'd told her we were getting out of here. I'd put her in the fucking car! I ran for the car's flaming metal carcass, but the boiling heat pushed me back.

No, not her too. I couldn't... I couldn't reach her. Were those her screams or the sound of metal twisting?

I'd done this. I'd put her in the car. I'd killed her.

"Dom..." Kempthorne touched my shoulder. I whirled and shoved him hard in the chest. He staggered, backing off, dark eyes full of sympathy.

"You fucking prick," I snarled, my voice strange in my ringing ears. "Was it worth it? Whatever you're doing here, was it worth her life?! You don't put bombs in cars, Jesus Christ, Kempthorne. This isn't a warzone."

His face fell. "Dom, I'm sorry—I didn't mean for this to happen. I just... Olivia's plan was never supposed to get this far. She had to be stopped." The glow from the flames danced over his face, cutting deep lines around his mouth and eyes, showing his pain. Good. He should hurt.

"Sorry?" *Sorry?!* I couldn't do this, I couldn't be near him. I'd lose it. The trick was already simmering at my fingertips. I could easily light up Alexander Kempthorne too, make him suffer like Penny must have.

Something in the car exploded, whirling me around to stare at the flames. Heat sizzled over my face, drying any tears as soon as they left my eyes.

She couldn't be dead.

I'd just been with her. I was supposed to save people now, not hurt them like before.

She'd been right there, worrying about *me*. She was just a girl in strappy sandals caught up in all of Kempthorne's latent bullshit and now she was... dead?

"I'm so sorry," I whispered.

A figure wobbled on their feet on the other side of the fire and wiped a hand across their bloody lip. They *laughed* at the flames. DI Barnes. I was moving before I could stop myself. Kempthorne grabbed my shoulder. I shook him off and plowed toward the laughing DI. The trick sizzled at the end of my fingers, pooling there, seeking flight without an artifact to channel it. Rage fed it now. Rage at the injustice, at the endless lies, at a world that saw latents as objects to be used and bought and traded. Fuck her, fuck Kempthorne, fuck them all.

"You're goin' down, bitch."

"Dom, don't!" Kempthorne yelled. "She'll absorb it!"

Mirth glittered in Barnes's eyes. "Do test me, John. That is exactly why you're here, after all." I swung for her, but the bitch moved fast, stepping aside with ease. Her hand clamped onto my right arm and my knees hit the dirt before I'd registered I was falling. Barnes's words tickled my ear. "That's it, darling. *Give me everything you've got. Burn for me.*"

Something clutched at my heart and tried to rip it out

through my ribs. Gasping, I scrabbled to fight her off, to shove her, do something to get away, but whatever she was doing sucked hard on my soul, making the world fuzzy and filling my limbs with lead.

I knew what she was... I'd met her kind before.

Her laughter rolled through my head. Her trick tugged in waves, sucking on my power like I'd drawn on Penny's, only a thousand times worse. Barnes's brutal attack ripped out everything that made me a latent, taking my soul too—if I had one left.

Was this what she'd wanted all along? The artifacts, the latents, she wasn't saving them, she was *feeding* on them. The bitch was the worst kind of latent—an absorber, a leech. The ones I'd encountered in Syria had left every latent they'd attacked spent and, in most cases, barely breathing hollow husks.

I gasped for air, but my lungs still screamed, deflating. My heart beat too hard in my chest and throbbed in my head, furiously trying to pump blood around my body— to move, to escape.

"Shit." She hissed so close to my ear its sound shivered through me.

In the haze and the dancing firelight and the smoke, I saw the main gate rolling open. Flashing blue lights joined the blurs. Sirens swallowed the crackling, spitting flames. Fire trucks. A distraction. People. Yes, she'd have to stop. But the world was blurring and fading and I fell through it all—going cold.

A girl in strappy sandals barreled out of the smoke with a two-by-four raised above her head. She screamed —coming *at* me. She swung that plank of wood, thwacking it hard into Barnes, knocking the bitch off me.

I flopped onto my hands, gasping.

"Oh my god, Dom?"

Penny. Her small hands cupped my face.

But she was dead.

Did that mean I was dead too?

Nothing made any sense. My head throbbed, trying to crack open, and my chest burned like I'd swallowed all the fire. This was bad. Real bad.

Penny's tear-streaked face peered into my eyes. "Dom, are you okay?"

Holy shit, was she crying for me?

Fire hissed, steam rolled, the fire crews set to work on dampening the flaming Lexus. Noise and chaos boiled all around, but I was still breathing, I was alive, and so was Penny. "You're alive?"

"Yeah, no thanks to you!" Her tiny fist punched me in the arm. "No way was I staying in that rich guy's car with you acting all weird about him. Good job I didn't. I nearly died!"

Shit, Kempthorne... I shoved up onto tingling legs and scanned the carnage. Fire crews swarmed the fire. But there was no sign of Kempthorne or Barnes. "Where'd they go?"

"He ran toward the river, that way"—Penny pointed out of the open gate—"after the crazy woman."

Oh, hell no. Whatever bullshit was going on between them, Barnes wasn't getting away and I couldn't trust Kempthorne not to let her. I staggered into a loping run, waved off the approaching firefighters, and broke into a jog. "Stay here!" I called back to Penny. "I'll be right back."

29

Half limping, half jogging, I crossed the road outside the yard and followed it downhill, toward the river. More of the yard's fencing ran alongside the old riverfront, earmarked for property development. The Thames was a huge, dark scar running through the middle of London. Light from the nearby embankment's buildings reflected off its inky surface, but the mighty river swallowed most light down into its swirling darkness.

The London Eye loomed close, its glittering spokes motionless. I hobbled along a broken pavement and spotted a gap in the fence, its edges yanked outward, making a hole large enough to slip through.

A flash of latent heat and light blipped beyond the fence, closer to the river. Barnes. More unstable than ever now she was fully charged with my stolen trick. The bitch.

I hobbled through the gap, trying not to think about

the creeping chill consuming my insides or the sticky wetness dripping down my back. I'd be fine, everything would be fine. *Stop Barnes.* That was all I needed to focus on. I crossed a flat area of scrubland toward the sound of echoing voices and lapping water.

Barnes glowed ahead. My stolen trick lit her up as though she was some divine being sent from the heavens, but the crazy on her face was pure evil. Kempthorne's retreating outline cut a striking figure against the distant blinking lights lining Westminster Bridge. A few more steps and he'd topple off the old dockside, into the river. Barnes had him cornered. She could burn him up with a touch.

The pair were so engrossed in each other, neither saw me creep closer.

Kempthorne had his hands up in surrender. Blood stained his shirt, right over the old gunshot wound. Barnes's glow washed over him, lighting up his ashen face and flickering in his dark eyes.

What did Barnes want with all that power? Leeches stole tricks, hoarded them, turning themselves into walking artifacts. I'd faced two in Syria, killed both, but with a trained Psy Ops team. Never alone.

"You don't need to do this," Kempthorne said. The wind teased through his hair, flopping that curl over his forehead. He glanced back at the thick, soupy waters and stopped at the edge of the dockside, right by the ledge. One more step and the Thames would swallow him. "Olivia, please. The research, it wasn't meant for this."

"London must be heard." Barnes's voice had turned eerily smooth and seductive, as though it wasn't entirely her own. She held her hands out, spread her fingers, and pooled the trick in her hands—my trick. "After what they did to you, how can you not stand with me? With the shadows?"

He stretched out a hand. "Olivia, you're sick."

"How dare you, Alex! You know I'm not. We're not sick, we're right!" Her trick flared, fueled by raging emotion.

"No, no... of course. Listen, I know what it is to be so consumed by the fight you turn into the very monster you're fighting. This isn't you. Let me help you."

She laughed like he was the insane one. "You help me? How can you be so naive? You were the first of us, after all. Come with me to the Eye, watch me raise London from her slumber. I have your authenticator's power—John's power—and so many others. They are all a part of me now. You see it writhe?" Turning her hands, the trick licked over her fingers like golden honey. Much of it was mine, but much of it belonged to the other latents she'd harvested. It was never about saving latents or mad experiments. It was all about her, and the power she couldn't get enough of.

Kempthorne's gaze flicked over Barnes's shoulder and fixed on me in my hiding place, striking deep into my thumping heart. A jolt of knowing drove determination through tired limbs and the aches and wounds and pain faded. A connection tugged between us. Familiar, soothing. The corner of his lips ticked and my heart sank. The heroic fool was about to do something stupid.

A strong gust of wind rocked him on the edge of the dockside. London's glittering buildings across the river cast him in moody silhouette.

"All right, we'll do this together," he said, offering his hand for her to take.

She stepped closer. "As it was meant to be."

A grimace pulled his fake smile tight. "Indeed."

She lifted her glowing hand and the trick spiraled from her fingers in golden threads, reaching for Kempthorne. He knew what she was—a dangerous, highly powerful latent, able to suck the power from artifacts and fellow latents and weave it together. He'd probably always known DI Barnes was a walking nightmare. And he knew she had to be stopped—by any means.

The fool was going to kill himself to end her.

But Kempthorne was *not* dying on my damn watch; Robin would have my balls in a vice.

If anyone was killing a copper, it was me. I was the East End lad, the criminal's son, the dirty latent, the tool, the mistake waiting to happen. If I went down for it, it wouldn't matter. Kempthorne would go on to figure all this shit out. He *had* to.

Barnes closed her hand around Kempthorne's. He pulled her close, like dance partners, and her crazy smile softened as she looked into his eyes.

The trick's glow crawled over Kempthorne's hands and lapped up his arms, wrapping around him, consuming him too, until the pair of them glowed like stars. It would have been beautiful if it weren't so fucking tragic.

Kempthorne raised a hand and cupped Barnes's cheek. Regret and sadness filled his eyes.

"Sorry, Alex," she said. "You *have* changed. I just can't trust you." She shoved.

Kempthorne reeled, teetering on the edge of the dockside.

My heart leaped. Adrenaline surged. I sprang, slammed my shoulder into Barnes—knocking her clean over the side—and snatched Kempthorne's flailing arm, catching him on the cusp of falling. Momentum tumbled us both to the ground. The thick, wet smell of river and mud wafted, too damn close. Had we fallen another inch to the right, the Thames would have taken us, like it had taken Barnes.

I let out a breath, and with Kempthorne pinned safely under me, I pushed up onto both hands and glared at him.

Kempthorne's chest heaved and his sparkling blue eyes held all the answers to mysteries I was still discovering. A tiny tic pulled at the corner of the bastard's lips. We'd both almost died, multiple times. I'd had half my power yanked out, and Penny had almost gone up in a ball of flames from his stupid bomb, and he was *smiling*?

Part of me wanted to punch that smile off his face, and another part wanted to kiss his sideways-tilted lips.

Instead, I peeked over the edge into the swirling dark soup of the Thames, half expecting to see Barnes clinging to the bank. But she was gone, swept away by the river. London could keep her.

"Is she dead?" Kempthorne asked—the words so close to my cheek that the moment became curiously intimate.

"Definitely." I faced him, still had him under me, still felt him breathing, maybe even felt his heart pounding.

"In that case, do you mind getting off?"

Rolling off him, I flopped onto my back, wishing I hadn't when the stab wound barked up my spine. Now it was over, my head was back to splitting open and my chest had remembered it was supposed to be fighting to breathe and the wound in my back needed attention. The hollowness Barnes had left felt like a gaping wound too, one nobody could see. Christ, leeches were horrible.

Kempthorne clambered to his feet, brushed his suit down, and ran a hand over his hair. Unknown to him, his curl sprang back.

He caught me watching him and his little smile returned. He offered his hand. "All things considered, everything turned out rather well, don't you think?"

I eyed his hand like it was a trap and clambered to my feet without his help. "I think, *Alexander*, you need to tell me everything."

"Oh, right. Yes. Well. Where to start?"

"The beginning?" A spasm tightened my chest. I doubled over to catch my breath.

"Olivia Barnes approached me a year ago to speak about our shared interests. I knew her from the academy we both attended. We met in latent studies class. After she recently approached me, I regained her trust and learned how she used her position in the Met to secure artifacts and latants, gradually harvesting tricks from both to increase her own, with the ultimate goal of summoning some kind of sleeping entity she believed resides beneath London—the source of all latents." He rolled his shoulder and winced, muttering a curse at the blood on his shirt. "As an unregistered latent," he continued, "her efforts went unchecked for years."

"So you knew your friend was a bent copper and a latent this whole time?"

"Associate."

Really, we were splitting hairs now? I limped back toward the road, trying to keep my back from stretching the wound open.

"I could not accuse a Detective Inspector of substantial latent crimes without evidence. So I suggested to her that my team, with her help, would investigate an anonymous buyer collecting illegal artifacts at auction. She knew of this person, and naturally wanted to secure certain artifacts—for her own personal use. She believed we were on her side and we were, to some degree. Anca was an element that needed to be removed."

I glanced over at him keeping pace beside my limping gait. Barnes hadn't orchestrated our involvement in her case at all. Kempthorne had done that, already aware she was on the slippery slope to latent sickness. He just needed evidence, which he'd planned to get while Barnes's attention was on the rest of us and Anca. He'd played everyone. Sneaky bastard.

"I suspected she was onto me when you mentioned a meeting at Cecil Court," he said. "And the deck of cards left at Cecil Court obviously weren't yours. Fifty-two cards, not fifty-one. The deck was planted. I knew you didn't attack Kage. Barnes's scheming was one thing, but taking you, harvesting your trick—trying to frame you for murder—" He pinched a speck of dirt from his sleeve. "That went too far."

His summary left a whole lot out and if he thought I was going to forget his involvement in all this, then he'd hired the wrong fool. "And Barnes wanted me because?"

"I may have dropped a few hints about your impressive trick. To an absorber like her, you're irresistible."

"You used me as bait?"

He frowned. "I don't know that I'd put it quite like that."

I laughed, because what else was there to do? At least I knew where I stood. And really, was I even surprised? "What about Anca? Where did she fit in all of this? Besides giving you something to distract Barnes with?"

"Hm, yes... I fear the cases are actually unrelated. Anca's benefactor has not been found."

"Or maybe the cases are related, through you," I said.

He fell quiet, suddenly no longer so talkative. Fine, we were playing *that* game, but when I wasn't bleeding and about to fall on my arse, we'd be having a conversation about exactly how Kempthorne fit into Barnes's insanity and the anonymous M trying to get to Kempthorne and his research from behind the scenes.

We hobbled on some more, almost at the road. He ducked back through the fence, and when I followed, the wound in my back chose the moment I straightened to set itself on fire. "Fuck..."

"Dom?"

"It's fine—" I waved him off.

"It clearly isn't. Let me see." Stepping behind me, he lifted my shirt without waiting for my agreement. Warm fingers danced around the hot, angry wound on my lower back. His touch tingled, tightening my skin. Instinctively, I pulled away.

"Stay still," he ordered. The touch firmed up, skimming and kneading. Was that necessary?

His strokes were distracting, part painful, part...

something else. I cleared my throat and endured. "Why didn't you tell me you suspected Barnes?"

"Because, Dom, you're many things, but delicate is not one of them. I couldn't risk you or Gina alerting Barnes before we had sufficient evidence. Any change in our behavior and she would have known I was aware of her scheming. And you were doing good work with Kage, rooting out Anca."

The fact he didn't trust us said more about him than it did about his team. He should have known we'd have his back. Peering over my shoulder, I caught the look of deep concentration on his face. His touch still teased, strangely intimate. "You need to work on your trust issues, Kempthorne."

His eyes flicked up and he huffed a quiet laugh. "I've heard that before."

"And you owe me cake."

"Cake?" He dropped my shirt and stepped back. "The wound isn't as bad as I thought. You'll be fine."

A tingling had simmered away the pain. Whatever he'd done seemed to have calmed it.

Blue lights from a passing police car flowed over us. Distant sirens warned more were incoming. Kempthorne watched the car disappear around a corner and slid his gaze back to me. "*Are* you all right?" The way he asked— softly, quietly—made it different from all the other times, and in the darkness, his intense gaze almost smoldered.

"Yeah." I swallowed. "You?"

"Yes. Fine. Thank you... for catching me. I'm not sure I'm ready to die, just yet. There's work still to do."

He was strange at times. He smiled, which had me grinning, until I realized I was supposed to be mad at him. I limped away, and when he fell into step, I said, "You'd better come up with a story for how we lost Barnes back there. You can lie well enough for the both of us, right?"

Secret knowledge shimmered in those hazel eyes. "There may be some truth in that."

30

I made it a personal rule to try and avoid hospitals. The sterile environments, echoing corridors, and beeping machines reminded me of events in the military I'd prefer to forget. But I wasn't there for me. I'd come for the guy asleep in the hospital bed, in a room all of his own.

Kage Mitchell was stable, lucky to be alive, and he'd make a full recovery, so the doctors said. Which seemed... impossible. I'd seen the card strike him, seen him on the floor, bleeding out. And I'd seen enough devastating wounds to know when someone wasn't going to make it.

Hollywood made it.

Slumping into the chair by the bed, I sighed hard. Kage's heart monitor blipped behind me, curiously comforting. A poster on the wall opposite demanded I *register my latent baby to give them the best start in life!* I rolled my eyes at it. Christ, the propaganda was suffocating.

The last two days had been full of questions about

Barnes's disappearance, endless statements regarding the sixty latents she'd kept contained for harvesting, and I was still recovering from having my trick yanked out of me. It would take weeks to heal from that, if it healed right at all. "Am I still a latent without a trick up my sleeve?" I asked the sleeping Hollywood.

Dreaming, he was oblivious to my presence, which was probably for the best.

A whole array of conflicted thoughts ran through my head. I was angry at him for his methods, and pissed at myself for caring. He had been trying to help, in his own way. And the one time he'd been without his gun, he'd nearly died. That was on me. Maybe I'd been wrong the whole time, and his way was the right way?

I wasn't even sure right and wrong existed. Or what was right was a matter of perspective. Like Kempthorne, who I didn't doubt had been trying to do the right thing by keeping all his secrets from everyone. We still needed to *talk* about things, like the coin, and why it kept coming up in conversation, and why Barnes had been so adamant she and Kempthorne were best pals. But Kempthorne had made himself even more elusive than before.

He was avoiding me—hiding at Ravenscourt. At least he hadn't sacked me. Yet. My past had taught me getting too close to the top brass didn't end well. The same applied to Kempthorne, and I'd seen his murder wall. His private obsession. He might come to regret that like my ex had come to regret sleeping with me, and I'd be out on my arse again, with nowhere to go but down.

Kage stirred in his sleep, looking fucking adorable.

"Barnes is probably dead. Not many people survive a dip in the Thames," I told him quietly. "All the crazy she stirred up to distract everyone from her plan to raise some latent god under London is over and the office phone has finally stopped ringing. Robin is pissed off about everything, but mostly me and the missing custard creams. We still don't really know who M is—you can probably help with that. Gina's treating me like I'm made of glass. She knows Barnes tore my trick out. In latent terms, I can't get it up. Even my cards don't sing like they used to—"

Annie breezed into the room, startling me out of the chair. In a deep sky-blue dress and colorful silk scarf, she looked amazing. "Oh sorry, I didn't realize you were in here. I'll wait outside—"

"It's fine, I was just leaving."

"Oh, don't go, please, Dom. I'm glad you could make it. I wasn't sure you'd take my call."

I almost hadn't, but if I'd ignored it, then I wouldn't have known Kage Mitchell was very much alive.

She tucked her golden hair behind her ear and approached Kage's bedside. "He looks okay... Thank God." Looking at me, she said in a hushed voice, "We didn't really speak before, at the party. But Kage has told me about you and him. That's why I called you."

There was a me and him? The two of us were a thing? "He has?"

She must have seen the surprise on my face because she quickly added, "It wasn't all bad."

I laughed and remembered this woman had kicked someone in the nuts for trying to gay-shame Hollywood. Annie was one of the good ones.

Her mood sobered as she gazed down at her friend. The love on her face was real. "How is he?"

"He'll be all right." By some miracle.

"He's a survivor."

"Aren't we all," I muttered, watching his lashes flutter. Even in a hospital bed, with his chest wrapped in bandages, hooked up to machines, he still looked impossibly gorgeous—now with added vulnerability that made my stupid heart race and my protective instincts kick into overdrive.

"How long do you think he'll stay in London?" I asked. He shouldn't stay at all. The Met would have it out for him and his methods clashed with the UK agency ways. But I didn't want him to leave.

"He doesn't have much in the US worth going back to —his words, not mine. But he didn't have much here either." Her tone suggested we were both familiar with that feeling of being on the outside. She was an unregistered latent. Kage wasn't a latent, but he was close enough to one to care. Life wasn't going to get any easier for us.

There could be a place for him at Kempthorne & Co, if I asked Kempthorne. But I was too close to *everything* to be objective. It also meant I'd have to pin Kempthorne down, and he was as slippery as an eel when he didn't want to be found.

Annie pulled up a chair and settled beside Kage.

"I'll come back when he's awake." I headed for the door, giving her some privacy.

"Dom?" She smiled shyly. Not the smile she used for TV, but the one I'd seen in the photo stuck to the mini-fridge on the narrowboat. "Meeting you, it helped him sort a few things out, you know? Things about himself. So, thank you, for everything."

I wasn't sure how I'd helped. He'd saved my arse more

than I'd saved his and when we weren't shagging, we were arguing. I nodded anyway, and left, trying to ignore the squirming sensation in my chest. Christ. I was falling deep for Hollywood.

Gina pinged my phone the second it picked up a signal outside the hospital, demanding I return to the office for a new case. Another downside of living over the office was a definite lack of vacation time. I needed a break. Maybe I could ask Kempthorne if I could crash at Ravenscourt? I wasn't done with his murder wall, and the time we'd spent going over it all together had been one of the better times in recent weeks. It would be worth it just to see him have another minor panic attack over preparing cereal.

Back at Cecil Court, Gina buzzed the door open. The building was quiet, except for Gina rattling a few cups in the kitchen. Climbing the stairs, I shrugged off my jacket and called, "Hi Honey, I'm home."

The sudden sight of Kempthorne standing on the landing stopped my heart. "Er." I winced. Had I just called him Honey? "Hi. That was, er... I meant for Gina to—"

"Good morning, Dom," he said brightly. He had his coat on, so he was heading out. All the shadows in the stairwell seemed to flock to him. This was the first time I'd seen him since the ride back to Cecil Court with my clothes smelling of burning Aston and my trick stripped. A whole lot of things were left unsaid between us.

"You good? Your arm?" I asked.

He rolled his wounded shoulder. "It's fine. How are you holding up? How's your back? And your... the other issue?"

"Uh huh. Yeah. Fine." I was not getting into the limp-power thing with him anytime soon. That shit was way too personal and we'd already somehow trampled over the boss/employee line.

He flicked his coat collar up and lifted his chin. "I was just—"

I was blocking the stairs and *staring.* I hurried up the last few steps and stepped on the landing outside the flat, giving him room to pass. "Sorry."

He frowned down the stairwell. "Ah, no," he said. "I meant—never mind. I was just—the kitchen, Gina and I—"

Christ, why was this so awkward? "Oh, the kitchen? Right. Sorry, I thought you wanted to get by—whatever —" I flung open the door into the main apartment.

"SURPRISE!"

The explosion of party poppers and tiny rainbow stars had me reaching to charge my cards with what little bit of trick I had left until I saw Gina's grin. Robin mustered something resembling a painful smile that came off as more of a grimace. They'd slung a 2 *YEAR ANNIVERSARY* banner decorated with horseshoes and bells between them that looked suspiciously like it was meant for a wedding anniversary, but what the hell, it was good enough.

My heart expanded.

"We didn't forget," Gina blurted. "We were just really busy and then things happened. Sorry it's late." She frowned and chewed on her bottom lip.

Holy shit, this was the most thoughtful thing anyone had ever done for me. "Is there cake?" *Please let there be cake.*

"There's cake," Kempthorne's voice rumbled. He strode by me into the kitchen, heading toward a large white box on the countertop.

Gina suddenly wrapped me in a bear hug that I had no hope of avoiding. "I'm so glad you didn't leave." Pulling back, she added with waggled eyebrows, "Kempthorne bought the cake."

That, I had to see.

Once I was free of Gina's bear hug, Robin formally shook my hand, her grip like ice. She let go and poked her glasses back up the bridge of her nose. "Congratulations on surviving two years at Kempthorne and Co."

"Thanks." Had she suspected I wouldn't?

"It's been interesting, Dom. Although, expenses have increased since your arrival. I'm not yet sure if there's a correlation." Her smile at the end suggested she was joking. Maybe.

But from Robin, that was a ringing endorsement. She was beginning to warm to me. In another two years we might even become friends.

Without flourish or ceremony, Kempthorne proceeded to unbox the cake. Robin handed him a single candle, and they muttered between them, conspiring while blocking the cake from my view. Gina rolled her eyes and folded her arms, waiting.

Kempthorne turned and presented a large Number 2 unicorn cake cradled in his arms. His crooked smile played on his lips, lighting up the humor in his eyes. His gaze caught mine. Oh, he was enjoying this.

The artfully designed number 2 in the shape of a unicorn's head came complete with rainbow hair and pink glitter lips. It was bonkers, and meant for a kids' party, but did I care?

Kempthorne opened his mouth to explain but my grin cut him off. "It's awesome," I told them. "You guys are awesome."

"Awesome attracts awesome, right?" Gina bounced toward the rack of knives with worrying enthusiasm and Kempthorne set the cake down on the table. Its single candle flickered.

"Oh, make a wish!" Gina exclaimed.

"I don't think that's—it's not my birthday." And I wasn't five years old.

"It still counts." She glared, brandishing a knife.

Taking a breath, I considered all the things I could wish for, flicked my gaze up to the man who, two years ago, had shaken my hand like I belonged, caught his raised eyebrow, and blew out the single candle.

"What did you wish for?" he asked.

Gina gasped. "No! You can't tell anyone or it won't come true." She gleefully stabbed the unicorn in the neck and carved the first slice.

Robin opened a bottle of bubbly and grumbled to Kempthorne about the cake not being paid for with company funds. We ate cake, drank wine, and chatted in the tiny kitchen of 16a Cecil Court, and it might just have been the most perfect moment of my life. If I'd told them, they'd think me pathetic, so I soaked up the chatter and the time with this new kind of strange adopted family I'd found, painfully aware it probably wouldn't last. Good things never did.

Gina and Robin were deep in conversation, on their second glass of wine each, when I sidled up to

Kempthorne. He had his sleeves rolled up and his arms in the sink, buried in bubbles up to his elbows.

After stacking the dirty plates beside him, I grabbed a towel and began drying the ones already clean. "So you bought me a unicorn cake?"

"The available options were limited at short notice," he said matter-of-factly.

"What would you have bought, if you'd had the time to plan?"

He smiled to himself and handed me a clean dish to dry. "I'll save that idea for next year." A sly turn of the head and a quirk of his lips, and he asked, "What was your wish?"

"It's classified."

"It's just you were looking over and—"

"Was I?" I shrugged, playing naive.

We both knew I was lying. My eager heart tripped under his suddenly intense gaze. Definitely time to change the subject, and seeing as he was relaxed, now was the perfect time to ambush him with something that had been bothering me for a while. "So now it's all over, are you going to tell me why the coin is so special?"

Darkness snuffed out the light in his eyes, and that part of Alexander Kempthorne I never could get a handle on looked back at me as though trying to dissect my motives. "Because of the secrets it keeps."

So many secrets. But this one, I was beginning to unwrap. "The murdered girl I saw in the coin. She looked familiar, a lot like Penny."

"Yes, she did," he said. No more, no less. He was trying to keep his face neutral, but that little flickering in his cheek betrayed him.

Was the coin lost in the Lexus explosion, or did he still have it? Clearly there was valuable knowledge in it—personal information. The man who stood beside me had been through terrible things. Things I'd had no choice but to know intimately. He frustrated the fuck out of me, but I respected him for surviving.

"She also looked a lot like the girl in the photographs you have in your loft apartment," I said carefully. "With the three Labradors and the bright smile?" And the same Kempthorne cheekbones as the rest of his family in their stiff family portraits hanging on Ravenscourt's walls.

His lips pinched, trapping words behind them. Regret and maybe fear shadowed his eyes. The girl in the coin's psychic burn, the girl in the photos spread across his table, the murdered girl... She was his sister, Charlotte Kempthorne.

A coincidence that Penny Montgomery just happened to look like her, or Barnes's idea of a game? A personal blow to Kempthorne?

The more I ventured into Kempthorne's murky world, the more unanswered questions bubbled to the surface.

He pulled the plug from the sink, took up a dishcloth to dry his hands, and checked over his shoulder to confirm Robin and Gina weren't listening. Dipping his head, he said, "I fear it's far from over."

"Meaning?"

"Barnes was formidable, well-connected, and she had the opportunity to collect artifact evidence from crime scenes, but she wasn't bidding against me at those auctions. She didn't roll the pen under the museum door in an effort to trigger you, and she definitely didn't try and kill you at the first auction we attended. She wanted you alive. She wasn't the puppet master—this *M* figure. I fear the only thing M wants is you and I out of their way."

Then, if she wasn't M, who was? His glance questioned, expecting me to have the answer, but if it wasn't Barnes, then we were back at the beginning, no closer to discovering who was collecting artifacts and who had an interest in removing me and even Kempthorne from London.

"There's a force at play in the shadows of London," he said, "one I don't know I can find in time—"

The door flew open. A ragged, filthy woman charged in, chest heaving, black pixie-cut hair clotted with mud, clothes askew, face all grazed up, and a manic look in her eyes.

I almost didn't recognize her. DI Barnes.

Robin yelled, "Artifact!"

A terrible, undeniable force screamed at me to *look, to take!* She had my lost Cecil Court key pinched between her fingers, but in her right hand, she gripped something so tightly her fingers had turned white from the strain.

The item thumped its beat through my head, its whispers hissed. The pen. She must have had it on her the whole time, and by luck escaped the Thames.

The artifact crooned and cried, screamed and demanded. It knew me. We had a connection, and it wanted me to *listen*.

Barnes's trick blazed in her blue eyes.

Surprise!

The dish slipped from my fingers and smashed into countless pieces. I hardly heard it.

Take it.

The pretty, twisted thing. Take it and own it and use it

and light up London forever. Burn it all away. Cauterize a million wounds. Memories pulled me down—trying to drag me into the past. Screams. Agony. All I had to do was take the pen. A sweet release for everyone. The pen knew, the pen had seen it all, and it wanted to show me its secrets. *His* secrets. The screaming boy on the table, the boy who did not belong. *The boy who was made.*

Barnes lifted her fist with the pen clutched inside. Her panting subsided and her eyes widened, her face fell slack. "If I can't have it, neither can *he*."

A tiny voice at the back of my head warned that she was about to blow all of Cecil Court to pieces, just like the shattered dish at my feet, and there would be nothing left of Kempthorne or Gina or Robin. But the tiny voice was easily ignored, especially when the larger, deeper, darker force began to fill the room—Barnes's trick bloomed. Its pressure popped my ears and pushed against my chest. It was bigger than me, bigger than this room, these people, bigger than the street, so big its presence flooded the absence left by Barnes's assault and burned through my veins, promising limitless power.

Light blazed from between Barnes's fingers—lighting her up like a beacon in the darkest of nights. The pen. She'd kill us all with it.

I lunged.

But Kempthorne was faster. He slammed into Barnes, tackling her clean off her feet, and fell with her into the hallway. She screamed, but her scream was a distant buzz behind her terrible, wonderful power spilling in from all around—coming up from below, beating through the walls, washing in waves. It tasted like baked earth after summer rain, like wet riverbanks and burned wires.

Kempthorne grabbed her hand and the light shattered like a thousand exploding lightbulbs—except we were all inside the light. Kempthorne let out a cry. His body bucked, his muscles locking up. Power tore through him—*into him*. So much of it.

"It'll kill him!" Gina screamed.

But it wasn't. Alexander Kempthorne was *absorbing* it —and fast. A few more thumping waves and the artifact's undeniable presence contracted around Kempthorne, quickly vanishing under his skin.

The pen was silent now, resting in his limp, open hand like any normal pen. He slumped against the wall, eyes fluttering closed, and lay there, pale and motionless.

"No, no!" Barnes screeched. "He can't have it! He can't take it from me!"

With the artifact spent and its terrible allure gone, I shook my head clear and dashed for Barnes. She tried to scramble to her feet and make a run for the hallway. Catching her arm, I yanked her back, slammed her face down on the floor, and pinned a knee between her shoulders. "Stay down! Under the Unregistered Latent Act of Nineteen Seventy-Eight, you're under arrest for multiple offenses, including but not limited to attempting to detonate an artifact. You do not have to say anything, but it may harm your defense if you do not mention when questioned something you later rely on in court. Anything you do say may be given in evidence. Do you understand?" Barnes sobbed under my knee, all the fight —and power— having been drained out of her—*taken* out of her.

Kempthorne hadn't moved. The pen lay in his open palm, his skin scorched. Was he breathing? I couldn't tell.

Robin dropped beside him and reached for the pulse-point at his neck.

I was falling, but staying still, my knee wedged against Barnes's back. Falling, with nothing to hold on to, because Kempthorne couldn't have survived.

"Is he alive?" I croaked, already knowing the answer.

She didn't reply.

"Robin—*is he all right?!*" He couldn't be dead. But he had to be. No non-latent could survive a psychic blast like that. The friction resonance alone would've fried his neural pathways from the inside out. His brain would be soup.

My gut whooshed, heart pounding. Nausea wet my tongue. Not Kempthorne too. More death, more bodies, more people I'd failed. But not him. He was Kempthorne. Untouchable. With his stupid hair, and his flashy watch, and the way he always tugged on his cuffs, the sly little knowing look in his eyes when he was thinking up his clever plans.

Barnes squirmed. Her sudden laugh punctured my mental spiral. "He's not dead, John! Didn't you know? Didn't he tell you? Alexander Kempthorne is one of us!" She cackled and clawed at the frayed carpet. "One of us. Made, not born. We were all *made!*"

"Robin—?" I snapped. "Is he fucking alive?"

"He's fine!" she snapped back, glaring over her shoulder. Her fierce green-eyed glare burned through her glasses and blamed me, like always. "He's just unconscious. Say a word of this to anyone and there are ways you can become *unregistered*, very quickly."

I exhaled hard, remembering to breathe. Wait, did she just threaten me?

"Do you understand?" she demanded.

I blinked. "Robin, w-what—"

"John Domenici, do we have an understanding?"

"Shit, yeah. Of course, yes."

But also, holy shit, Kempthorne was okay? Only a latent could absorb a mountain of power like the one coming off that wretched pen. So who and what the fuck was Alexander Kempthorne? If he was a latent, and he absorbed power... that made him a leech, just like Barnes.

Could he be a latent? Had I missed it all this time?

Every time I'd almost lost control, he'd been there, a hand on the shoulder, a voice in my ear. He'd talked me down again and again. The touches, the smooth words, his soothing presence. Had he been subtly managing my trick this entire time? Manipulating me for two years? No, he wouldn't, not deliberately. That would be a step too far, even for him.

But if he *absorbed* power, he could steal it without permission too. I tried to think back, to remember if I'd ever let him close, but he'd always been distant, always kept himself away—until recently.

And Robin's reaction to what we'd all just seen... She was protecting him. Because she knew the truth; she'd always known.

Kempthorne *was* an unregistered latent.

Shit, it was obvious now. Everything the pen had shown me from his past, the experiments, the way he was distracted by artifacts, how he kept them safe—kept me safe. Artifacts were more than a job to him, they *were* his life.

We were the same. Anger simmered. He could have

bloody well told me! Damn the man, he could have *trusted me.*

"Idiot." Barnes chuckled. "You're in too deep now, John. In too deep! The shadows are rising for him! For you all!"

I dug my knee deeper into her back. "You're going to prison for a very long time. Not the safest place for a copper. Or a latent. And my name is *Dom.*"

Her cackle grew more insane and shrill and the worst of it was, she knew a whole lot more than me, and despite her ramblings, she was right. I'd only scratched the surface of Alexander Kempthorne's life, but I was beginning to fear the darkness I'd uncovered went all the way down.

To be continued in Tide of Tricks.

Dom, Hollywood, Gina, Robin, and Kempthorne all return in
Tides of Tricks, Shadows of London #2.
Buy today!

TIDE OF TRICKS SNIPPET

Shadows of London #2
Excerpt

"What'll it be?" a voice beside me asked.

I turned my head to find a guy leaning on the bar, smiling. Kind brown eyes skimmed my face before dropping lower, not-so-subtly drinking me in.

On another night I might have been game. "Sorry, mate."

"Just a drink?" He shrugged. "You look like you could use it."

At least he was honest. And persistent. One drink wasn't going to kill me. "Okay, thanks."

He waved over Rick, and while waiting, scanned the bubbling crowd. "Is it always this busy?"

"Fridays, yeah." He wasn't a local, or he'd have known which bars to avoid on a Friday if he was just out for a quiet drink.

Rick breezed over, took his order—same again for me,

and a Stella for my new friend. With the drinks poured, Rick slid mine over on a napkin, tapping a finger on the bar to draw my eye. A single word stood out in black ink on the white napkin: *careful.* I thanked Rick as though I was thanking him for the drink and folded the napkin over, hiding his warning.

Careful.

"You're welcome, sweetheart." Rick dove back into serving his bleating customers, leaving me intrigued.

My new friend, James, who didn't look the sort who came with a warning, chatted about his job, some finance thing that sounded like it sucked his soul out, although he smiled all the way through telling me. Rick's warning should have had me backing off, but now I was curious, especially as James appeared to be harmless.

James asked about my career and I skimmed over all the details—stint in the military, now private security. Telling people I was an agent usually resulted in them ranting about latents, and how they should be locked up for everyone's safety, which got awkward, real fast.

James was easygoing, a nice guy, and the more he talked, the more I wanted to know why Rick had warned me off.

He finished his third beer and made like he was thinking of moving on. "It was nice to meet you." He dug into his pocket, as though digging out his phone or a business card. "Maybe we can do this again?"

"Yeah, it's been nice." It had been nice. It wasn't often a guy just wanted to talk over drinks with no strings attached.

He offered his hand to shake, and my alcohol-addled brain didn't see anything suspicious about the gesture. I closed my fingers around his and felt the press of a cold card against my palm.

When he let go, a playing card lay in my open hand. The King of Hearts. My heart stuttered, then tried to clog my throat. The noise of the bar—laughing, chatting, chinking glasses—it faded behind the deafening thump-thump in my head.

James smiled, like we were best mates, and leaned in. "He knows." He held my gaze and the charming, easy-going James I'd just met suddenly peered at me like he knew me—the real me. Not the soldier, and definitely not the agent at Kempthorne & Co. He knew me from *before*.

James left and I stared at the playing card, feeling my gut churn as the rush of a hundred unwanted memories poured in.

"Hey, Dom... you okay?" Rick was far, far away. The noise of the bar rose and fell in waves. Sickly heat rolled over me, prickling goose bumps across my skin.

I swallowed, but more saliva pooled around my tongue, nausea rising. "Yeah, yeah." I slid off the stool and fought my way outside through the crowd and slumped against the wall, struggling to keep my guts from climbing up my throat. *Breathe*.

A group of girls laughed as they teetered along the pavement in heels and short skirts. Bubbling and bright, their ruckus brought me back, grounding me in the now, surrounded by cold night air and the thump of muffled music.

I still had the card in my trembling hand. The King of Hearts.

He knew.

Fuck.

I tossed the card to the ground and twisted it into the grit under my heel, but the panic didn't fade. Standing on the street in Soho, surrounded by laughter and light, I felt exposed. My lies, my life, it was coming undone. I'd been so focused on never going back to the East End, it had never crossed my mind that the East End might come for me.

Dom, Hollywood, Gina, Robin, and Kempthorne all return in
Tides of Tricks, Shadows of London #2.
Buy today.

ABOUT THE AUTHOR

Born to wolves, Rainbow Award winner Ariana Nash only ventures from the Cornish moors when the moon is fat and the night alive with myths and legends. She captures those myths in glass jars and returning home, weaves them into stories filled with forbidden desires, fantasy realms, and wicked delights.

Sign up to her newsletter and get a free ebook here: https://www.subscribepage.com/silk-steel

CPSIA information can be obtained
at www.ICGtesting.com
Printed in the USA
LVHW030903250222
711994LV00007B/158